THE PASSIONATE KISS
OF ILLUSION

SCOTT SHAW

BUDDHA ROSE PUBLICATIONS

First Edition 1990
Fifth Edition 2025

Library of Congress
Cataloging in Publication Data:

Shaw, Scott
The Passionate Kiss of Illusion
    1. Title
    PS35669.H38627P37 1990 813'.54 89-71261

ISBN: 1-877792-04-7
ISBN-13: 978-1877792045

10 9 8 7 6 5 4 3 2 1
Printed in the United States of America

the wind it grabs you
        it spins your world around
the raindrops fall into the ocean waves
       the one
           merges w/ the whole
the essence of silence
holds your soul transfixed
and you see that life
it has no meaning
the holy
they know nothing at all
realization comes w/ your eyes open
and enlightenment is found
in the arms of the
Passionate Kiss of Illusion

TABLE OF CONTENTS

INTRODUCTION

Shaman is my name, Sandy Shaman and what we will be discussing in the pages that follow is enlightenment. No, not the traditional path to obtaining cosmic freedom, but a road which veers over to one side and a road which can only be consciously traveled by a very few.

When I showed the initial text of this manuscript to one of my babes, she commented, *"What pornography."* No, it is not pornography. This text outlines a spiritual path. Its techniques are no less valid than the Tantric Yoga Schools of Khajuraho, India.

People often feel that if something does not fall into their own framework of knowledge, then it must be wrong. Wrong, there is no such thing. Each person must find their own way to progress towards the ultimate understanding of enlightenment.

With all of the particulars out of the way let us proceed with a story or two of my life— occurrences which have led me to a far better understanding and a far deeper realization of man, woman, human nature, God, and the universe.

Remember, read between the lines and stay conscious...

CHAPTER 1
TAIPEI

I landed in Taipei in the early afternoon on a mid-July day. Off the plane I get, grabbed my suitcase, *no problema.* I'm out-a-there. So, exit the terminal and on to the airport bus stop for the central train station, I'm planted.

This is the place where most of the people entering Taipei head for. Taipei is a small city geographically speaking and the train station is a central location.

The bus pulls up. As I get on, a Chinese teenager bumps into me and in perfect English he says, "Excuse me sir." Obviously, a kid from L.A. on his way to visit relatives.

Sir, that always makes me annoyed. Here I am twenty-five years old, and everyone now calls me sir.

Anyway, the air is hot and to my nearest calculation in the Fahrenheit scale it is probably five hundred degrees. The bus is air conditioned though, so the ride, well it isn't too bad.

In the seat in front of me sits two Chinese men. In fact, the entire bus is full of Chinese; I, being the only non-Asian, honky, *la-way, quai-lo,* in tow. That's what I like about Taiwan. It is not an Americanized tourist haven yet. No other westerners to compete with and have steal my spotlight.

But so, as it goes, these two forward sitting dudes decide to close the curtain on that bus ride into the city central. Thus, blocking my view; un-cool. Now, not only is the fact of a bus with curtains annoying but I like to see the scenery, if you know what I mean. Even though I have seen it many times before—like things are always changing, you know.

Not being in too forward of a mood this day, I decide to just let it hang/let it ride and check out the scene from opposite/other side of the un-closed curtain window of a bus ride view. But, in general, I was none-too-happy with this situation. But, it's like what was I going to do, go and blaze them up over a stupid closed curtain?

Next to me sits this mid-twenties Chinese lady. She is not all that *beau-ti-ful,* in fact she is verging on the ugly. So, in this case, at least, my attentions were not drawn outwardly, inward, or upwardly, if you catch my meaning. Yet, as she falls off to sleep and her head falls upon my shoulder, my occasional glances take me to the thoughts of momentary fantasies. Well, I wouldn't marry her but perhaps I could spend a moment in time ...

As we get closer to the city, buildings begin to pop up and the smog becomes denser. Now, they say that Mexico City has the worst smog of any city in the world, but I don't know, from my experiences of the two places, nothing compares to Taipei.

The bus makes a few quick stops along city streets to drop people off. One old man argues in Chinese with the driver that he wants to get off at an unscheduled stop. The argument goes back and forth for a while until the bus driver finally concedes and slows the bus down just enough, as he passes the man's desired stop, that the old dude can jump off. With that, there he goes flying—jumping off into the streets of Taipei. Bye bye...

I thought that the old dude was going to kill himself, end up as street pizza. Taipei streets being packed full of vehicles as they are and the general

10

tendency sociologically, stereotypically speaking—well, the drivers, they are not what could be called, uh, too courteous. But anyway, he made it.

We finally arrive at the rail station terminal. The amusing thing about this place is that a rail station does not exist. It is under construction. It has been this way for several years and the only thing that has been accomplished, that I can see, is that a few steel girders have been put into place—stroking upward like phallic symbols into the Taipei smoggy sky.

The actual rail and bus station, I mean the ones that work and are in operation, are over there across the street.

Off the bus I get, grab my suitcase and I notice that a Taipei taxi has just pulled up. I throw my bag in. I join it. I tell the driver the name of my hotel. He turns and looks at me with his half-rotten gold-capped teeth smiling at me. Obviously, he didn't understand a fucking word I had said.

Now although I had been to Taiwan at least once or ten times, this was the first time I was to stay at this particular hotel. And though it's supposed location was near this nonexistent bus and rail terminal, I had not seen it before, so I could give little in the department of direction, in my very poor Mandarin Chinese, to this bad taxi driving dude.

He hands me a piece of paper and a pen, desired me to write it down. While I'm writing away, he fires up a smoke and offers one my direction. I just shake my head, "No." I continue writing. Once the etching is accomplished, he tries to read it. But, still no-go.

So, he starts up the ride and we drive about two blocks away to the local po-lice station. Now this place I had seen before. He shows a meter maid, who is standing out front, the piece of paper. No luck, no-go, she didn't know where the hotel is either. He then jumps out, grabs this po-lice-man who is walking out of the door. He, the po-lice-man, points to the building that encompasses the entire center block between where we were and where we are. Long ride *por nada.*

So, you learn something new every day. I could have walked half a block and been there. Oh well, next time...

The driver, back in the car, drives me the one block and pulls up in front and center of the hotel. With a smile on his face and no desire to charge me for his and or my folly, he waits as the hotel doorman opens my door and carries my suitcase inside. I whip the bad lad the equivalent of U.S. $5.00, which in Taipei is not just a pittance. I gave it to him for the ride, for his time, and for the joke on the both of us.

Leaving my suitcase at the bell station, but keeping my eye on it—I don't like leaving my stuff Asian unattended, I go to check in. Room 711. Yeah, good luck, seven-eleven.

Up to the room I go, my suitcase following me. Here I am Taipei, as the evening approaches and a new chance.

With every dance there is another chance.

Well, I sat back for a while, listened to the English-speaking radio station that was full on songs, long forgotten, from the 1970s. It was the type of radio station that I would never allow myself to listen to back in L.A. But, this was Taipei and it was nice for the time and the remembrance.

I unpacked, scratched out some poetry, wrote in my journal, and noticed how the hotel, supposed to be one of the finest in Taipei, had a surprisingly unclean vibe. It reminded me of the hotel I stayed at my first time in Bombay, minus, of course, the massive cockroaches. Back there/back then, rebound/recoil from monkhood: celibate, swami, sinner, and saint; all a point of view.

I learned it way back there, that no one is without desire. And when you think that you are something, you are never that. Take off the robes, take off the collars, take off the uniform of ego(s), what do you have? It has been a long time on the hard road since then. Anyway, somehow this hotel had a somewhat homey feel to it.

Six o'clock rolled around and Taipei T.V. returned on the air. It is kinda funny I always thought, me being of western breeding and all, how in many Asian countries; I mean, even the ones that have massive T.V. production, programming, it is only on and functioning certain hours of the day. I often wondered, was it financially based or did they not want the people to become addictively pre-washed and brainwashed and thus would not work hard enough. None-the-less, nothing was on that interested me—no good kung fu movies, so out to the streets I went.

The streets, yeah, that is where I am at home. That is where I belong.

I strolled around seeing the city once more. What a city, millions of people pushed onto one another. The smog so bad that at times you lose your breath if you walk too fast. The cars honking. The people pushing. What a mess. What a great city.

Taipei, though similar in population numbers to Hong Kong, varies so much. Hong Kong is on the ocean and, thus, is not burdened with all the smog that Taipei hpossesses. The people, though in both places Chinese, look very different. Taipei, formerly known as Formosa, had the majority of its vast population move from Mainland China in the twentieth century. These people were basically Han Chinese, which explains the lighter skin tone one finds here, than in the predominantly Southern Chinese based population of Hong Kong. One occasionally will see one of the indigenous dark-skinned people of Taiwan, in Taipei, but it is rare.

The walk continued. As the nine o'clock hour approached, I began to think of my returning to the hotel to ready myself for the nightlife upcoming. I just had one more stop to make, the outdoor food stall street over by the train station— the real train station, not the aforementioned, under construction, train station.

I arrived there and looking at my watch it was 8:47 in the P.M. It was still crowded and the scent of the food smelled good. Should I eat? Should I take my life into my own hands? *'I am a little hungry,'* I thought, but it is getting a little late. I couldn't decide. Oh well, *what-the-fuck,* why not? It will put me more into the vibes of the city. So, I ordered up, sat down, ate quickly, then was back on my way to the hotel.

As I was walking through the street, nearing the end of the food stalls, my eyes came upon, coming up, this western girl walking my direction, in the opposite direction. Her eyes were full-on glued to me. As I studied her, her nature and her look, she seemed to be from Australia. Well, here we have a *New Wave* Aussie, I realized.

She was obviously checking my scene. I do suppose that it is a bit unusual to see a blond haired bohemian *New Wave* guy with several earrings in both ears walking down a street such as this in Taipei. I mean it is not on the main tourist thoroughfare or anything.

With her was this Asian dude wearing tight black pants, a black tee shirt, and his sunglasses at night. He was obviously so caught up with himself that he did not even notice that his babe was seriously drooling all over some other guy. Namely, me.

Inside, I laughed to myself as I analyzed this couple. I figured that he was obviously Taiwan born and was there visiting—putting on a show for his family. So, he brought his chick from Aussy with him, where his parents had probably moved a decade ago to find fame, fortune, and the good life.

We passed each other, the girl still all over me. As we passed, I looked in her eyes and smiled and thought to myself, ah another time, another place. But for me, for the most part, white is just not right. I prefer those of Asian stock. I moved on.

I continued my walk back to the hotel. I got caught up by a passing train. Thus, the road is blocked generally for about five minutes or so. The cars, the motorcycles, and all the people caught up breathing the exhaust and waiting. Millions waiting for the moment, the moment of motion, as then they may resume their movement into the abyss of the Taipei night. The movement into their own dreams of glory, of fatal passion, of lasting love, and mostly of the movement that this world so strongly pursues, to no-where fast. Man, Taipei, the fucking smog is bad.

Me, I stood. I looked around. Anything of interest? No, no young ladies to focus my LOVE attentions upon. So, I just waited and looked forward to the evening ahead—the usual daydreams, the usual fantasies.

The train went by. The gates, they rose, and I made my way back to the hotel. The night was young. It awaited my arrival.

Back in my room, I powered down a couple of quick Heinekens out of the hotel room refrigerator, just to take the edge off the evening, if you get my meaning. And, oh yes, to catch the slightest of a little buzz to get the evening started off right.

I got dressed and decided to look at least semi conservative, not yet knowing the scene of my proposed nightspot of and in focus. I put on my typical baggy cuffed pants, my thin lapel sport coat, and a pair of red adidas tennis shoes. To keep it really conservative, I mean you know, feel out the situation, I took out all of my earrings, leaving only one in my right ear.

I guess I should go into a little paraphrase here concerning the old earring in the right ear and all. You see, when I was coming up, right was right and left was; well, like you know... So, my first earring went in the right ear. Now-a-days most dudes, who have the one side pierced, go for the left. Why, I don't know? Why, it changed, I don't know that either? But you know, like in India, dealing with the *kundalini* energy and all, right is the *suriya* or sun side—the male side. It also is the side where the *pingala* current flows. The *pingala* and the *ida* current are subtle nerves, *'nadis'* related

16

to the breath; running right/left, respectively. The left side is the moon side, the feminine side. So... Earring in the right ear. Anyway, if you have the interest, read some books on yoga and you will find out a lot more about it than I am going to get into here.

Well, I'm ready for the night. Oh, I forgot one very important detail. I reopened my suitcase, dug through the mess and found my handy supply of travel ready *con-troseptives* (rubbers). Never leave home without 'em.

As is always the case as the evening approaches, I place one or sometimes two in a nearby the bed handy location. Tonight, being no different, the same is done. I find a good spot. I place them between the Taipei phonebook and the Bible. What a holy gesture, I thought. I had to cross myself once just because...

I relocked my suitcase and I am ready to strut. Down the hall I go and into the elevator. My destination being the third floor and the discotheque.

Now there is a very important point I feel needs to be brought out here. I dislike discos. Aside from the ones I go to while traveling, I rarely go to them in L.A. I mean, I do not like the type of people or the mentality of those who frequent them. You know, it is just not intellectually stimulating. Yet, in Asia, where people have little other means for musical indulgences, and one does find a somewhat different type of constituent than in the states, and even though age is creeping up on me, well, I do love to dance.

The disco in my hotel is considered, by most, to be the best disco in Taipei. Compared to what, was always my curiosity? None-the-less, it is closest at hand, so arrive I do.

It has been open an hour or so when I got there. The music is pumping and the floor is jumping. I plant myself at a bar stool on the side of the dance floor and up comes a sweet little waitress inquiring as to my pleasure. I tried to explain a greyhound to her but no luck-chuck. Now, there is a drink I can drink like water, still getting eventually fucked up and in the morning wake up feeling like a champ. But to my dismay, and her lack of understanding, I must settle for a New Taiwan Beer, bottled, of course, by the Taiwan Wine and Tobacco Monopoly, as it is so eloquently written upon the bottle. I drink it down as I check the action.

The floor was moving. The dancers were dressed in semi modern fashion. Somewhat to my laughing amazement, several of the people were wearing wayfarer style sunglasses. The reason this was quite amusing to me is that six or seven years back, we involved in punk rock and later *new wave* invoked this style of the indoor, nighttime, sunglasses look. Now here are our bastard children following our lead and example, when we, the forerunners, have long ago given this up in the passing of time. It would be like now in L.A., in 1984, seeing someone wearing a skinny necktie and doing the *pogo*. Anyway...

Dreams to be found and dreams to be lived for no other apparent reason but the fact-u-lat-ion of false self-worth and deadened self-dreams. Where the source of all pain lies; seeing who we are and remembering who we have been forced to become. So few ever take the time to wonder why.

Out there on the floor, there was this couple dancing; he in his fifties; she, maybe in her thirties.

18

Him, well he was dressed in this white tux, and she was dressed in a sequined gown. Their dance simply involved pointing their fingers to the sky. I mean which fucking way to Saturday Night Fever? I laughed both to myself and at times quietly out loud as this man, obviously of the Taiwanese upper echelon, got out there and kept changing sides pointing his finger to the sky.

To paraphrase Bruce Lee from Enter the Dragon, "Don't look at my finger, look at where it is pointing to."

The night was still young, and I began to catch a buzz on the more serious side. Slide another New Taiwan Beer my way, baby. The waitress kept bringing them as I finished the last.

To the left, the left of my barstool, sat a table; a round wooden table. There at this table was a group of seventeen or eighteen year olds. Myself, being the old man that I was, all of twenty-five, and seeing the younger people sitting, sent my mind back to my younger days and the L.A. club scene.

Punk was given birth to back then; now new wave disco was flourishing. In the mid-to-late seventies and early eighties you wouldn't catch me dead in a disco scene but now here I was Taipei, in a disco and remembering my seventeenth year and all the presence and purpose that I once felt.

The funny thing about it all was that here in Taipei I had the feeling of no age. It always comes over me. I don't know what it is? I am just not held bound by that horrible knowledge of impending maturity, even as I stared at the relative youngsters at the table to my left. I didn't quite know what it was, and in fact it did not matter. For here I was, Taipei, a wild young buck on the prowl in the night.

Immediately, I noticed sitting at the far side of this table, a girl who seemed never to take her eyes off me. Well hey, what's a guy like me supposed to do?

Now, she looked AOK to me. So, my interests were necessarily aroused—naturally…

As I sat there, studying the situation, checking out every angle of attack. What move was the first move? What move would be the right move to make? Which at times of semi-soberness and being as my reclusive nature is, is generally never quite all that definitive and/or clear. Before I could do anything though she got up with the other girls at the table and hit the dance floor, girl-to-girl.

Now, there were a few guys at the table who also eventually got up and joined in the dancing group, but she kept her focus on her dance-mate girlfriends and not on the dudes at hand.

In Taiwan, they have an interesting habit. At least I think that it is interesting. In the middle of the floor they have a pillar. No, not of salt, but it is painted black and it has mirrors on it. Women who wish to dance, and if their love-stallion is not willing or if they are riding solo, they go up to these mirrors and boogie while watching themselves. To me, it seems boring. I mean it's like fucking jacking off—taking matters into your own hands, if you know what I be-a-talking-about?

I mean you can only fantasize so much. Along with this, it is not unusual to find chicks only dancing with chicks and dudes with dudes. Boring, boring, boring, in my mind. But there she was, dancing away. Me, I wasn't worried, the night was young and the situation wide open.

Now this young beauty, well not exactly a total beauty, but she definitely had an interesting look about her, she looked to have a bit of Caucasian blood running through her veins. Her hair was, oh so slightly, almost blond, and her features were a bit rounder than the average Taiwanese. It was dark though, and I was not quite sure if it was the light, the booze, or really her.

She had a *'do'* similar to mine: long in the front, parted on the side, long in the back. She wore flooding pants, a plaid shirt, and a belt. Overall, she was a bit chunky, maybe fifteen or twenty over. But, my emotions, let's just say, they had been stirred…

I sat there looking onto the dancing evening. Asian bodies moving to a mid 80s disco beat. Lights flashing as a man in a tux pointed to the sky.

What should I do? Ask her to dance? Maybe, yes? Maybe no? Should I? Shouldn't I? Maybe dance with one of the other available women on the floor. Would they dance with me? Maybe dance alone? NO WAY!

I sat there not knowing what to do. Better have another brew-ski that was for sure.

My focus of interest, after dancing for a while, left the group and sat down and fired up a cigarette. She grabbed the bottle of rum sitting mid-table and poured it into her coke. I thought to myself, this is my chance, I will let her sit down and rest for a while and then I will move on up and ask her to dance.

Ah, the confusion of the moment. Most of us have been there. Should I? Shouldn't I? What should I do? The confusion of momentary infatuation, I love it. I love to hate it.

About that time, one of the men who worked in the disco, dressed in this fine gray tux and red bow tie came up to me and said, "Good, no dancing.

You stay out of trouble." I laughed, but inside I knew, maybe no trouble but also no fun. And danger being my middle name, well...

At that point, the music shifted to the slow cuddle up stuff and her friends rejoined her at the table. I was slightly unhappy with this occurrence, but it was one of those situations—not a damn thing I could do about it. *Yeah, so let's like woe, just flow man. And like hey, contemplate the universe...*

I thought how easy it would be to take a woman up to my room from this disco. Just a few floors up on the *el-e-va-tor*. No front desk to pass. No dirty looks from the hotel assistant night manager when he knows a babe is in tow for one reason and one reason alone. No taxi rides, no fees, payable in advance, just clear and simple con; the con to lust.

The slow music was playing; my initial game plan had gone to shit. So, I order up another New Taiwan Beer, one sipped it and as the waitress passed by again I lifted my empty bottle to let her know, slice another one this direction, baby.

The music went on at that pace for maybe twenty or thirty minutes. As they picked it up, they played a song that I completely hated and there was no way in the fucking world that I would lower myself to dance to it. The next song, I said to myself, *'I will ask her, the next song...'*

Halfway through the song I hated though, her and her friends got up and started to dance. Fuck!

The night went on in my confusion. Past the twelfth or thirteenth new Taiwan beer, I mean they are large size, I could hardly give a shit about dancing and started ordering up the hard stuff. Her stare was still there all over me but my confusion about the, *'To ask or not to ask,'* no longer permeated my feelings.

Late night/all night, they left. I hammered down a few more, was sent off with a smile from my waitress who had her eyes focused on the pure lust direction all over my bod—warm for my American form. No, it can't be tonight, I thought and hit my room solo. My spinning room. I was definitely laced up.

*   *   *

Morning, oh man does it hurt. Got to get outside, walk some of this hell off, but the heat was killer, the day put me under. I walked. I did not want to walk. Taipei: the streets, the heat, and the smog like nowhere else in the world. The day passed, one of those days that should just never have happened.

Night two, my shit relatively together. Will she be there? I don't know. Give me another shot at the poison, another shot at the love. Give me any dream that is worth its desiring. A desire that is worth its weight in gold. Give me anything, anything will do just fine. Spread your love disease upon me; leave me no room for escape.

Inside, ten o'clock. Led to my bar stool, which awaited my return, by the gray tux-ed, red tied, "Good, you're not dancing," disco boy.

The dancing, it was there. And yes, the babe, she was there too. Oh yeah! My waitress comes up, love in her eyes, and though they didn't have grapefruit juice, as it turns out, they did have OJ. "Why the fuck didn't you tell me that last night, hit me with a screwdriver, baby." It's almost as good as a greyhound.

Up from the table, the group, her group, the babes group, she and them, them and she, they did dance on. Should I, could I, another night lost in the same old fucking indecision.

I sat there, powered down several. I did, as I usually do, lose count. Time to make my move; fuck, slow music on again. Sit this one out. Pour another one of those bad dudes my direction or better yet make that three.

I hate indecision. They say it is from insecurity. I don't know, maybe it is? But where does insecurity come from. Ah fuck, all this introspective psychological bullshit. Give me another stiff drink of liquid security.

As the music slowly picked up, she and her group of disco aficionados got up to move.

The next song came on. My kind of song, heavy down beat and moveable. Being more than slightly intoxicated, I said to myself, "This is it." I got up to dance. Look out!

Ah, how I do love to dance. Immediately that feeling of the rhythm and the bliss hit me. It had been a long time; too long.

The L.A. clubs had become a joke over the past year or so. With all the mid 80's people trying to catch the last wave of new wave. They didn't even realize that it had washed out long ago. Being the musical ethnocentric that I am, I would rarely go to the clubs in L.A. anymore. But here, *on the road,* the hard road, I would wine and dine, I would move.

I rather pushed my way into her field of vision, moved right into her dancing group of friends. I was doing the crawl and I wasn't wasting any more time. As I was dancing, I began to look around and to my amazement the eyes were all on me. Was it my paranoia or was it my dance. I concluded that they had never seen anything like the moves I was throwing before. A few fingers pointed and there were a few giggles but most of all there were the eyes. Then everybody began to try to imitate my moves. Give it up chumps.

As my young lady friend and her attentions became more and more focused on me, she let her friends slip to one side and we danced, oh how we danced. Within twenty minutes or so I was covered with sweat. It soaked through my shirt and my hair was dripping. It felt great. It had been too long since this had occurred.

It is just not in my nature to do things half assed. I never believed in the middle path; it is too safe. The Buddha was wrong. One should either do something all the way or don't bother. And the dance, ah it so cathartic.

The set went on for maybe forty-five minutes or so before the slow tunes started. The previous forty-five had been full of eye contact, smiles and I knew we both could feel it.

The slow music began, we looked at each other, smiled, and I returned to my stool, her to her table. I could see that much conversation was to come accompanied by stares by her and her friends over in my LOVE direction.

As I reached my stool, I was met by waitress, who was obviously digging my scene, as well. She had on her tray a glass of water for me, accompanied with a brew. I powered them both down, ordered up another screwdriver and the evening, well, it was opening wide to a million new fantasies, a million new possibilities.

I sat there making occasional cool eye contact with my love of the night, just to keep things happening. Mostly, I kept my eyes on the floor, the dance floor. I did not want to look too obvious.

I knew if I were to hope for anything from the evening, this evening, I must give her the slow dance as well. So, I sat there for fifteen or so, waiting for my liquid courage to build up, waiting for the moment of motion; it was time, I made my move.

Though my white shirt was still wet, I went over to her table and extended my hand to her. She looked at her friends for what seemed to be a very long time. Seconds turn to hours in moments of indecision when your life is on the line. Then, our eyes met, she smiled and got up. She was mine.

I pulled her close as we went on to the dance floor. Too close I knew for a first close dance with an Asian lady, but I wanted my cards on the table. As we danced, I could feel my wet shirt against my skin. I wondered if she could feel it too.

My mouth, it tasted like orange juice, it tasted like beer, but the dance it moved on. She was a smoker, I was not and as we moved. I could smell the tobacco on her clothes, on her hair. Well, I guess you can't have everything. We danced on.

She was not too small, maybe five feet five or so. Maybe it was the heels, but we fit together good.

I thought to myself of a time my friend Venchenzo and I had gone out dancing in L.A. a while ago at some bullshit disco scene. We had just finished dancing with these two babes, to the fast-paced music pounding in the night, and as the slower stuff moved on and as we left the dance floor my eyes caught sight of this, oh so fine, babe on the Mexican side of the picture and I went right up to her and asked her for a dance. Generally, it is not so easy to get a chick to dance to melodic music on the first time out, but she agreed. My buddy Venchenzo, seeing what had happened, stood there saying loudly, "You be bad, you be bad."

The thought made me laugh. As I did, I pulled my body slightly away from hers and asked in my best Mandarin, which is none too good,

"What's your name?"

She just looked at me and smiled. I then asked her in English and she replied,

"Ming Shao."
She smiled, "What you?" she asked in bad English.
"Sandy, Sandy Shaman."

As the beat picked up, we continued our dance, and the evening went on. At times her friends would dance on up. I could tell they didn't dig my moving in on their local scene, but hey, *'Fuck 'em,'* I thought.

One of the male macho dancing dudes, one of her friends, spoke near perfect English and he would dance up occasionally and ask me stupid questions. Ming Shao could not speak much English herself but seemed to understand well enough. That was AOK for I was the same with Mandarin.

Well, the games and the dance went on and on. Time to rest; not for me but the weak of spirit, the weak of heart they always seem to slow down their pace. Me, I was covered with sweat, wet through and through. My long hair looks like I just got out of the shower. I-LIKED-IT.

I decided to make myself right at home at their table. I mean forget my lonely bar stool. Leave that to the poets and the drunks of which I am periodically both. I guess I chilled one of the homeboys out of his seat but hey, if he can't take a joke, fuck 'em. And anyway, all is fair in love and war.

They were drinking the rum and the coke. Order up a bottle, keep the new cokes coming. Sorry, that is just not my brew, nor my style. Hit me with a screwdriver, better make that *dos*.

My waitress put the jealous love stare upon me, none too happy with my move into this zone of affection. She brought the drinks my way though. I thought maybe now, seeing this, the girl and I, she may have poisoned them. But hey, if you want to play you have got to pay.

A few more drinks, another dance session, a lot of stupid questions from the dude on the English-speaking side of the situation, and then closing time, 2:00 AM. Early for my late-night blood. In L.A. there are a lot of spots that I would have chosen to trot on to at that hour of the night, but...

We are up, we are moving out. I get the look from the waitress as we pass her at the door. I wink, her direction. No pain, no gain.

Motoring down the elevator, the group, them, she, her, and I. I had to make a move, had to do something fast. If anything could be done at all...

Ground floor,

"Would you like to talk for a while?"
"Talk?"

Moving towards the late-night taxi, parked by the door at the front of my love crib central.

"Would you like to talk for a while?"
"Talk?"

What the fuck is this, *déjà vu?*

"I will take you home later."

At the taxi door, she began to rap something. I really didn't understand, it was spoken way too fast. But, I could hear to the effect that she was going home or somewhere with me. Then, it got heavy: the fast, the almost loud, the back and forth, then the dude who spoke good English, "See you tomorrow." She was mine!

My cock got hard. Like a meat-eating high school student with hormones running with the wild and the free.

Back in the hotel, back past the late-night front deskman with his dirty look, thinking he knows what the fuck is going on. So much for getting a babe to my room unnoticed.

"Would you like to go have coffee in the coffee shop?"
"Okay."

Cool ploy, for I knew that the coffee shop, it was closed.

"Oh, it is closed but we can have some from room service, up in my room; alright?"
"Okay."

The mirrored glass elevator ride into the lost realms of the night. Damn, I love being in Asia, where with every dance there is another chance and everything it is just so fucking haveable.

We cruised it room side. I open the door, in we go, in we dance. Forget the coffee, I grab her a rum and coke out of my hotel room refrigerator; uck. Let's loosen up what is already loose. I power down one, well maybe three, of those little shit hotel room refrigerator bottles of vodka straight, and we sit back into the conversation.

My room toned in red: red carpet, red upholstery, red bed spread, red, almost erotic but I don't really like the color.

Here, in the more light of a likeness I could stare into her eyes. Yes, she had to be part *Anglo*. I sat on the floor, leaning against my bed, she sat in a chair. I inquired to the fact, the honky fact, no answer. She looked out the window for a time and then just leaned down and kissed me.

The meeting of the lips. A feminine touch leads a man to a thousand deaths, a thousand births. Alive, in a life just too fucking short. And, the world it pulls us away, feeds us its lies; like the lie that a kiss will last forever and love it will never fade. But, it is only the believer, the fool who listens to these words. Believe me, nothing last forever. But, promise me that touch anyway.

She sat herself atop me. Young, yes but she was no fool to the passion. A kiss leads to a, *well you know,* like a push to a shove.

She was plump. She had an almost blond tint to her brown/black hair which was definitely shorter than mine. A plaid, yes plaid shirt, covered by a red, matching the interior designer belt, and jeans. I mean we're talking real fashion passion here. Yeah, right.

Slip off the shirt. It came off like it was greased. Her kisses were poured onto me like wine. Bra, covering small breasts. Reach around, unfasten it. A bit of a gut, let it hang low. I don't understand why people don't keep themselves in shape?

Her shirt off, her bra down. I move my lips from her mouth to her breasts. Her small little nipples; obviously from the Asian side of her bloodline. They tasted like sweat; sometimes it tastes oh so sweet.

Lift her up, off of me, give her the roll onto the sheets. Her shoes, they already were kicked off. I pulled down her jeans. Anybody got a crowbar around here?

My love machine, I mean my tool of love, it was in motion ready for the kill. Sport coat off, necktie off, white shirt off, red tennis shoes off, baggy pants off; she knew what she was doing at least in the clothing removal part of the negotiation(s). But, the proof is in the pudding, if you know what I mean.

Love in the moment: love, lust, fire at will. A kiss, a touch, a lick, a feel, plant it, sink it, stick it deep. We are one.

I was just enough inebriated to pump it full on with no worry of the quick blow off. That semi numb, dick numb, if you know what I mean. I am sure that you do. Upside, downside, all around side. Give it to me once, give it to me twice, make me feel alright...

She had a slight scent: pussy scent, stinky beaver, fish chops. I knew she had to have some *Anglo* in her. I mean, stereotypically, on the whole, honky chicks just seem to have that scent. You know, a funny little story here; the first chick that I ever was really spending time going down on, well actually the first *dos,* I mean I could not understand how dudes could dig their face into that sour smell bush of putrefied fish. I mean it stunk! It wasn't until I met my long time Spanish love, that I even considered spending more than a few muffing seconds down on those wild bushes. A later realization, stereotypically speaking again, of course, that Asian ladies, well, they just don't smell bad. I don't know what is it? Hit the douche factory baby.

So, it was good, it was, well... Mediocre. She pumped me on top. I put her under the meat grinder on the bottom and so on and macho dude so forth.

5:00 AM rolls around, bail time for her. She had to go. I asked her if she wanted to stay. She declined. "Hey, see-ya-later."

I roller over, rolled off my partial remaining duds, drifted into sobering too fast sleep. Another day on the horizon, another chance to dream.

*　　　*　　　*

Three or four in the afternoon I woke up. Pulled it out, my head basically in the mode of clean. The liquor was clear, not tainted dark. I always wake, well usually, post the drinking of the bad vodka clean and clear.

Shower, I took it. Breakfast, well lunch, (I call it *dunch.* You know like all the wild and the way too cool call breakfast/lunch, *brunch.* So lunch/dinner, *dunch.* Right?) It didn't go down easy. It was American on the Chinese side of the picture, and they served me up some desert which turned out to be full of worms. Fuck, it makes me sick even now to think about it for I had eaten a few bites before I realized the dirty deed.

Anyway, still some hours of daylight to kill, I hit the streets. The streets and the heat and the not knowing where in the Taipei smog to go.

Walk fast, walk past, what do I see, who sees me. Lost only into the realms, the spectrum of my fading memory. It all means so little. Let no other person lie to you and tell you that life means something more.

I ended up at the Taipei art museum. AOK, it was AOK. Good show on, a photo here, a photo there. Toss them into the nowhere of somewhere realm of all the millions of journey photo slides that I have taken.

The heat, the smog, and mostly the night coming on. Fuck the walking, I grabbed a taxi, ride on ... Hotel hell, a kiss in my mirror, time to kill and money to spill. I awaited for the later hours of the dancing evening to come upon me.

Chinese T.V., on the T.V., fuck it. I wrote some poetry, drew some pictures, listened to the sounds pouring out of a time warp English speaking radio station, playing songs of choice from the nineteen seventies. Again, it was almost fun to hear all the stuff which I was way too cool to listen to back in L.A.

The sixties stuff was always cool, but seventies platform shoes and do a little dance, make a little love, well, anyway...

Ten o'clock, dressed to kill. A plan for a *further-ment* of my love, a dance, a chance; Ming Shou. Down the elevator, I ride. Into the discotheque I strut. The red tie, gray tuxed dude greets me. The waitress in love, complete with smile in hand, walks me to my bar stool, following up with a screwdriver. No more need to ask.

The table, the table it was over there, lost and longing in the dimly lit disco evening air. Empty, it stood alone. Alone, except for a bottle of rum, bottles of coke, and cigarettes in their packets. Lost to no one's eyes, no one's lips. My love, she was dancing, her friends, they surrounded her. I sat back staring out onto the dancing floor thinking how cool I was. I'll have a drink or two, let her come to me. I'll wait for the dance, in the chance, any chance that may ever be.

Time passes slow when the world is not revolving around you. I did not like the feeling, did not like it at all. She, Ming Shou, was out there dancing, dancing paying no attention to me. I like to be the center of my babe's attention, if you catch-my-meaning. I mean, come-on, she should have come over and been drooling all over me.

The dance went on, the drinks they kept a coming. I poured them down at will. Water and wine, it feels so fine. Kiss me elixir, kiss me tight, kiss me deep.

Finally, the music slowed for the first slow session, the dancing crew came/went and sat down. The lovers remained engulfed dancing in one another's arms. Love, it is for suckers.

'Okay, here she comes,' I said it to myself. Here she comes and there she went. She didn't even bat an eye, went and sat down. Well, fuck this.

I ordered up another round, one round maybe two. Where were the eyes from the two nights before, embracing me, lost but never found.

Finally, enough was enough. I walked over, stood next to her, asked her to dance. A head shaking, "No." NO! What the fuck is that. After what we had last night. No! Fuck you too. And, except for the smile of the young soul boy who *rap'd* the English, I got pure *negatory vibes* from the whole crowd.

Another drink, if you please.

Sit back into the evening, let the evening pass on by. A drink, to no stare. A never alone at the table, sweet young thing of a miss that I asked for a dance one more time just to confirm that I was a catching the right vibes and no. I fucking hate the word no.

Hey, I don't need you either. This reasoning, however, did have a haunting effect on my mind. Past the point where the pain ends, past the point where the pleasure begins.

Up comes the waitress, the waitress with a gleam of love for me in her Chinese eyes. Unknown to her was the night before. She had seen the dancing, seen the leaving, but as the music moved, the pedals pounded, she had no idea of what had gone down, or should I say who had gone in. In tow she had another, another waitress, seemed to be the upper echelon hostess. Speaking better English than my dreamy eyed mistress,

"Would you like to meet two ladies?"
"Two ladies?"
"Yes, those two."

I looked. Well, how can I say this nicely, whores, hookers if you will.

"They are busy right now but will be free after twelve. They saw you dancing last night and liked the way that you moved and wanted to meet you."
"Sure, whatever," I answered.

Over my shoulder, there they sat, Arabs arm-in-arm with them. Yeah right, just what I need, Camel Jockey, "CJ" sloppy seconds.

Power down a few more, power them down as I sit. I look onto the dance floor. I would prefer to be dancing, but dancing *so-lo* to a mirror, well that is just not my style.

There was this little princess though, man she did have the jam. Move and groove, make love to her own reflection; reflections in the night. Yeah, the mirror it was like a phallic symbol, large and square, black, and her. All those shit head psychiatrists always say we want to make love to ourselves anyway. Dance on baby, dance on...

She was early twenties. Her dude struts up, forty-five plus. I could see why she needs to wack herself off. Old man probably can't even get it up. She swung, he tried. Ah well, fuck that story, you can imagine the scene.

Up pulls the dude, red bow tie of warning. By this point, me, I am seriously tilted.

"Good, you are not dancing tonight, keep yourself safe."
"Fuck safe," as I slurred my words to him.

No babes were really single and on the scene. I sat there choking the chicken, making love to that oh so serious bar stool. You know, like the poets, like the drunks.

I have heard about shit like this, as the babe of the night, my babe of before, dances off with her friends as the music now pounds down. I don't know, maybe she got it from her parents, the late hours coming in and all. Maybe from her friends.

Who keeps the tabs? She danced on, walked on, her friends left to the realms of the night. Hey, if they don't want to know, then forget 'em.

A little pushed passion, I was Chinese eyed. Sliding, I was sliding onto the floor. Better pick myself up off of it. Walk out cool, walk out straight, walk out alone.

Waitress in love, very bad English and all,

"Where you go?"
"To my room."
"You no wait for ladies?"
"No, I like love."

I said it plain. I said it simple. I saw her melt gently into my hands. I said the magic words, the words of love, the promise of forever.

Maybe I was just too drunk, maybe not drunk enough. You know, you never quite know in those situations. But even in my very simple English, I painted a picture abstract. Love, not lust. Yeah, that is what I am looking for. Melt into my hands baby. Melt into my crotch.

Out the door to the doors, elevator; push the button. Open door; step in to the stepping out, the two ladies of the evening they were there. I guess they had just now/just then completed their *rendezvous*. I was booked in their appointment book. Well, what can I say, I did invite them up.

Now *dos* is fine when you got the time and my dick full-on; full-on way wasted drunk. Somewhere in that space between the too drunk half-mast and the too drunk full-on erection, where there is no way on God's green earth, (I think it is more blue than green though, don't you), that you are going to cum. Well, the second way makes one feel mighty potent; *im-por-tant* if you catch my drift. That was where I was at.

There was no discussion, my drunken Mandarin Chinese was for shit and they, they couldn't speak English. Black was their color, the clothing clothed upon the skin. Black, like all the best whores in Asia wear. Well, they didn't wear it for too long.

I grabbed at it, they removed it. I ripped the buttons from my shirt. They did their business, letting me do mine.

I reached for my rubber, crossed myself as I removed it from its holy place. Put it on, eventually took it off. It grabbed way too tight; a definite no go situation. Huff and puff, mostly I let them stay on the topside, stimulating my form.

One was pretty, one was not so much. But who was counting and, in that state, I guess it really doesn't matter much anyway. *They all look good through the bottom of a shot glass,* as the old saying goes. One had a seriously tight pussy; had that muscle vice grip action up and down. One was stretchy, a little bit of flab around the waistline; way side, waste side. Move and groove, who gives a drunken fuck.

So, with their damage done, $500.00 U.S. a piece, for the night. Hey, I didn't want them to stay, "Bye bye."

Me, I was out (asleep) before the door even fully closed.

*   *   *

Morning comes as morning does, felt Okay. That was until I went down and had a little on the breakfast side of the picture. One of those creeping hang-overs dancing through my day. The heat and Taipei, mostly I slept.

The nighttime came: dues, and duds, all were paid. I had thought to hit another disco scene that evening but this one, it was so close. Down the elevator I ride. There was the babe, table sitting, her and her friends. I felt kind of a gloat, *'Like hey, who needs you.'* A drink down, the hangover gone. I was ready to party.

There was the same old crowd, the same old faces. There was Ming Shou and her group, they were there every night. Others came every night as well. Damn, don't they have anything better to do?

Some of the *disco-ites* were tourist, some were new locals, and some were the distant, the further, and the maimed. To party, age has no barrier. Party, but just stay away from me.

My hooker friends came a little late, later and alone. No new meat on the action table. Did I want to dance? Sure, I always want to dance. We got on down.

They were looking at five hundred more, per. "Thanks, but no thanks. Been there, done that."

A drink, a dance, the evening wore on. I even brushed up against Ming Shou once on the dance floor who had spent most of the time nursing her table. *'Ha,'* I laughed to myself.

I had declined the monetary invite for the evening and was nursing my drink at my private reserved bar stool, alone, when about closing time, this guy came up to me,

"Do you come here every night? Do you have any female action?"
"Yes and no, respectively. I don't know, you can try those two over there. Oh, they have left."

Mohammed was his name. Mustached, like all of those C.J.'s from Dubai. He seemed AOK though. Post a short *convo* he bailed with a,

"See you tomorrow."
"Yeah, whatever."

About to split the scene, (split-the-seams, man), waitress with love in her eyes comes up to me and says,

"You know there is other discos, Taipei has many."
"Yes, I do know that. I come here because it is easy, for this is where I stay."
"Would you like to go out with me tomorrow night? It is my night off."

I have edited her bad English, and my bad Chinese.

"Sure, why not."
"I will call your room tomorrow," she said.
"Okay."

She turned down my tip. Handed it back to me. Promises for another time, another dream. I went to my room alone. Alone and not too drunk. It felt good to just lay back in the surrounding red, lights off, and listen to the sounds of the alone late-night Taipei.

Excuse me while I go crack open another bottle of the grape before I finish this story. . .

*   *   *

Morning calls; well it actually did, a ring upon the telephone lines. A ring unanswered. Unanswered, why you ask? Well, let me describe my love of a cocktail waitress to you.

Twenty-five, I would say that she is give or take my age. A college graduate; yes. So she said. A new wave *'do,'* like the sixties kind of shoulder length. A bit longer on one side, kind of bob style. And oh yes, ugly. Damn she was ugly.

She had posted herself with the English name Mimi. Ugly and a stupid name and myself getting more than enough pussy. And, with the passionate inability that I have to say, no. Anyway, escape I did not answer the telephone.

Now I was in and out all day, not hung over. A Taipei gift or three to buy for my main back state side, L.A. babe. When I was in, songs from the nineteen seventies blasted on the radio and the telephone rang.

As for me, well I had a sincere and serious *pre-fer-ance* to just go dancing at the in-house disco rather than to go pavement hopping with an ugly babe that I no doubt would have had to partied all over in the closing moments of that evening. Post a dose of my charm, post a dose of the drink, of course. I mean, come-on, it would have been one of those sessions of waking up to, *'Oh fuck, what did I get myself into.'* ThanX, but no ThanX.

So, the calls they haunted me and I did feel a bit bad about them but... You know how the love pup rides and my cookie did not need be dipped in rancid milk.

Nighttime, my time, dressed to kill and money to spill; disco time. Mohammed, he was there, pulls up a seat next to me. We sat back and checked the action, acted like old drinking buddies. We grabbed a table, pour down a few and discussed the staleness of this place and how he thought Manila partied so much harder.

I spoke of Seoul and a sweet little thing waiting for me and my current thoughts of bailing this trap and going to her. He said the flights were all booked to Manila, he had checked, or he would be a heading out too. Not enough on the party line here for him.

It got me to thinking though, time to bail. Go to where the climate is a bit cooler and the love, well, a bit warmer.

But, there they came, dancing goddesses of the night. Mohammed, he was shy, I was not. Will you, she would. We got down to it, as that chick over there at a table, Ming Shou, looked on.

Now me, I like to *boog-a-loo,* when I dance, I mean I do get down. Off goes my coat, unusual not the norm. Somehow the impending heat of this evening was coming down. I kept prodding Mohammed, finally he went for the sitting friend of my dancing babe.

"Why don't you slow down?" he asked.
"I can't," I answered, as the sweat poured from my now soaking wet hair.

Singapore, they were from Singapore. Funny Mohammed and I had just, unbeknownst to each other of course, flown up from there.

Dance a dance with a stranger. Dance a dance that equals a life. A moment lost is a moment gone and forever is too big of a word for me. So, kiss me in your reason, forgive me for all of my

42

lies. Move with me in fields of rhythm. Dance until the dance will dance no more.

The dancing evening proceeded. About closing time, in a blue oversized work shirt by the distant looks of things, Mimi, (the waitress), in ugly; red, big, valley girl sunglasses, she had come looking for me.

She moved a slicing beat over on the side of the disco floor. Me, I moved and grooved with Miss Singapore. No, dance for the employees. Yes, I know. I have heard it all before. Oh well. Your loss baby...

Closing time, going time, the S'pore babe promised to meet me in L.A. in one month. But, that's another story.

Mohammed none too happy, didn't get his claim to fame. I mean who goes to Dubai anyway? He wanted to get a hooker and take her to my room for he was staying at some cheap hotel. Fuck that.

Good night all-right, a kiss for a Singapore stranger. A kiss for a dream of hello to be lived a month away. Mimi, all she could do was smile as I sliced my way out-a-there and make excuses to her fellow employees as to her reason for her presence. Yeah, she must have really dug me.

I woke, day next, with the situation getting stale, with Mimi closing in, with love and illusion on other shores waiting, I made a telephone call. I got a plane to South Korea, *no problema,* First Class. I was gone. I was out-a-there. See you Taipei, see you another time.

CHAPTER 2
UP IN FLAMES

"So, what do you do with the paintings that you like?"
"I burn them."

Those words, they still ring in my ears as her memory comes to mind, as I write her tale, the little that I know of it.

It was an art opening at a museum. One of those scenes I occasionally go to and check out the action up on the walls and on two legs, as well. You never know what you will find...

The rafters ring with their silence now as I remember. What was it, maybe five years ago?

Art openings, especially here in L.A., are always full of those pompous, pseudo cool art archetypes, who continually claim to be bohemian in one regard or another and I have yet to see one who is what they have titled themselves. That is except for this one solitary case.

Solitary, I feel it. I sit here in it. I write in it. She lived it too. Her name... Well, is it really important? I don't know? But, maybe her story is. For a name, a reference point, I will call her Suzette.

*　　　*　　　*

As I stood there scope-ing the scene, art and otherwise, into my visionary field came to dwell a goddess from another plane.

Green, she wore green, the most mystical of colors. It was drab green: dull, olive. Her skirt, long and flowing, her top to match. Her hair long, almost merging into the fading distant auburn red of the neo-expressionist art piece which she stared into. I saw only her back and yet I knew.

It was one of those situations in which I forever wonder if I am approaching it for the impeding possibility of love or the necessary and completely programmed sensations of lust. I have come to philosophize about this issue far more as the years have continued. None-the-less, I moved in.

I stood behind her, slightly to her left, a degree to the right of the painting. There, I saw her face. White, it was very white—porcelain white.

I hadn't had the chance to plaster my, "Let's fall in love vibes," upon her, when she turned to move away and without really looking, walked directly into me. Is my presence so unimposing or was her interest in the painting so directed? I do not know?

Live the first kiss, alive in its own perfection, so our meeting was.

I, then and there, felt the impending destiny, the destiny of destruction. I should have listened more closely to my intuition. I did not.

"Oh, I'm sorry."
"No problem," I said.

We spent the rest of the evening together, viewing the statements of art hanging upon metal nails in the wall. We proceeded to discuss the realities of art and its purpose, there of and there for. I, at the time being of the firm belief that if an artist was a true artist, as opposed to simply a business-person, they would not exhibit and sell their creations at all. *Art for art sake.* Her definition was not far from mine.

She asked me,

"How much of your art do you really like?"
"Maybe half of it."
"Have you painted a lot?"
"Yes, a lot."
"What do you do with all the pieces?"
"Keep them here or there."
"Why do you paint?"
"I guess I seek forever. I attempt to grab onto eternity."

We both laughed. Then, I inquired,

"Have you painted a lot?"
"Yes, every day."
"Do you like what you paint?"
"No, almost never."
"What do you do with the paintings that you don't like then?"
"I don't really pay any attention; they just seem to disappear."
"So, what do you do with the paintings that you like?"
"I burn them."

Her responses to my questions pulses to this day in my mind, as does her perfection of her noted reality. Her answer(s) so much purer than mine. Freedom, she was the embodiment of artistic freedom.

*   *   *

There she was, a true artist. I have met so few. She, like I, believed that art was completed in the moment, not to be created over a period of days, weeks, months, or years. She unlike me, far more free. She held so little attachment to her art that post the creation of a piece had no real care what happened to it. During her bringing into being a piece of art, she could just walk away and forget it. She believed that if she never painted again, it would be no loss to herself or the world at large. Total art, she was so much more of an artist then I.

*   *   *

Days drift into nightmares of all the creativity that must be accomplished in the passive mind of this artist. Sometimes it really drives me mad; all the creation(s) left to create. Yet, time is only a boundary created by our own perceptions and I know it is I who desires to seek fame/fortune; the passions of a fool. Sometimes I even go into the mode of full-on creation and hermitize myself.

Solitary confinement, it has been passed off as the dream, the destiny of the artist, since the pages of history have been written.

Solitary, but not alone. Alone, but not solitary. Let them tell that to those who are alone—really alone. Those who the world has shut out, shut down. Some, like Suzette, could deal with it. Me, it drives insane.

Some try so hard for acceptance. Some realize that they will never achieve it, so seek it never more. Suzette, yes Suzette, she was like that.

A wondering child, lost and all alone. She never fit in, so she never tried to fit in.

Somehow, I always love the distant, the alone, the worldly losers, the separated due to artistic vision. Yes, I love them the most. I guess I like looking in a mirror.

*   *   *

I had not seen or heard from Suzette for several days. I had given her a few calls but to no answer on the telephone lines. Momentary dreamy dreariness in an artistic reclusive life. I cut her some slack though. *'Maybe just a re-treat,'* I thought.

*   *   *

Pull myself out. The alone was coming down way too hard. I went out, decided to go over and see what she, my only *pure-on* artist confidante, was up to.

She and I by this point, well we did go back a ways; maybe a year. I guess a little more. Time it does tick on. All a perception, remember.

As I drove in the direction of her abode, I remembered the gallery, the night we met. I remembered a comment that someone had made as Suzette and I walked about the place, feeling the abstract impressionistic energy of the paintings upon the wall. There was some guy, you know the real asshole type talking loud, saying that anyone could do this shit. It looks like a child's painting. The dude had finally gotten on my nerves and I said,

"Hey, if you don't like it, why did you come?"

"My wife made me come and this stuff is trash, anyone could do it! The artists just do it for the money!"

"If it is so easy, then why don't you do it?"

"I don't have any goddamn time to do this shit, but it is easy!"

"The obvious is easy," I said, "Copying landscapes or people, but a camera does that much better. To have the vision to create this, you need to be more than a camera. This is feeling, something a photograph can never capture."

"You are about as full of shit as this art," he says to me.

Now, don't piss me off *mutha' fucker*...

"Why don't you just crawl back into your fucking suburban life with your twenty-five-dollar Sears paintings and quit ruining the energy of the art and keep your idiot comments on art to your fucking self!"

Now let me put things this way. Those were a bit younger days. I didn't like what he said. I was about to take the loser out of the telephone book.

"Let the mindless be mindless,"

Suzette calmly interjects. What could a forty-year-old Neanderthal say to that. Suzette took my arm and pulled me away.

She always did have a calming effect over me.

For us, it was love. We had been very close since that night. She was my lover, my friend, my inspiration, at times even my enemy. But always, whatever emotion she touched off, it vibrated like the hand of a sorceress in my heart, in my soul.

I arrived at her apartment. It was an old square structure over in the Wilshire district. I had arrived with a bottle of, *'The Dom.'* I mean it had been a few days of self-reclusion and more than a few days since I had seen her last. Love, well it did seem to be eminent and passion, well passion is always a must.

I parked. I walked towards her building with visions of love, lust, momentary diversion, anything would do. As I began to get closer, I noticed that there was a note thumb tacked, (white thumb tacked), upon her white door.

As I got closer, I saw Sandy was scribed upon its face.

At the door, I removed it and began to read.

Dearest Sandy, it said. As I know it will be you who is reading this, for you are my only friend, the only one who ever comes over, I am forewarning you that it is better that you do not enter my apartment. I have chosen to end this life, and I do not wish you to see me dead.

The emotions swirled in me. It was like the feeling of love and how it hits you over the head. It was like the feeling of hurt or of anger, when you want to control something that you know that you can have no control over. My heart started pounding, my stomach went into knots, then it just all went numb. A lack of balance overtook me like my equilibrium had been pulled away. It was like my senses just shut down. I was in a haze; there was no feeling.

I could not feel my head. I could not feel my mind think. Time became slow.

Eventually, I sat the bottle of champagne down and continued to read.

This is a choice I have made. People like you and I are different from the world; apart from the people who lose their vision or never had any to begin with. We are people who live our visions but there is so few of us, Sandy. The world keeps moving farther and farther away from the artistic and soon there will be none left.

How I remember how she and I used to sit and at times cry because it was so hard for us to make our way in the world. Sometimes we would sit and discuss the games we had played that day, the way we acted to other people in order to be looked at as normal and acceptable.

She knew it, felt it, so much more than I. The difference, our difference… Me, give me some finances and I could play it off so much better than she. She was always distant, always removed, like a lone yellow sunflower in a vast green field grown atop a glacier.

We would speak of others, of the importance they placed upon their possessions, their jobs, their cars, their homes; all of their toys as we called them. It was so much more important to both of us to have someone who truly understood us. To move into the visionary mystic space together. To discuss the abstract, feel the unknown. It made the world livable.

Even though the prospect of our living the artistic mystic dream began to seem more-and-more impossible; we still had each other. Someone to go and focus with and still believe that there were some visionaries left.

I mean, look at Rimbaud, considered to be one of the world's great poets, but he stopped writing poetry at the age of nineteen and went and took a job in Africa. He was just like all the rest. An artist, perhaps in his youth—as most youths are less restrained, thus more creative. But, he came to believe that lie just like all the masses. We would never allow ourselves to do that, not Suzette and I.

We would hold each so tight at times when the world was way coming down on us. Though we both knew it held no answers, at least we had each other.

The note finished by saying,

This is not an excuse, not a plea, it is simply my choice, and I have the right to choose my death.

Suzette and I had talked about this fact several times and we both agreed. So much of life is pre-set for a person; where they are born, who their parents are, how they are raised. All of these things affect how they reacted to the physical, material, and spiritual worlds. With all of these factors already in place, pre-chosen, a person assuredly has the right to choose the time and method of their own demise.

*   *   *

I stood there on the steps of her apartment very confused. What should I do? What could I do?

Confusion plays deep games with the mind. It tells it what to do, how to do it. When, in fact, confusion is the worst boss of all. Believe it, it lies to you. Listen to it, it will destroy you.

Movement from nonexistence to false existence, on to the great abyss. Not much of a choice...

Suzette had suggested that if she were to kill herself that she would lay down on a canvas and slit her wrists. This would be her last work of art, her last artistic statement.

If I were, as I was, her only friend, then should it not be I who was to see this last creation?

Creation at the hands of destruction, sounds almost too Zen for words. But, then Zen is not words. Zen is feeling; the feeling of no feeling. The statement of no statement, which is the ultimate statement. Life and death, death and life. Movement into the no movement. Abstract reality, the saying of the perfect nothing. Nothing, which it all equals anyway.

If I did not go in, even in my now tearful confusion, I knew that if this, in fact, had been the case, if she had ended her life upon a canvas the paramedics, agents of the world, would have no understanding or appreciation for this final statement and would simply destroy it.

The obvious is simple. The physical is simple. The subtle, few will ever understand. I knew I had to go in.

I do not know if anyone can comprehend this without the experience, but try to imagine the intensity of having to walk into a place, an apartment, a room, where you know that there will be death awaiting your entrance—death meeting you at the door. There can be no lie in absolute truth.

I reached for my key, and for a moment, I hoped it was just a joke, just a method to make me see deeper into myself.

It is always hard to tell a person how to feel or how they should be in any given situation. To actually experience a moment though, that is so much more enlightening. Demonstration by action. I hoped it was only that.

As that thought crossed my mind, I realized how angry I would be if this were the case. For on the other side of the coin, who is so all knowing to think that they know what another person needs to experience or needs to know?

I began to pull the keys from my pocket and move them towards the lock. I dropped them because my hands had become full of sweat. But, for some reason, I continued to reach for the door handle with my other hand. I began to turn it. It was open. It was already unlocked.

*   *   *

What had seemed to be hours of my standing there was actually put into its proper context of seconds as the smell of death filled the air.

The smell of death, there is no way to describe it. I remember visiting a butcher shop in my youth; death permeated the air then, as well. I always thought of that anytime I wanted to eat meat.

This was worse though, human death. I knew this was no joke.

The ultimate test. The ultimate lesson. Movement into a space of no space. Movement into death.

I opened the door expecting to see a pool of blood upon a canvas but there she was. Suzette, laying on the couch, her right arm hung over and opened. A razorblade lay on the floor, next to her hand. Her skin, a whitish green.

The blood, the life fluid that had flowed through her veins, had now poured out of her precisely slit wrists and was stained, coagulated into her dress, onto the couch, upon the rug. As I walked closer, I saw how it had even found its way and blended with her hair, forming its beautiful texture into knots.

*   *   *

I guess I should have known it, known her; she was far too nonattached to her art to ever have the necessity to do something that I would do, make that stupid kind of forever, look at me statement—canvas and final life blood.

More than noticing the smell or her color, I saw a vague smile on her lips. She had found what she was looking for.

I have thought of this many times as I remember her. I had always believed that if one were to kill themself, that it would be best done with a large caliber gun. Something fast, something painless. For I always thought that if one were to kill themself with a knife or by taking pills that there would be that last moment when the body, when the mind tries to hold onto life and decides that it was not all that bad and not worth dying for.

It would be like waking from sleep when your mind wakes up and your body is still sleeping. That hell of a feeling of lack of, of no control. But then, it would be too late, for there would be no foot that you could shake, no hand to move to make yourself wake up. If there was any remaining desire, not that total release, then one would be trapped by the hands of hell for eternity.

She must have had no desire for this life left though. This fact has comforted and assured me when I have thought of her, that smile upon her deadly face.

*   *   *

I was standing there. I could feel myself crying the tears of numbness, the tears of the love that I had for her, they were running down my face.

Crying for who, it is always the question. Not for the dead, for they are free. It is the crying for our loss, the living's loss. The attachments of a fool. The fools that we are. We hold on. The dead do not.

I know now that it was not for her, not for her death that I was crying. For I could see that she had moved into a happier realm. It was for myself. For the loss of the closest friend I have ever known.

I stood there for a few minutes, but she was gone, there was nothing that I could do to bring her back. I left, closed the door, and made the necessary telephone calls.

I made the mistake of going back and letting the police speak with me, blame me, interrogate me, until I finally told them to fuck off and walked away.

There was no family to call. If Suzette had any, she never mentioned them to me. I was the sole survivor, *'Soul survivor.'*

Her possession added to little. I guess the apartment management handled them. Her body, I picked up the cremation ashes, released it in the divine mother ocean.

The world had won again but it was no achievement. A visionary was lost.

Time has passed as I sit here now writing her story. I feel the aloneness of my life. The constant battle I must fight to be who and what I am, who and what god and destiny had led me to be.

There is so little room in this world for artists or mystics. Never believe that they are revered. The name, the title may be, but the name, the title does not pay the rent.

The businessmen, they are the *czars* of this planet. If an artist or mystic cannot do it by the financial books, then they are damned to a life of art and of mysticism alone and broke.

Money is a fool's passion, but it sadly dominates this world.

Suzette made her choice to leave this ship of fools.

Energy flows to energy. And though I no longer have her physical presence, I have her memory. At times, I think that there was so much more art that she could have created, so much more that she could have given the world. But, the world is blind. There is no vision for art. There is only barely the vision to read stories about artists.

Her story/our story, it was short, not long lived. Her life, Suzette's life, the same—short.

For some, it just seems that they were not destine for this world, for this space, or for this time. The philosopher, the psychologist, or the fools may tell us that it is them, they who make themselves uncomfortable in their own skin. Me, well... I disagree with that. For they, the philosopher, the psychologist, or the fools; no, they are not the artists, not the dreamers. Their vantage point, well, it has no room for judgment, for they have no understanding.

So, I pray for people like Suzette, people like me, who have difficulty finding form in day-to-day hearsay living or nirvana in the mundane.

May this world someday find its truth. Though I doubt that it will. And, may it stop lying to itself that it honors the poet, the artist, the dreamer, for it does not. It only honors the entrepreneur who pushes and makes money from the vision of the fatal, the passion for the seers, and the love of those who know how to dream.

Good-bye Suzette, I will love you forever.

CHAPTER 3
ZERO ZERO

The punk rock era had met its maker. That is not to say that were not still many of the neo-punks around. And, it is true, new wave/mall wave had become quite acceptable in this modern-day western society, which decided to title this new music, "Dance orientated rock." But, those of us who were there at the inception had seen the change and made our own moves out.

L.A. was lost. There was not the rebellion of the sixty, the punk rock of the seventies. The city was empty, like a lost child emerging onto the horizon of fear. Nothing meant anything at all.

With the end of all eras, things change. The feelings, they just somehow become different. Things change, yes. But we, the alive, the living, still remain seeking, searching in the night, scouring the illusion, hunting for the dream and all it has to offer. For it is not time to die; not yet.

When there is no era, people struggle attempting to find meaning—they look to religion, to jobs, to friendships, to marriage. All of the things which promise, at best, temporary fulfillment but guarantee to stab you in the back like a bitch the moment you turn around.

Venchenzo and I, were two of the damned, still out swinging the bat, attempting to find enlightenment in the L.A. night.

This evening, the club scene was dead, none worth going to. We, in all our desireful desirelessness, longing for a distraction, sat at Venchenzo's Hollywood apartment, killed a few twelve packs, watched silent T.V., listened to old Thin Lizzy LPs, and basically hung out until we had finally pulled our shit together enough, at about 11:00 P.M., to bailed out of his crib and cruise onto the night.

We decided to hit the streets. We drove by the local liquor store and picked up two more sixers and a couple of short dogs. Short dogs, you know, the one-pint bottles. With the purchases in hand, back to the streets we went. Where the dead live and the dead-end people play.

We drove around Hollywood and basically continued our submersion into drunken stupor. A subject which we were both experts in.

We had time to kill, for on these nights of indifference the only calling was the dream of the very late night where there was always a bottle of Jack Daniels awaiting us—a societal freedom in a land so lost.

Hollywood is a weird place to cruise around. Well, it is a weird place anyway. It is a fashionable hang out. All the East L.A. and the Valley kids come to look, to pick up, and exhibit their wares. But, for people like Venchenzo and me, who had grown up in the filth of the city, it held little promise for us; simply the reality of a life we had been forced to live, forced to accept. A life that had taken its toll on the both of us and in the process taken hold of both of our souls.

The cops were out in full force checking the cruisers, checking the whores, and checking for IDs. But we sidestepped them and kept our driving down to the back streets—with an occasional gander at the fools dancing their dance on the boulevards. As we drove, we found time to pound down the sixers.

Time passed, as time tends to do. The cry of the night whispered softly in my ears, and I knew there was no way home and never an easy way out for two of the damned.

As we cruised the streets to nowhere fast, it came up upon the 2 A.M. hour. Ah, the arrival—for here in the city, this was our time on a Saturday night. All the tourists had returned to their suburban worlds and we, the lost, dug down deep and entered our realm—the after-hours world. We knew it was here, at this juncture, if there were any dreams still left to have, any passion still available to hold, it was here that it would to be found.

Now, at 2:00, there was this little more or less private club that would open. Private, for if you didn't know where it was, no one would tell you. But, it was placed on the verges of the lost inner city barrio wasteland—where we could haunt the sleep of all the indigenous winos, gang-bangers, and old Latinos who were certainty lost in their dreams.

Venchenzo and I pulled up about the same time as the owner was unlocking the place. The door opened, as the droves flooded in. We kicked back for a few in the car finished the last two brews.

I stashed the still unopened pints of Jack in my inner sport coat pockets. I mean, hey, the evening was young.

We strolled in—in all our pagan glory. As we settled down, scooping the situation, we immediately noticed there was a lot of new people roaming around; definitely more than usual for the lost late night. But, the Blues they were playing over the sound system, playing loud, and there was a lot of new faced babes in the room, so we were not complaining.

I cracked open a bottle of the Jack and kicked back a few hard shots. You know, to get in the mood.

I handed it to Venchenzo. He did the same.

It wasn't long before we noticed that these two babes were sitting over at the table where all the free after hours cheap two dollar a twelve-pack beer existed. They had their hands on a brew and their eyes on us—and the thought of lust, I have to admit, well it did cross my mind. So, over we cruise, and the rap began to be laid down.

As it turned out, all the new faces were the product of a nearby art college. I always wondered how you could grade art. But, these two young ladies had also come to our domain of the night via this school, so I didn't want to scare them off by becoming lost in the philosophizing department.

To accurately describe these women, is a bit hard, for I had begun to become quite inebriated by this point. But, the one I was putting my moves on, to the best of my recollection, had bushy red hair, was a bit plump, and had come to L.A. via a life of a child of a father in the military stationed in Hawaii. The other chick was dark, a bit plump herself, shorthaired, and from New Orleans.

"Would you like a beer," was inquired of me.
"Personally, I'd rather have a case of the crabs, than a case of that beer."

Yet, if the truth be known, there had been times in sobering desperation that I would partake of that bad, sorely on the cheap side, beverage.

Our conversation quickly moved as the Jack Daniels was passed around between the four of us. I begin to give them the rap. When they asked our ages, I was forty and that Venchenzo was forty-two. Now, the truth being, Venchenzo is two or three years younger than me, and I was twenty-three. But, the words continued, forming their own path, in their own abyss. Does a word mean anything anyway?

I begin telling them of Venchenzo and my involvement in Vietnam and all the gruesome stories that went along with it. I told them that Venchenzo couldn't talk as his tongue had been sliced out when he was in a POW camp. He hard stared at me, in laughing disbelief, that I would have come up with such a line. The chicks, becoming intoxicated themselves, believed it all: the age, Vietnam, and everything. In truth, Venchenzo and I were both way too young to have ever gone to Vietnam, militarily in the 1960s, 1970s war, that is. As all lies have their truth, truths also have their lies. I simply spilled out a divine offering to the goddess of the rap.

My words were moving good. I had saved Venchenzo from that fate.

As the ride continued, the sweet young red headed thing, who I never knew her name, was drinking right along with us. Her friend was sticking basically to slowly sipping the cheap beers. Fuck that, it gives me a hangover.

Women always amaze me, the ones that is, who claim to drink. For I have never met one who could back up her claim; two beers and they are out-a-there. But, this young red headed lady was slamming the Jack right along with us. I watched as her conditioned was deteriorating.

The moment of truth came as the moment of truth always does, for she had to hit the head, and I was to show her where it was. So, in she goes and in I go—and the rest will be recorded in the *Akashic Records* for eternity.

I laid one slob on her and she was immediately mine. We are in there, tongues touching tongues. My hands slipping her bra up. I was much too drunk to unfasten it. I begin licking her large boobs as my hand moved up her mini skirt, slipping down her panties.

She was wet, available, ready, and I wanted a taste of the goodies in her medicine chest. I slipped her up on the sink, pulled down my zipper and tried to shove my dick in. She said,

"It's locked," as I begin having troubles getting it in.
I said, "Well unlock that *mutha' fucker!*"

What she meant, I never really knew but finally I got it in and began the power pump.

I was not up to my usual pro status yet, the all-day alcohol had taken its toll and the truth being told, I wasn't all that much into her. I told her,

"You have to excuse me here; I'm flying half-mast."
She said,
"Oh if that's half mast, I wouldn't want to try it at full mast."

My ego soaring, my mind saying, "Yeah right." I slammed away as I kissed her and felt her tits. And, oh yes, that comment did make me full-on hard.

*   *   *

Now, this building that we were in, it was old. I mean old and run down. So, there was only

64

one bathroom and no lock on the door. People keep opening the door trying to use the head. This got a bit annoying to her, me I didn't give a fuck. But finally, after she kept complaining, I did unscrew the hot light bulb. Then, at least, those wishing to enter, realizing that they could not, well they didn't get the full-on show of my Love Pup in action.

One young lady did come in. I mean, hey, I understand, when you got to go you got to go.

I *pronto* realized that she was ever so fine, as she sat down to do her business. And, I was more than willing to dump my current engagement for her. I even suggested it to the newcomer who had entered my domain of love. My momentary mate, however, was not into that at all. So, I stood there fucking her on the sink and talking to the other chick as she was taking a piss.

She, the girl pissing, suggested that my friend and I go out on the couch in the other room, but I said, "No way, I might get lice out there."

We pumped for a while in private. She kept saying to me, "You scoundrel." Stupid word, I thought, what the fuck does that mean, "You scoundrel?" But, none-the-less, we went at it until I finally came. In my condition, I was amazed that I blew the cookies off at all.

Did my deed. So, I pulled it out, left her there on the sink, and headed out to see what my party bud Venchenzo was doing.

I told him about what I had been doing, though he already knew. And, he joking whispered to me,

"Oh man, you are my hero."

You remember, his tongue had been cut out.

65

We both laughed. Red eventually came out as I polished the last few shots of the Jack that Venchenzo had saved for me. So, now it was on to the last of the, now warm, cheap hang over beers. Fucked up, I didn't care anymore.

I slammed down one real quick and about that time the other babe had to hit the head. Now, I hated to be a cold monk to Venchenzo, and for the most part there is honor among thieves, but this evening led me to the bathroom. After her, I went. My only worry was, could I get the wild pup up again, so soon after my last ejaculation. Me, being in my drunken state and all...

The joke of the matter was, like there was no battle. These were way haveable art college students, and she did nothing to halt my advances. I was in no space to play games, so I went right for it. I started to lay some serious slobs on her. I could taste nicotine breath. Uck. I felt the breasts. Yeah, they were there. Dick was rising to the occasion, so I went for her crotch and notice that she had something tight around her genital region. I later realized this to be a girdle. I told her to pull that bad baby off.

Just as she started to, my young little red head must have realized what I was doing and into the bathroom she pounces and by my arm she yanks me out. Being the gentleman that I am, I just laughed and left.

Now, the two chicks went into the bathroom to talk. Looking at my watch and seeing it to be 4:30 A.M., I knew it was our chance to bail. So, even though Venchenzo didn't get any, he was so drunk he didn't really care anyway, and was ready to leave. So, out the door we go. We left, at the same time the chick who had been taking a piss as I fucked, left with her dude. She yelled out,

"See you in the bathroom."
I answered, "See you in my dreams baby."

Venchenzo headed over to my ride. Just as we were getting in, out came the two babes yelling,

"Where are you going."

I look at Venchenzo and ask,

"You want to fuck her tonight?"
He slurred, "No man, I'm too fucked up."

So, we drove away, as we laugh our way back to Venchenzo's crib.

I dropped him off and headed on drunkenly back down to Hermosa Beach. As I pull up to my place, I saw the ocean. As I opened my car door, I could hear it. The sun it was just coming up behind me. I got out of the car; my head was spinning and I knew that when I woke up I was going to have one fuck of a hangover.

Another kiss felt and unforgettable reality lived.

CHAPTER 4
BURMA

I had been in Burma a day or two and had jumped on up to Mandalay with the intention of seeing a few friends that I had made the last time around and just hanging out in the Southeast verging on the South Asian reign of the divine mother, *Burma Mata.*

I had arrived the night before, checked into my hotel, slid on over and had dinner at this tasty little restaurant I know. Kicked down a few Mandalay beers; quite good actually and rolled in about 9:30 P.M. or so. Most of the people of town long ago asleep.

The day, it was a new day, a moment cast into a civilization who desires no contact from the outside world; so says the government. The people, however, with western fashion and gossip magazines on the newsstands, dressed in their dhotis. The men with their modern hairstyles, the women with their *'do'* styled feathered back, say the opposite. But that, of course, is a matter left up to destiny, politics, and society. Three issues which few can change and fewer choose to question.

Post the breakfast, post a walk-up Mandalay hill, post a nap, out on the streets again...

I was walking down the street, it was maybe 2:30 P.M. or so, in the early afternoon, and I had the basic intention of going over to my friend Myint Myint Kyi's crib. She was a sweet young lady, twenty-eight at the time, who lived with her uncle and each day took the long bus ride to a pagoda far from the city where she would dutifully sit for two hours in meditation.

The meditation of escape. Ah, he is a dastardly fellow, who lures one into believing that they are accomplishing something, when in fact, well...

Sometimes I had gone with her. Taken the crowded bus ride far out of the city. The Burma buses not being made for a six foot one-inch-tall westerner. I had to crouch or bend over the entire ride. But, Myint Myint, she and I, that was a different time, another reality.

The early December day was warm, high eighties, but one could feel the winter coming on. Of course, winter in Burma is not quite winter at all. The humidity was a bit high, but I had found after a week or two in Southeast Asia the temperature or humidity doesn't really bother me anymore. You simply become accustomed to it.

I walked my way down the street. It was paved initially by the British, no doubt. People were everywhere: some walked, some rode their bicycles. And, the air, the air smelled like Burma, *Burma Mata.*

As I walked, out from this building with a restaurant sign, comes this young lady wearing a western style white tee shirt and a wraparound dhoti. Unusual dress for a woman in Mandalay. I hear, "Hello, Hello." It was obviously me who she was trying to contact. I stop, she walks up, "Peace," she says.

Now this is a very funny tradition in Burma. The first three English words people seem to learn is, hello, peace, and money. Now hello and money, I understand, where they get peace from, complete with the two-finger sign, is way far beyond me.

She comes up,

"You want food?"
"No thanks."

Of course, this is always my initial reaction to people's offerings.

"Have you eaten today?"
"Not since this morning."
"Come on, come on," as she grabs my arm and pulls me in.

Well, what an invitation. How could I refuse?

So, in we go. It was a house type structure; two story. Over to my left, as we walked through the door, I noticed a couple of couches in a receiving room type setting. To my right, in a much larger room, were wooden tables and chairs.

She sits me down under the ceiling fan at a wooden table, sprouting four wooden chairs, and goes off to get me some food, I surmised. I looked around and I was the only one in there. *'No wonder she was trying to hustle up business,'* I thought. But, I could not help but wonder what type of food I would get in a restaurant with no customers.

I sat and looked out the open windows. They had no glass, simply an opening which had wooden shutters that could be closed in the rain or in the night. If I kept my head turned a bit, I had a good view of the street and the people walking by.

The people, content to focus on their own predicament, not noticing the watchful eye of a western dude observing their every movement and wondering about their every thought as they passed. But, I was inside and they were out.

The lady soon came back with a small woven basket filled with what looked to be potato chip type things. But they were a bit larger, a bit whiter. Almost like the size of a small *chapatti*, the Asian version of a *tortilla*. I asked her what they were, for I had never seen anything like them in Burma before. She appeared not to quite understand what I had asked.

What was more striking than the basket of Burmese potato chips was that the girl had returned without the bottom half of her clothing. The tee shirt she wore was a bit long and it covered her nicely, but something obviously was in the works.

I sat there for a moment. My vision, I believe, a bit transfixed on her legs. My thought, "Fuck," I wonder what I have gotten myself into this time.

I had a chip or two and then yes, I had called it. It was not going to be a, *'let's just let me have chow session'*. She lifted up her tee shirt a bit, exposing an off purple faded pair of underwear and her belly button. She then moved into a bit of a dance. I was thinking, *'Un-huh.'*

She danced around moving her belly almost like a belly dancer but not quite so precise or proficient. I sat there more than a bit intrigued as her body swayed only a bit, she let her stomach do most of the action. Her tee shirt held up by her hands, just under her breasts.

As she moved, she made a comment quite casually,

"You know, I'm a virgin."

'Hum,' I thought to myself. *'Now one way or the other this is quite interesting.'*

Either she takes me for a fool and simply wants an American love stallion who will take her home to mommy in the good old U.S. of A or maybe, just maybe, she is a virgin. A commodity which no doubt is for sale at a price, a very high price. Or even and/or perhaps she is one of those flirty women who needs male attention to the *max-a-mum* and goes to all possible lengths to get it. A Burmese P.T., *'prick teaser.'* Make your choice from one of the above.

At any rate, there I was. I laughed at myself, as I often do, with the situations I get into. I thought it was funny that all I had planned was to visit a friend and maybe do a little cultural observation, but here I was, being danced to by a Burmese Goddess. Illusion by any other name... Well, maybe this is cultural observation.

Soon, she stopped the dance, grabbed my hand, pulled me from the chair upon which I sat and walked me to the left side of the dwelling, passing the two couches in the receiving room. One was funky red, the other faded brown. I said, "Hey, what about lunch," realizing that I had probably walked into a den of iniquity. I mean, after all the only thing I had in mind was a bite to eat, but up the stairs we went.

Now, I am not one who is easily taken in. My *naiveté* wore away long ago on the streets of Hollywood. Nor am I one to casually go to places I am not familiar with, such as upstairs in a house in Mandalay. But, I said to myself as we approached the top of the stairs, *'Come-on, this is Burma and the dudes, little and weak as they are, are no threat to you—a bad street fighting dude from L.A. And* *hey, no one has any guns here. And, if the best hotel in Rangoon, the capitol of Burma, is priced at only $25.00 U.S. a night, how much can a whore cost you?'*

So, we strutted up the wooden stairs. Walked down the wooden painted white hall to a wooden room about mid-house, and in we went. I mean how could I say, "No."

The room was not so big, not so small. The only furniture in it was an end table and a bed which she led me over to sit upon with her. Not exactly a bed really, it was wooden and framed from the wall, with a type of sheeted pad upon it. My thoughts and/or questions of her possible virginity were fading rapidly.

She began to talk in broken English about Burma. She said that Burma had disappointed her, so she didn't care if she disappointed Burma. *'Interesting premise,'* I thought. She asked of America. She had never heard of Los Angeles but knew of California.

We sat and talked for a time about life and love and god and things in general. I thought it was all heading to the basic, you know what.

After a time, she got up and said that she had to go for a few minutes and to wait for her. So, I kicked back, thinking she had to go hit the outhouse of a head or something. Again, not so cool. I mean, my hotel crib came complete with a real, as opposed to unreal, bathroom. Not a great one, but it existed in actuality, none-the-less.

Two minutes turned into five and five to ten. I said, "Well fuck this." So, I bailed out of the room and headed downstairs. Surprisingly, there were a few people there now, but no sign of my new friend named, Pa Noon.

On the red couch sat a man, a black man. I only mention his race because this was, in fact, quite a rarity to find a black man in Burma. He looked to be British by his attire.

I stood there looking around and he said to me, "Who are you with?"

By the way he spoke, I knew he was, in fact, British.

"Pa Noon," I answered.

He said, as if surprised, "Very expensive."

Well, there they went, all the illusions I had were shattered. This place was indeed a whorehouse. I had thought, almost hoped; well call me a romantic, I had almost wished it was not.

When it all hit me, the whole situation became quite surprising. I mean there I was in a whorehouse in Mandalay, Burma. I had never before seen a *house of ill repute* in Burma. The government being so strict and all. Once I had bumped into a couple of hookers who had taken their style right off the street of the Pat Pong in Bangkok. But, I had never encountered a brothel, let alone even heard of one here.

A bit dumbfounded, I sat down with the Soul Bro and we rap'd a bit. He wore black slacks, a cotton print shirt, and wired rimmed glasses. There was a dude sitting on the other couch, looked to be German. He sat there and didn't say a word as we spoke.

As we sat there talking about America, the U.K., Burma, how he worked for an oil company over Thailand way, and life and situations in general, he throws in the comment, "Virgins must be expensive."

Now, was he referring to Pa Noon? Maybe he had heard the con, too. And what did he mean by expensive? I mean in a country where one could live like a king for a hundred dollars a month…

Anyway, my mind lost itself in the complexity of the question, the uncertainty of the unknown. I sat there, wondering. I mean, fuck, who knows, maybe he even had gotten taken upstairs for the few minutes of nothing.

Pa Noon soon walked up. She still had the same tee shirt on but now had re-covered her bottom half with her dhoti. She said nothing but simply grabbed me by the hand again and began to lead me up the stairs once more. I nodded, "See you later," to the Burma *bro-ham* and went along quietly. I felt a bit like a puppy dog as Pa Noon pulled me along.

Just as I was asking her where she had gone, we meet this guy halfway up the stairs. He is dressed in a cheap blue two-piece suit, (a suit, an unusual commodity for a native Burman), and begins saying something in Burmese to Pa Noon. I have a very rudimentary knowledge of the language, but I could not understand at all what he had said.

He then looked at me and told me that I must leave my bag with him. My bag, as he referred to it, is what I carry my cameras in. And, while traveling and often times otherwise, I have it/them with me. I mean one can never know when that perfect picture will present itself. The moment in time where you can isolate the singular instant and hold its soul transfixed for eternity.

I said, "No way, Jose, these are my cameras."

It went back and forth and he insisted that I must leave them downstairs. I told him that I had them upstairs a few minutes earlier and they had brought no one any harm. But, this just pissed him off and it continued.

Now Burma is an interesting country. I think that there is no other place in Southeast Asia where the people who speak English do so with such fluency. And, the number that do so speak it, percentage wise, is quite high. Obviously due to the British Empire and the missionaries and all their lingering foolish effects, etc.

Finally, I conceded and gave him my bag after repeated assurances that it would be okay. Normally, there is no way that I would have backed my guns down, but the situation and the curiosity of and for Pa Noon, it was so intense. I had not looked for it, nor even desired it, but there it was, and it was so crazy that I had to check it out. As in all cases, you have got to live things out if you want to experience anything.

Down the hall we continue, this time we headed past the first room we were in for the rear part of the house where the roof of the first floor becomes the balcony of the second. We sat there outside as the evening slowly crept up on us and the air began to cool.

I looked at Pa Noon, studying her face, her movements, her energy. She had golden dark skin, black hair that was almost to her shoulders, and the high cheekbones so commonly found among the people of Burma. I listened as she spoke. I watched the movements of her body, obviously not the movements of a virgin but those of a more than partially experienced Southeast Asian whore. But, that was alright, too. She was nice. I liked her. I do seem to have a certain affinity for whores.

As twilight came on, she looked at me and said,

"I don't want to fuck you, Okay? I don't like you."

Those words rang in my ears and though I could see in her face the total opposite; that she did in fact like me a lot, and that is why she said what she had said. My natural sense of pain and emotion into play.

But, I mean hey, *'If they don't want to know that, forget 'em.'*

So, we stood up and she led me back to the upstairs room that we had initially been in. She told me to wait.

"How long," I asked.
"Just a few minutes, really."

Now, this waiting stuff was getting to be bullshit on the serious side. But, I waited.

In my mind, I was not sure what to expect; post the initial invitation, post the rejection. I knew one thing though, that a few minutes were all it was going to be and then I was out-a-there. I mean that playing game shit gets old fast, real fast.

I put in about twenty very long minutes, more than I had expected to. Finally, I said, "Well fuck this," out loud again. I decided to head downstairs, claim my camera bag, and go surprise my friend as I had initially planned.

As I walked down the stairs, I heard voices and as I reached the bottom, I looked into the restaurant section and there were now about ten people sitting at tables. They were all Burmese or Burmans as they prefer. I looked for my black friend, but he nor the Garman dude were anywhere to be seen. I surmised that they apparently were upstairs, a-partying.

I checked out the room there she was, Pa Noon. Strategically, she had placed herself in the company of about three men. She now had put a loose-fitting shirt over her tee shirt and had applied some make up.

Normally, a situation as such would have caused me just to leave. My camera bag, however, was not in hand, and more than that, I was a bit pissed.

I walked right over to her, and though no words were spoken, I looked directly into her eyes, and we both completely understood the dance, the game, and each other. I was in no mood to fuck around.

She—she was the whore who didn't want to be a whore, bound unsparingly by the lies in her own truths. *Me*—well I was the dreamer, the lover of experience, wine, women, and song; not necessarily in that order. She was cast in a world that offered absolutely no way out. Me, I was lost in the endless search for a perfection that has long been destroyed by time, life, and modern man. Both of us were trapped in a fool's game, a fool's passion. I was in no mood to perpetuate the illusion any further.

This time, I grabbed her hand and back up the stairs we went. We enter the room and I lay her down on the bed. No times for playing games. I lifted up her sari type dress, pulled down her light purple colored faded underwear and exposed her partially hair covered beaver. I put my hand on it. On to the tender zone I began to make finger movements.

For a moment, the thought went through my mind to whip out my bad pup and do the full-on power pike driver, cum real quick, and get the fuck out-a-there. I mean one of those total use the *ho* to the max, make them feel like shit, like a real whore, type situations.

There we were, a dance; brought on by the promise of lunch. Something that I had not yet even received. Us and the allure of love, glanced at in the eyes of Burma, *Burma Mata.*

Given to the lie. Given to be stolen away. Lost in a moment of a fool's passion for something that never was and never could be again.

I looked at her and lifted myself up. I stretched out my right hand to her left hand and pulled her up from her lying position. I asked her if she would like to go and take a walk. She smiled, pulled up her underwear and said that she didn't know if she could.

Just as I was about to ask what she meant, there was a knock on the door. The dude in the two-piece suit came in and they began to speak in Burmese. They seemed to be arguing. He then looked at me and said that I would have to leave. I asked, why. He just said that I must.

I began to get mega pissed at this point. I never did like being told what to do even if it was the little pimp's whorehouse and his country.

It went around and around for a bit. I watched the guy reach into his pocket. I knew what he was going to do. Had I wanted to take him down easily I would have done it then, but out comes this silver knife, which he had to open. I mean, what a fucking idiot, pulling out a knife and having to open it. Anywhere else, they would just pull out a *gat* and blow you away.

He obviously thought that I would be scared. If he had only known how many times that I had taken much bigger knives away from much bigger men than he and given them back to their owners the hard way, he might have thought differently.

Knives, guns, cool cars, and all that kind of shit, are all nothing but penis extensions to men whether they be Burman, American, or whatever who have no *huevos* inside. I mean, it makes one feel like they have so much fucking power, so much control. Life in all its temporary-ness. And power it is so fleeting. I love it, watching the fools who feel they are controlling the situation but in fact are the ones who are being controlled.

I was just at the point of saying fuck it all and leaving. I mean, this was their melodrama, not mine. They continued to argue in Burmese and I heard Pa Noon mention my bag. I said,

"Damn right, where the fuck is my bag, anyway?"

The guy pretended to know nothing about it.

Time to stop fucking with me. I angrily told the dick that I was not going anywhere without my camera bag. The dude finally caught my vibes and said that he would get it for me if I promised to leave. "Leave. Fine with me, *mutha' fucker."* I was in the middle of a situation that I had no desire to be in, just give me my fucking bag and I would be out-a-there.

As I walked from the door, I looked back and saw tears coming to Pa Noon's eyes. Tears for the life she had not chosen. Tears for the life that had chosen her. Deeply lost in the powerlessness of a power-full man. At least so he thought.

She was tied by the ropes of destiny and the desires of the gods that we so seldom can make understand and virtually never convince to change our fate. As the man closed the door behind me, I thought that I would never see her again.

We began to walk down the stairs, the man in front of me. He still held onto the open knife. I thought, *'What a stupid fuck, I could cold-cock the bastard and he would never know what hit him; letting me walk in back of him like that.'* But, I walked on. My hands were not clinched in fists, my hands and my mind were open. I wondered about the whole purpose of this seemingly purposeless situation.

At the bottom of the stairs, I again asked the guy why I had to leave. It went back and forth for a few minutes until he finally said that if I really wanted her that bad, I would have to pay more money. I guess he thought I had already paid the standard rate, whatever that was. Bad businessman.

I asked, "How much?" "Fifty khat." *'Small change,'* I thought. So, I laid him the money and back up the stairs I went.

Into the room, there was Pa Noon extremely happy to see me again. I told her the story in brief and asked, if she would like to go for the previously discussed walk. Her only answer was, "Can I fuck you?"

By this point I was in more than a boiling mood and in no disposition to fuck, make love, or any of those things of or in between.

"Walk?" I asked.
"Okay, if I can."
"Oh, you can," I answered.

Down the stairs I once again traversed. This time hand-in-hand with Pa Noon. I see the main pimp on the wooden porch and notice there in the corner is my confiscated bag, along with a few others. I went right over to my bag and picked it up. The dude asked where I thought we were going.

"Out," I said.
"No, No!" he muttered as he grabbed my arm.
"Let go of my arm."
"No, no, you go."
"Listen asshole; let go my fucking arm!"

He didn't let go of my arm, his mistake.

At this point I was in no mood to play anymore games, so I broke his hold, shoved him back and delivered a stepping side kick straight to his face. This put his lights out pronto.

I looked around me; ready. No one else even attempted a movement. They just sat or stood there and stared in disbelief.

As I look in retrospect, the Burma pimp was probably only trying to protect his merchandise, us being the bad foreigners and all. But youth, power, control, penis extenders drive us foolishly into all kinds of frenzies. I am no exception at times. A fool and his power...

Off the porch, camera bag and Pa Noon in hand, down the street in Mandalay we walk.

Back at my hotel that night I did not sleep much, expecting at any minute a bunch of local guys to come busting in and I would have to kick some serious ass. Pa Noon on the other hand, quietly, securely slept. By daybreak though, I thought it was strange, no one had come.

After discussing the issue with Pa Noon and her having no desire to return to the house of ill repute, I decided the best thing for both of us to do was *Get-Out-a-Dodge*. I went to the Tourist Burma office which was located in the hotel. The only place, in fact, where one can buy air tickets. Luckily, two seats were available. So off to the airport, we were bound for the capitol, Rangoon.

We sat waiting at the excuse of an airport. I admit doing a little sweating, not just from the heat, but the thought that there I was kidnapping a whore from her main man. And, I could not have just quietly stolen her, I had to ace her pimp in the process.

As the previous night had passed to no confrontation, I worried as to the local police view of the issue. But, the plane landed, picked us up, almost on schedule—very unusual for Burma, and we flew away.

Pa Noon had obviously never flown before, through the whole flight she held on tight. As the air below us spread to distant strands of suchness, I have to admit that I gloated into dreams and fantasies of where her and I might go together and what new love we may find.

We landed in Rangoon and to the hotel we went. An old colonial British structure that once inside one feels like you could be living a hundred years ago.

I knew one of the receptionists, intimately, if you catch my drift. So, there was no problem getting a room.

The next few days went by with us just hanging out, talking, learning, and taking walks in what was a small backward city to me, but a metropolis to her. We made love like we were sixteen-year old's—engulfed in a newness, a love never before felt. A love we believed would last forever. A love, like all loves based in lust—that never could.

On the third day of our stay in Rangoon, Pa Noon said that she knew where some friends of hers lived. She said she had memorized the address from letters they had exchanged and that she would like to go and visit with them if I didn't mind. Of course, I did not.

Off she went in a taxi that I gave her money for. I spent the day in the bazaar and going to pagodas where neon lights surrounded the head of Siddhartha Guatama, the Buddha. They flashed their waves of *nirvana* on and off.

Returning to the hotel in the late afternoon, she still had not come back. So, I laid out, took a nap, had a few *cervezas* in the hotel bar and waited. At about 8:00 P.M. she rolled in. Not talking much, she went and took a shower.

That night at dinner, she spoke of how much she liked Rangoon and how the people, especially the men, were so nice. Well, as I sat there reading between the lines, it did answer my question. Her friends, obviously hookers. Friendly people, well when a person has a particular one-pointed reason to be friend; sure they are… When I asked her what she had done, the conversation was naturally avoided.

My seven-day tourist visa had run its course. Seven days, such a short time for a country like Burma. But, that is all the government allows at one visit.

Pa Noon and I drifted apart. She had stayed out. Me, I moved in. Moved into the space, the space between my own lines. Lost in a drama of a fool's moves in his own movie, where a whore who I had loved, was forced by the gods, by destiny, and by years of programming to be nothing more than a whore. I knew it would be impossible to un-make what had long ago been made.

As it had been before, as it was to be again.

So, I lived a moment with her. She lived a moment with me—just a moment with a man who wasn't after only her pussy. But, then destiny's call was far too strong, she went *back to the chain gang.*

She moved her way, I moved mine; to the airport and my plane which was nine hours late. I headed back for Bangkok, my main town. Where it is clear who the whores are, who the virgins are, and what they did and did not want and more or less what it takes to get IT.

CHAPTER 5
NICHOLETTE MARCELINE

Well, it had been a month, in fact exactly one month to the day, that I had been hanging out, living on and off with, and in general wasting a lot of time with this sweet little American born Japanese girl named Michelle.

It wasn't that she wasn't nice enough, but the spending five or six hours in bed after we would wake up and living all this non-productive time with her had just gotten a bit old. My wheels had begun to spin in her presence, no new knowledge was being gained, paintings were not being painted, or music played. I had begun to search for a way out.

It was Monday, about 2:30 A.M., the telephone rang. As it rang, I thought, I felt, *'Ah, this must be one of my people, the people lost in the late night.'* It rang again, up off the couch to answer it, "Hello." No answer. I heard the sound of two taps. "Hello." Nothing. Two taps, they came again.

It came over me. It hit me like the taps upon the telephone—a rolling pin across the head. What was it now two, maybe three, no four years. The tapping, the telephone, the silence, the beauty of the moment where there was nothing that could, that would be said. Nicholette Marceline, ah it must be Nicholette Marceline.

I guess she needs a little bit of an introduction at this point…

Nicholette Marceline, this beautiful Indonesian girl with eyes that pierced my soul and skin the color of the misty caramel night. She was one of those loves that though you separate, the world pulls you apart, you never, ever, ever stop loving or stop caring about.

The tap on the telephone, I could feel the vibrations in the air, she was asking me, "Do you remember me?" I wanted to tell her, "Yes, I remember you." "Yes, I still love you." I wanted to tell her but due to life, destiny, karma, and the world, beautiful Nicholette Marceline was quite one hundred percent deaf and could not speak a word.

Even when we were close; yes, the years had now gone by, I never had one of those machines that a deaf person could type their message over the telephone lines.

When there was no one on her side to translate her message to me, she would just tap. In fact, we had a bit of a Morse Code. As the taps came over the line, I struggled to remember. I could not remember. What a joke, for it was I who was a Boy Scout; Senior Patrol Leader—still have the diploma.

In one ear came the taps, in my other Michelle saying, "Who is it? Why do you have a smile on your face? Who is it!"

From the taps I believed that she was saying to meet her at 4:00 A.M. I had hoped that was it for if it were not, I had no way of re-contacting her.

The last few years had been pretty crazy, a lot had gone on, and I was not sure of what had become of her. I hoped I was getting that secret code straight.

My mind flashed as it often did, way back when, when we would communicate on the telephone lines: how she felt, what she felt; for she had no idea, no confirmation as to whether I was listening on the other end of the old *co-ax* or not.

My answering machine would pick it up sometimes, some of those times in the distant past.

Sometimes I could still make the *pow-wow*. Sometimes I know she waited for my no-show.

She never complained. Somehow what we had was all so much deeper than all of that; show, no show, to be or not to be, see or see you later. Maybe she felt it, maybe her intuition was strong; shoved into motion by her other senses being shut down, not up to modern standards. I really do not know, I can only speculate.

There were three quick taps. The three taps, "Goodbye." I hung up the telephone, Michelle quickly,

"Who was that?"
"Just an old friend."
"It was another girl, wasn't it?"
"Maybe."
"Why didn't you tell her that you had a new girlfriend now?"
"Because my words would have made no difference."

Ah women, how they love to love, put the chains of love around you so tight in the late night; forever. Forever, speak to me of forever. Forever, I never understood that word.

"Why didn't you tell her that you were spoken for?"
"I'm spoken for?" I ask.
"Yes!"

Wrong words to say, baby. Babes, they are funny, you know. I have only met a few who were different, but it seems any woman by the time they turn twenty-one they begin to think seriously about getting married. Those who are twenty-three and still not committed begin to worry big time. By this point they are grabbing onto the first average adult male that comes along. Michelle was way—into this mode and direction. But let's face facts here, I am hardly an average male and marriage, well fuck that. I am just not the marriageable kind.

You know, but this marriage consciousness seems to permeate all women. Why, I always wonder? I mean, relationships are just not like they are on T.V.

This geared up for marriage shit is especially true with women who have been former sluts, or the *there-abouts*. Michelle being the perfect example. I mean, their logic always is, they have had their share and now make the excuse that they were always looking for love and this dude or that dude did them wrong. And now, dick-list in tow, they are ready to settle down. But I mean, who-the-fuck wants to marry a former slut anyway? There are too many old situations that you would probably have to run into—fist first, if you catch my meaning. And, I just don't' fucking need that type of aggravation. And, I do not know what it is, but this slut shit seems to be mega common in terms of the American born Asian chicks.

Now call me not a modern or self-actualized sort of guy. Because in truth, I am not either: neither, either/or; of that type, of those things. I mean, I just don't dig it, don't go that route of, "Hey, let's hang out with my old main squeeze, etc." Once a dick has been planted, that is previously owned turf. So, say I am animalistic, call me insecure, but fuck all that. What is, is; what wasn't, never was, and what is mine is only mine.

Anyway, I know I am getting off the track here, the story to be told... Back to the center.

Michelle, that was the case in point of her, a former slut, twenty-three, looking full-on for that band of gold.

But, as I told her, *"A slut, like a rose, by any other name, is still a..."*

She had grabbed on tight though, tied herself to me. Jumped into my mystic daydream and here lies the problem.

Another woman, another chance in the dance. She saw a man, but she never saw me. My life, my lifestyle: a new and different way of thinking, a new and different way of living—of viewing life. She saw it, as others had before. She became engulfed in it, wanted to hold on to it, to me. Lose her-self in the dream. But, as all those from a distance—watching only the screen of the melodrama of life, it can be observed by them. Seen, but never touched.

But, soon the questions began to come, I had watched them come to view before,

"Why don't you get a job?"
"Why don't you start dressing, looking like everyone else?"

This is the stage we were at, Michelle, she and I. The let's settle down and slip into the mundane stage. But, fuck the mundane. The mundane is boring. And, there certainly is no art living there.

As said, I was looking for a way out. *Exit, stage left.*

"Who was it," again she asked.
"Nicholette Marceline."
"Then, it was a girl!"

"Yes, it was. But not just a girl."
"Oh, so you loved her! Why didn't you tell me about her?"
"It's a long story."
"But you love me, remember?"
"I am finding that hard to remember."

At this point, she grabs me and kisses me, then begins to take off my clothes.

"I'll remind you," she said with all that bullshit love in her Asian eyes.
"Ah, Maya Devi," I said.

This is what I often called her, Maya Devi.

"I am not an illusion. I wish you would quit calling me that."
"You're holding me back," I said. "Anyway, I have to go."
"Go, where to see her? No way!"
"Yes, there is a lot of ways."
"Then you can forget about me."
"I have been trying to do that for the last several days."

So, with that, she bailed for the door, slammed it and was gone. Ah freedom, it does taste so sweet.
Yes, I knew that I would get the typical, "Why don't you love me," telephone calls. The threats of suicide. The eventual banging on my door, that she was famous for doing. But the step, my step, it had been taken.
Another move into the night, stepping off to nowhere fast. The place where illusion, it is quickly

lost and the truth, it becomes unveiled. Knowledge gained here is knowledge kept deep.

I re-buttoned my shirt, from Michelle's vain attempts. I headed for the door; outside, I locked it. Got into my bad little black '64 Porsche 356 SC, I was out-a-there.

Nicholette Marceline and I, whenever we would meet in the late night, we would do so at this little greasy hamburger stand over on Virgil and Santa Monica Boulevard in East Hollywood, *'Jay's'*. Though I could only at best guess that is where she had intended our meeting to take place; it was, *how-you-say,* our place.

It was unclean and unsafe. I loved it. And, though our destinies had been barely saved there many times, it was a step into the violent night. A place where only the strong, or the fools, can survive.

I drove, listened to the radio, remembering her. Remembering our times together. It had been a long time, a lot of change had come and gone. I wondered who and what she had become.

Getting there maybe half an hour early, I sat in my ride awhile listening some more to the late-night radio. Then, I went up and ordered a double chili cheeseburger.

I sat there eating, reflecting how I had known her at a very different time, a different space of life. A time when I was much less cynical. A time when I didn't give people my opinion and just simply let them be who they were, who they wanted to be. As I sat there thinking, I realized that perhaps one of the impetuses of my change had been her.

Nicholette Marceline was a more than beautiful girl and though she had grown up in the suburbs of L.A., the night had pierced her soul. She became one of those, like myself, with that knowledge of the streets. That destiny that sinks in so deeply into the heart that you can never leave it. *The love of the last.*

Nicholette Marceline had taken the pains of this life and the knowledge of the nights, with all its eminence of death, one step farther than I wished that she would have gone. For you see, she was quite a hardened junky.

And *The Dog, The Chinaman;* he is an evil master.

I sat there realizing that was probably what had separated us and had made me wearier, less trusting, and accepting. From there, it had all been downhill.

It kept coming to my mind that I hoped it was in fact her who had called and not just a sorry joke of destiny—a faulty telephone line. I hoped that this was where we were, in fact, suppose to meet. Where her tapping hand had hoped to lead me to. The paranoia began to set in...

I began talking to this obvious wetback of a Mexican dude, who had planted himself next to me at the food-serving bar. He was quite amused at the fact that I continued to refer to myself as a *pinchie weto* and the occasional local Santa Monica Boulevard faggot love punk as *pinchie maricones.*

Out of the corner of my eye, in my peripheral vision sight, I see the shadow of what appears to be the silhouette of a woman driving a more than a few years old Japanese pickup truck. I looked, I watched closely.

The seconds rapped, lost to eternity, waiting. Waiting for the moment of motion.

The truck pulled up to the curb. The door opened. Out she stepped. I looked at my watch, she was three minutes early.

There she was, the same beautiful woman: long black hair, dressed in jeans, tennis shoes, and a tee shirt. Complete, with a look of mysticism in her eyes.

I rose from my stool, walked gently, softly, slowly over to meet her.

We hugged. As I pulled away. I saw the tears form in her eyes. One more tear lost to this pagan night of the streets with no meaning and no one to catch it.

I looked deeply at her and with my right hand I told her I sign language that I loved her very much. She pointed to herself, indicating that she loved me too.

Our communication had always been a funny one, though she could read lips and had taught me some sign language; and, of course, there was always the handy pen and paper...

In fact, stashed somewhere, I have in a box just about every note she ever wrote to me. But, beyond all of that, we didn't really need physical communication. It is hard to explain but it is something that has happened with no other person in my life. We could communicate; understand each other with our eyes, with feelings, call it intuition if you will.

Somewhere though, all this communication had become lost for us. Somewhere in the moments of the needle in her arm or my running to Asia, we had moved apart. Why? I always wondered.

I asked her, if she wanted something to eat. She just gave the thumbs down. At that moment, I stopped wondering why I had never run into her, at

94

this hamburger stand, over the years. As I would often go there, late in the L.A. night.

She motioned to come on and so into her truck I got. As I did, I noticed that she has this killer stereo system in there. I had to laugh, as she wouldn't have even known if it was on full blast.

Off we drove into the night. A silent moment, lost to the sound of the truck and the screams of the horrified streets.

She drove a few minutes and then pulled over and stopped. She grabbed a pad of paper. She wrote down that she didn't like that place anymore and that she was glad to see me again.

She wrote, it had been a long time and that she had hoped it was I who she had contacted and that I had picked up the telephone.

I stopped her writing and said,

"Here we are. It is good to be with you again."
"You too," she motioned.

We sat there silently conversing for a time, ended up driving back towards the beach, which we walked on as the sun rose behind us in the eastern sky.

She leaned over to me and asked me in sign language,

"Does it still sound the same?"
"The same, but always different," I answered.

She smiled and signed that it felt the same to her.

I then realized something that I had never taken the time to understand; that she could obviously feel the vibrations of the sea, the movement in her feet.

Mostly, it was good to be walking arm in arm with her again. Feeling each other, knowing that we knew one another, but yet, it all felt so new.

Eventually, we drove back towards the city as the morning go-to-work traffic grew. Ah, the great American wet dream, waste of time, pass the time; a job. No-thank-you.

As we approached Hollywood, she asked me if I wanted to go over to her place. Sure, and that is where we ended up.

It was a loft style place, one story, probably an old factory of some sort off of Santa Monica Boulevard. It was old and brick and big and nice. It suits you, I told her, as we walked in.

I went over and sat down on a pillow for there was no real furniture. She headed straight for the bathroom after picking up something in the corner by her refrigerator.

I sat there studying the brick walls, the lack of furniture, the two windows at one end of the place and no others. It was large, a large place, large enough for two. Yet, there she was, this beautiful dancer of the night living there alone. All those feelings of love had returned. But, she had obviously gone to shoot up.

I sat there calculating, it was almost 8:00 A.M., so she probably had popped the arm four hours back, just before meeting me. That meant she had a pretty strong habit going.

The monkey paw on the back, the monkey was too large. Bigger than her, definitely bigger than me. Walking a tight rope into infinity, into abyss, into death, into the night.

It was like being stabbed in the stomach as I sat there. All those old feelings of love that had just poured into me, maybe even more than I had chosen to remember. Maybe even more than before. Maybe even more than I ever let myself believe. And there she was off in the bathroom, *dogging down,* shooting up. It was a killer, the killer I had tried to forget. The love and the agony. In love with a junky.

I sat there thinking what could I do, but I knew that there was nothing, for I had tried before. So, there I sat, watching the blood flow from my heart, the blood drip out of my soul. The same feelings all over again...

Soon, she walked out of the bathroom, obviously much calmer than she had been before.

I guess I too was lost in my own form of poison, my own reasons my own rhyme. For I was so trapped in all those re-lived waves of love that I had not realized that she was gearing up and needed the puppy chow.

She walked up calm and clear, kneeled down over my legs, which were stretched out on the floor. She looked at me and signed, "Tired?" "Yes," I said. She stood up, grabbed my hand and led me to her bed.

Junkies are funny... There are those that just want the head rush, then there are those who like the alcoholic want to be totally plastered, and then, there are some, who shoot up several times a day like most people drink liquids and they seem to be fully normal but their heart, their soul, it is ripped out and torn into shreds. This was the case of Nicholette Marceline, she had developed, added another need.

We stood by her bed, and I watched her without question unbutton my shirt slowly. Then, she leaned over and kissed my chest. *Heaven in a moment of remembrance.* She unfastened my belt, my pants, and then left the rest to me as she began to undress herself.

It still remained, that beautiful caramel body, perhaps a little thinner, but ecstasy perpetuated. We lay down in bed and without a thought began to make love.

No time had passed, nothing was different. It was all just cast to the momentary foolishness of our tears. She began as she always did, when we made love, to breath heavily. I thought to myself, "If a deaf person breathes heavily and there is no one there to hear it, does it make a sound at all?"

We made love. We eventually fell asleep in each other's arms.

*　　*　　*

I was awoken at about four o'clock by her going to the bathroom, obviously to shot up. She came out, seeing I was awake, grabbed me by the hand, pulled me out of bed, took me to the bathroom and began to draw a bath.

There was no shower and the bathtub had obviously been added later, by a not so professional plumber. But, it did have a style.

As she leaned over to adjust the water temperature, I grabbed her. I held her, held her tight. Forgetting the distance, the years had brought. It was tight, very tight; we held each other tight. One of those needed hugs when the world has been ripped from you. Taken from her, in her way, from me in mine. We were both so empty, so lost. Yet, in this second of embrace, it was all forgotten. A need momentarily fulfilled.

When we released, she got immediately into the tub, on the faucet side. *'That was nice,'* I thought. But, I saw her wipe a tear away. Life, it had been too hard.

I got in. We sat there staring while the tub filled. I made a needle in the arm gesture, "Is it good?" I asked. She just smiled, turned off the water, turned around and leaned on me.

Time passed in the silence; true silence for her, inflicted silence for myself. I heard the water move, the water drip, the sound of the street outside, but to her, there was nothing. I always meant to ask her if there was a sound, any sound that reverberated in her mind. Perhaps the sound of *OM,* the eternal, the unborn, but the forever living. I always meant to ask her. I did not.

Maybe it is better, silence in its purest form. To never have to listen to the wicked words, the ways of the world. I don't know. I guess I never did. I suppose I never will. But, as all things are to the eyes or the ears of the beholder; it is just a point of view, a point in fact of individual definition. Who knows the answer? Who knows the cause?

No words needed to be spoken, at least none between her and I. Feelings were all that mattered and words though they try, a feeling they never can describe.

We sat in the tub, in the warmth, in the feeling. Nicholette Marceline's energy was good. It was not like most junkies who I found had very erratic energy. Most were driven mad by their strong, burning desire for the junk. Just like the whoremongers, the hounds of hell on the street. A need is a need—a desire, just that. Energy spins and spins driven by the two. But, hers was simple, centered, and clean, unclouded though I knew it obviously was in control of her life. A master stronger than even I. But, our silence spoke to me.

The evening passed quickly, lost in lovemaking and moments cast to the eternal essence of simply feeling. We decided to go and have dinner at one of our old haunts. In fact, my favorite restaurant in L.A. A little Italian place I had been going to for years in Santa Monica.

Out into the night, the night that holds no prisoners, takes only the fools into its confidence. My mind had worried, was my sweet passion of a Porsche of a rider still intact, in its position of parking. I had forgotten, we had left in alone. Alone, and for so long, out there on the extremities of the East Hollywood civilized world.

We cruised over, it was there; dumped her stereo ridden ride back in the direction of her place and we were off. Santa Monica to Wilshire and dinner and the night.

Dinner, love, her, and her junk; to bed 6:30 A.M. The next day was the day of the birth of my good friend's daughter. I stirred all night, or should I say all-day, that I would not wake up in time to make it to the birthday affair.

To the keeper of the facts, posterity and let the record be know, for you, Nicholette Marceline had no alarm clock. Nothing to arouse me from my sleep. But then, I hate alarm clocks anyway.

*   *   *

Ah, how I love the life, the life where no moments pass. Where there is no need to be awoken at a given and or specific time. Sleep ending into

100

the unfolding of nothing. For whose day is better spent, the worker who is dying for the boss who becomes rich from their labor or the visionary who allows the wind to blow through their hair?

Here I was though, living in a time of foolishness, a time when it was necessary that I had some place to be. Rise at ten o'clock. I rose at ten o'clock. I dragged Nicholette Marceline out of bed—literally. And she, drug(ed) herself into an acceptable frame of mind—a needle in the arm; she was off, we were off.

On the way, we stopped for a quick dose of morning cappuccino—sitting outside, of course. Then we picked up a few presents and headed in the direction of the Valley, over the hill.

We were in her truck. She was driving. I had the killer stereo system kicking full-on. I suggested we take Mulholland: the view, the city, and all. Just before we were to go up Laurel Canyon, I had her pull over at this little liquor store. I picked up a sixer of some imported dark brew, *Saint Pauli Girl,* my favorite. Cracked some bottles open and on we drove.

Drinking beer, listening to the radio, moving in a semi smog ridden westerly direction. The San Fernando Valley, home of Johnny Carson, Michael Jackson, and my friend. In fact, there was a time long ago, when even I lived there for a spell. Went to the local university, ran a martial art studio, and spent my time wanting to move. Move, but never back to Hollywood; the place of my birth.

Before long, the sixer was down and I had a vague buzz. We had just come upon that part of Mulholland where the pavement turns to dirt. Now, the decision here; it can be made, either to go downward into Encino or travel on into the dirt and the possible mud abyss.

She was driving, she made the choice. We traveled westward. The dirt road. I moved close to her and her gear shifting movements.

I put my hand on her soft denim covered oh so fine leg and began to move my hand gently up and down. She obviously liked the intention. She leaned over and kissed me upon the lips. One of those soft, one of those gently, drive deep down kisses. The ones that go straight into your soul. One of those that you watch coming, coming in your direction, with your eyes closed. Upon impact, upon embrace, one is taken deep into the lost/last moments of love. In love with a junky.

There it was, then I realized it. I was still longingly, deeply in love with her. It had never stopped. It had never ceased. I had just hidden it, somewhere lost in the recessed of a vault that makes up the feelings of a fool.

If love is love, it never dies even when it is over. Long ago I realized that, wrote that.

It hit me deep. It hit me hard. I knew that she felt the same.

'How does life get so messed up,' I wondered? How did hers, how did mine? How is it that the fucking stupid things of this world take control of us, take control from us. Burn our souls and leave us out of/away from the arms of something so special as this kind of love? How?

She pulled over off to the side of the dirt road and jumped out, motioning me to follow her. She jumped in the back of her pick-up truck with all the grace and perfection of the perfect gymnast. One sweeping motion and laid down on her back, arms outstretched, eyes closed tight, laughing; silently.

The sky, it was perfect blue. The weather, just warm enough. Even getting undressed, generally the hardest part of making love, was smooth as butter. The trucks movement flowed into love making time.

We lay there for a while once we were finished. I began to feel a certain uneasiness in her and soon she began to get dressed. I took this as a sign not to question but to simply join her and put my clothing back on too.

She got out of the back, looked over and smiled at me. She reached into the cab of the truck and pulled out the backpack that she always carried with her. She began to walk off. I yelled, "Stop." Then my mind realized that she couldn't have heard me no matter how loud I might have screamed.

I ran and grabbed her, knowing what she was going to do. She indicated that she knew I didn't like it, but I said, "I love you no matter what." She hugged me and went back and sat down in the driver seat.

It had been a long time since I had watched the process of the soul being stolen from a vein in the arm. But, here it was again, confrontation with the dog.

I could see that she was well equipped to do what she was doing. I could see that she knew just what to do. She didn't even have to strap off her arm to bring the vein up, just a slap or two and she dropped the needle right in.

I also noticed that it was only occasionally that she used her arm, for the tracks didn't run too long or too deep. All good junkies prefer much more casual placement anyway. Hidden, it cannot be seen. Hidden, it cannot be known. Therefore, in Aristotelian logic, it does exist.

She finished. I watched the emptiness embrace her eyes. Her need, it had been answered. Her spirit, it was gone.

She began to start the truck. I stopped her, kissed her once and got out from the passenger side and walked around. Decided it was far better if I were to drive this bad pup.

Well, we got to my friend's house, obviously a bit late. All the family and friends were there talking, barbecuing, and doing all the basic suburban life party type things in the backyard. Personally, I was more than a bit burned out. So, after all the basic hellos, I retired into the living room, laid out on the sofa, and tried to knock out for a few.

Nichollete Marceline not really knowing anyone, and not being of the social type, pulled herself up at one end of the said piece of furniture and stared off into only the silent oblivion that only she could know.

I tried to sleep but every time I got close, someone or another would walk in and say, "How's it going?" "How you doing?" "So, who's your friend?" Etc., etc., etc... I would have to go through the basic explanations every time, until finally one my soul bros commented, "Damn, can't a guy catch a few Z's around here," referring to me. "But, it's a party," was the answer. So, I tried for a few more but *nada* in the *nada* department. Well, we may as well go outside and see what there is to see, I decided.

I sat around with Nicholette Marceline realizing how far I was away from all of this. How distant I felt from this suburban family life.

I kept getting it from all sides as tends to happen at these family type of functions,

"When are you going to get a job?"
"Never."
"When are you going to get married?"
"Fuck that."

This one lady pulls up to me, who I have known for many years and says,

"How old are you now, twenty-seven?"
"No, twenty-six."
"Come-on now, you are old. I had my first kid at twenty-three. When are you going to give up that lifestyle you live and settle down, have kids, and get domestic?"
"As domestic as I want to get is a sleazy whore in a dirty motel room," I answered.

Nicholette Marceline obliviously reading my lips picked up her napkin, crumbled it up and laughingly threw it at me.

"See Sandy, there you have someone who wants to marry you."

The party went on. I felt lost and distant. I never was much of a social guy. We, Nicholette Marceline and I, stayed for the cake and left soon after.

Just as we had begun to drive off, Nicholette Marceline had me pull the truck over. She opened the door, leaned out, and threw up. Obviously, the Chinaman and all the sugar we had eaten had done her in.

We drove back to her loft. It was good to hit the streets again, to be out of the suburbs. The streets, where a man often meets the pavement and dies. One embraces life in these zones of unwilling consciousness. Where you see beyond the need for suburban gardener or a water sprinkler system. In this zone where the turf is not so soft, the turf it is not green at all. Where the poor, the lonely, the crazy, the life-full, and the life-less meet the not so soft, not so green, pavement of existence. Where the tough meet the turf.

I laughed to myself as we entered her loft. This is my world, the streets. I love them. I hate them. Only a fool would love them, but it takes hate to make them real. Yes, this is my home.

The night went on; it was spent with a bit of lovemaking and a bit of watching Nicholette Marceline go into the bathroom to shoot up. The time passed slow. I knew we were once again where we were a few years back, in love and her in junk.

The next day we rambled around the place until the afternoon came on, at which point Nicholette Marceline was about to run out of that bad powder white. She suggested that we go and score some. I didn't like the idea, but I knew from past experience that there was nothing I could say or do except go along for the ride or just walk away. And, I had walked away several years back. Obviously, it had proven nothing.

She pulled a brick from the wall, which revealed several hundred-dollar bills. My mind raced to the curiosity of where she had gotten that much money from, with no job, no support. But, I knew it to was far better if I didn't let my mind dwell on that subject for too long of a time.

Though I tried to talk her out of going, she just grabbed my hand and pulled me towards the door. There was nothing I could do, just let life take its course.

We got into my 356 and drove over near Melrose and St. Andrews where this guy, a dealer, a man I had vaguely known of for the last few years, lived. I will just call him Ben.

I choose to wait in the car. Nicholette was in and out in a couple minutes and we were back on the way to her place. As we drove, I was reminded by the radio that there was a concert that evening which I had tickets to. I asked her if she wanted to go. She did.

Post a *puppy chow* session back at her place, the remainder or the previous *dog* placed in her veins, we headed out.

Standing room, standing up, it was a stand-up concert. We stood; we held each other tight. Though the music pounded, the lights shown, and the band it did play on, she placed her head into my chest, arms around me, as I swayed to the beat, the rhythm, the sound.

As others around us danced with the music, she swayed in my arms to an inner sound, a sound no one else could hear. And while the music was playing, while she was in my arms, I cried a tear for her. I guess it was a tear for me. I just pretended it was her and how life had dealt us the cards it had. *A flush hand with a no draw deal.*

After the show, we walked out arm-in-arm. I saw that they were selling tee shirts. *'How cosmic,'* I thought. I bought one for her. She immediately put it on over the tee shirt that she was wearing.

Ah love, what brings us up to it? What brings us away from it? Only a telephone call in time.

We drove back to her place. It was much closer than mine, way down at the beach. I could see that she needed a fix. It had now been several hours. I had begun once again to count. I remembered how it used to be. I remembered my hour counting, trying to chart her addiction, trying to know her mind.

Engulfed in the moment, those thoughts of time passed reborn, reliving; calling me again. The past it was watching, forever. It would be calling, calling me out, calling me back, away into the night.

We got there; inside, I went and sat down. I preoccupied my time listening to the ringing in my ears. I hated that sound. I hated it, the ringing and yes the junk, too. I hated them both—both had control of me. Neither could I beat, nor win.

She immediately grabbed the bag enclosing her new supply, went into the bathroom: with junk, the needle, the cotton, and the spoon. I was thankful I had never become lost in that passion in the form of the powder white. I was glad it was one poison that had controlled my body not.

She came out soon. Soon, but the look on her face, the feeling, it was strange and different. She almost staggered over to me. She sat down, almost fell down into my arms, onto the pillow on the floor. Her body felt strange. It was like all full of goose bumps. My initial thought was, it's just the power of the powder coming on. Then, there was a jerk, then another. I became very worried. I didn't know what to do.

There was another jerk, a really big one. I was scared, crazy scared. I held her tight, she was semi holding onto me. I leaned her head back. I looked in her eyes, they were open, but no one was home.

What was happening? Was this normal with her sometimes? If so, I had never seen it before. I tried to make her read my lips, was there anything that I could do? She saw nothing.

I thought to call the paramedics but then she kind of grabbed my arm, more like it was a jerk, a contraction of the muscles. I looked; her eyes were wide open. Wide open like a scream, wide open and gone, totally.

I freaked out. I checked for breathing, there was none. I picked her up, tried to move her, even did a little Boy Scout C.P.R.; nothing, *nada,* zero. I screamed.

Nicholette Marceline was gone, had died, O.D.'ed. Dead, gone forever right there in my arms. It was not like I had seen on T.V.: no moans, no groans, no puking, nothing. She just had laid down in my arms and had died.

I started to cry. I held her, kept checking for breathing, checking her heart. I wanted to do something and there was nothing that I could do, nothing that I could change. The Chinaman had claimed another victim, taken Nicholette Marceline right out from under my grasp, right from inside my arms.

I loved her. She was gone.

I sat there for a time wondering what I should do, when there was nothing that I could do.

I got my things together. I left her place. I left her physical body. There was nothing, no price that I could pay, no promise that I could make that would ever bring her back.

All I could take with me was her spirit. The part, which was still pure, the part that was lost to fool's eyes who beheld only the external image. I took the unseen; that beautiful spirit, that beautiful heart. I have held onto it forever since that day. No one, not man, not the Chinaman, not the cards dealt in life, not love, not pain, not age, nothing will ever, has ever taken her spirit of purity from me.

I left her door unlocked. Walked to my car, drove to a pay phone, and called the paramedics. Obviously in tears, I told them that someone was O.D.ing. They wanted to know who I was, where I was. I gave them her address and hung up.

Now, she would, at least, be found. Her body taken care of, for I had her final possession—her spirit. God had the final possession of her soul.

I drove home in tears, wondering if she knew that this was to come to pass. Was this the reason that she had contacted me? I realized I never asked her. I realized I never knew why she had called me after so long a time.

Sometimes people are so knowing and they don't fight, they just let destiny take control. Sometimes those who have had no chance in life, made no choice in their physical make-up and design, just lay back like a sacred monk in a holy cave and are cast to the silence, cast to sightlessness, cast to other things that we can never understand. Sometimes it is they who have the truer insight, the truer intuition, the truer knowledge of mind, of god. They just let the hand of the divine take control and let go. Maybe Nicholette Marceline too, I don't' know? She knew, I do not know. But, I did love her. I do feel the loss.

The cards that are dealt us; who can say where or why. Some say it is all what we make of them. But, how do they know? Me, I don't know. I will tell you that I don't know. I have not been there, I cannot judge.

Those who have never seen the hard side or never lived the hard road, they think they know. They are the ones with all of the advice. I think that they don't know shit. They only think that they know. Nicholette Marceline, she knew, she knows; for she lived it: the good and mostly the bad. She was the one who felt the feelings so few of us will ever feel.

I got back to *mi casa*. I hadn't even realized it had been three days since I was last there. Three days that seemed like a lifetime. Three days I can never forget.

I opened the door, the place a mess as usual. I went and grabbed a dark imported brew out of the refrigerator. I listened to the thirty-nine messages, all from Michelle on my telephone answering machine. She wanted me to call. I passed...

CHAPTER 6
ROSA

I had been hanging out with this rather rich chick, on the millionaire side of the picture, who lived over San Marino way. For those who don't know, that is on the *bucks* side of the Pasadena tracks.

We were supposed to meet, mess around a bit on this one Sunday. So, I headed over in the direction of her mansion style house—owned by her parents, of course. Daddy's money and all...

I got there, went up and knocked on the door, and no one was around, not even the maid. So, I figured that she must have had to go and do something real quick and would be back *pronto.*

Now, it is not at all in my nature to wait around, especially for a chick. But, I was in a very temperate mood this day, so I walked back to my ride, which was parked across the street and gave myself fifteen minutes. I sat back, cracked open a dark brew that I had sitting in the back seat. Though it was a little warm, it went down right. Gave me that subtle edge of illusion that I needed right then.

I was there probably five minutes when up in front of my little love child's house pulls a mid-seventies rather funky sports sedan. Out of the car jumps this girl who was a friend of my rich little *familiar.* I immediately notice her out of the corner of my eye. Being as cool as I am, I, of course, could not acknowledge her presence.

She immediately saw me and springs in my direction, full of smiles with a friend in tow. She stuck her head up to the window of my car, her arms resting on the door.

"Hi Sandy, how's it going?"

"Okay Christine. What's up?"

"Just driving around and thought we would stop by."

"Isn't Melinda home?"

"Nope."

At this point, I begin to notice her friend. Notice her seriously, if you know what I mean?

She was obviously Latina, with dark brown skin. Her hair was long, very straight, very black. Just the way I like it. She was wearing this lightweight loose and flowing skirt and blouse. Obviously made of cotton with vague pastel prints on the both of them. I thought to myself how it almost looked like a summery outfit. Summery, for us being lost into the deep realms of autumn. There was no doubt she was a serious babe.

She throws a smile my direction and pushes her way right up to the window with her friend.

"Sandy, I want you to meet my friend, Rosa."

"Hello Rosa. It's an honor to meet you."

"Hi Sandy."

Christine then asks, "Have you been waiting long, Sandy?"

"No, just a few minutes."

Rosa immediately says, "Sandy, will you take me for a ride?"

Now, I thought this almost funny. You know, when *my scoot,* my motorcycle, was my main and preferred form of transportation, often times babes would ask for a ride; a motorcycle and all. That, I could understand it. That is, of course, before I introduced face to cement, kissed the pavement as it were. Was smashed off, *my hair blowing in the wind,* wild ride. And, my skull fractured in too many places to count. Luckily, the bad dude that I *be* walked away, post a minor hospital stay and a dance with a brain surgeon or two. But, that's all-other stories, in other books still to come. Anyway, as, *"Boss,"* as we used to say back in the sixties, as my bad little 356 was, I had never been asked to give someone an invitational ride in it. But… First time for everything…

"What about Christine?"
"Oh, that's Okay, Sandy. Really! I have other things I should do."
"Are you sure?"
"Yes."
"If I see Melinda, I will tell her that you took Rosa for a drive."

I looked at her out of the corner of my eye and laughed.

"I'm sure she will love that."
"Okay Sandy?" Rosa asks.
"Let's go…"

I tossed down the last swallow of the brew. Throw my beer bottle in the back. Reach over and open the door from the inside. She jumps in, all smiles.

I fire up the ride and away we drive. As I am cruising down the mansion lined street, I look over at Rosa and exactly at that moment she looks at me. The connection was made. Love in the making.

"I've never ridden in a Porsche before," exclaims Rosa.

"It's just a car. So, where would you like to drive to," I question.

"The mountains. I want to go up to the mountains and sit by a stream."

"Well Rosa, what mountains would you like to go to and sit by a stream in, perhaps the Sierra Nevada? I hate to tell you, but it's fall and there hasn't been any rain yet. These are desert mountains around L.A. so most of the streams up in Angeles Crest are dried up."

"Okay, let's go to the Sierra Nevadas."

'Busted,' I thought.

Now, for the most part, I live totally as spontaneous as possible and it certainly is not above me to head for distant locations at first provocation. My mind foolishly went to Melinda, my rich little friend. And, to only having a sport coat on and it being October and all; well... I might need more, etc., etc., etc.

I then remembered where my buddy, Saturday Jim and I used to go fishing sometimes, we never caught anything up there but...

"You want to go up past Azusa? I am sure that the river is flowing up there."

"Sure, let's go."

Busted again. This was definitely not the few minutes ride I had in mind when I left. I definitely caught myself up in this one. My current state of mind being far from in the perfection of the moment—it was dwelling elsewhere, on far less—a far less worthy woman. But, as I always have had a problem with saying, "No." Well, I headed up towards Pasadena to pick up the 210 freeway to head on and out to Azusa.

As I drove: the moment, Rosa's beauty, and the spirit began to take hold. She had rolled down the window and was letting the cool wind blow in her hair. If there is one thing that really moves me is a lady who is not so caught up with her hair, trying to look oh so perfect every second.

The freedom is the perfect perfection— perfection in the imperfections.

I realized; there I was with the most perfect woman that I could be with. Freedom in the making *sautéed* with a pinch of spice.

Black hair blowing in the wind. Skin that shined in the reflection of the early afternoon sunlight. If only I had a camera with me, a video to record the beauty for posterity, for all eternity. But, all I had were my eyes.

Pulling up next to us, pulling up past us, was this *diaper-headed* looking guy in a new little Alpha.

Cruise up, cruise past, weave in, weave out, shoot the curl; he wanted to play tag. A.O.K., I do like to play tag. So, there the two, well three counting Rosa of us were, shooting down the 210. In, out, down, and around. Utmost maximal, at the maximum speed. Mega velocity, upper limit, overdrive. In and out of the traffic around. Call it suicide. I would too. Call it dangerous, unconscious, endangering the lives of others. Well, there are too many people on this plant anyway. I like it; the heart pounding, adrenal flow potency. Where the slightest wrong turn, missed calculation is your last. The last, always being the first; a new beginning. Twenty miles deep, he finally bailed the freeway,

116

somewhere out there along the way. Somewhere back there, behind me; a few missed calculations if you know what I mean...

As we drove further and my hand was resting on my leg, she reached over and held it. Held it and just smiled.

I looked at her,

"What's your full name?" I asked.
"Rosa Isabel Del la Paz."
"That's a very beautiful name."
"Were you born here?"
"No, Mexico. Guadalupe. Have you been there?"
"No, not yet. I haven't traveled in Mexico much. I guess I'm a bit paranoid. Will you take me there?"
"No, I don't want to go back either," she replied.

We both laughed.

We got to the off ramp and headed up the road into the mountains. By this point, I was way into the situation. *'Fuck Melinda,'* I thought. *'Where else could I be that would hold any more importance than this drive and a beautiful girl holding my hand?'*

As we headed further up, Rosa said,

"You know that Melinda is out with someone else today."
"Someone else?"
"Yeah, a guy. I think his name is Peter."

Now, I briefly met this guy once. Melinda had said he was an old friend from school. He was a total yuppie want-a-be. He had short dark hair, dressed with zero style, in traditional cheap suits, and had a mustache; uck. As I have always said, *men and women just cannot be friends.* Sooner or later one or the other will put the moves on.

But let's face facts here, it is not hard to find a better man than me. At least in the department of security and the fulfillment of promises. Melinda probably had realized that I was already dipping my cookie in other milk. And, that my words... Well, talk is cheap...

"Are you mad?"
"For what?"
"That Melinda is out with another guy?"
"So... I'm out with you. And you are so much more beautiful."

Instantaneously my rap kicks in.

"I mean, can't you feel it? We are made for each other. I'm what you have been waiting for all of your life. I'm talking serious matrimony here."
"But aren't you jealous?"
"Of what?"
"Melinda being out with another guy?"
"Look, I'm out with you. Melinda and I are only friends."

My bud Saturday Jim always tells me I get myself into all kinds of trouble due to the thickness of my rap; *kinda* like maple syrup, you know. He says that I should just have it on tape and play it for each new chick that comes along, for it's always the same rap anyway. Hey, but if they want to play, they *gotta* pay. But, I mean double standards and all, it is AOK if I go out on the extremities, but if they do...

In actuality, I was quite pissed. Me, being the mega possessive person that I am. The truth of the matter was that Melinda was just a woman to pass some lost time with. To lie to. Promise her marriage, love, and forever and ever. But, the whole idea of her being out with some other *love stud* did piss me off. She had always claimed such love and monogamy for me, the whole week or two I had known her. What can I say, you hand a woman what they want to hear, all that matrimony bullshit and they mega love you back. It gets you into their pants mighty fast, if you dig my vibratory level.

"I'm really glad you and her are only friends and that you are so interested in me. I have seen you before. Did you know that?"
"No."
"Yeah, I saw you at the movies last week. I was with Christine and you were with Melinda. I thought that you looked so neat, so interesting."

'Interesting and neat,' I smiled. I mean, let's grow up.

"Why didn't you come up and say hello?"
"Well…"
"Never mind," I said, "We have found each other now and that is all that matters. By the way, are you hungry?"
"Yes, a little."
"Good, I have just the place."

There was this restaurant I knew of, up the hill a bit.

As we drove on, no longer was she just holding my hand, but I also held hers. After every shift, my hand found its way back into her grasp. You know, all that LOVE bullshit. It was not long before she leaned her head on me.

Love. Ah love. It only takes a second to form, and when it does, there is nothing like it. I do love love.

As we approached the restaurant, I noticed that there were more than a few people there. Some were even waiting outside.

Sunday, farmer's day and night to eat out. Me, if there is one thing I hate to do is wait for a table at a restaurant. It is rare that I will ever do it.

I suggested to Rosa that we wait until later to eat and just head for a nice spot by the stream. She was agreeable and said that she would rather be by the water anyway. So, on I drove.

We got up a ways and I noticed a seemingly nice little spot.

"Is this good?"
"Great."

So over I pulled. And out we get.

"It's warm today," says Rosa.
"Yeah, a little bit."
"I love warm weather."
"That's because you're from Mexico," I laughingly tell her.
"Me, I love the California winters. When I can wear my long coat and walk in the rain. I guess I don't' make a very good So. Cal. Dude."

Rosa comes over and puts her arms around me. Our first hug.

"See, we're made for each other Sandy. You are winter and I am summer. Perfect, don't you think?"
"Perfect," I said as I held her tight.

We stood there hugging, rocking back and forth a bit. It was the first hug, the perfect hug. It was like all perfect first embraces. It's a shame that they are so far between. But, the feeling, the total feeling of love to the maximum. Ah… It doesn't matter how long it lasts, for in those moments, who can think of anything else? Ah love, I do love it.

We were standing on a bit of an incline. The river had forged its way through the rocks turning it to dirt millions of years ago. Now it flowed perhaps twenty feet below us. Abruptly, Rosa jokingly pulled away and down she jumped into the reddish colored dirt, landing on her butt. Obviously, it had more than a hint of clay in it.

I looked at her as she sat in the dirt laughing. She was free, perfectly free. She didn't care if her dress had gotten dirty, all that mattered is that she was by the water. I looked and her skin almost matched the color of the dirt. I thought if she had been naked and if it had been night, perhaps I would not have even noticed her. But, noticing naked women is something; well, I have a keen eye for it, so…

I, being in a bit stuffy of a mood, elected not to try to make the jump but, instead, follow what looked to be a path the five or six feet down to bring me closer to the bottom, thereby not having such a far jump. I walked it to no avail. Once at the end of it, I found the dirt there to be much looser and thus down I slid to join Rosa.

She was sitting there laughing.

"Care to join me Sandy? Have a nice trip, see you next fall."

What could I do but laugh?
We sat there in each other's arms for a long time, just watching the river flow by. I too was very much into the water; the rivers flow to the sea.

"I would like to take you to this place in Big Sur sometime Rosa. There is this special spot where the river flows into the sea and if you sit in just the right place, and if you put your finger in one ear, all you can hear is the ocean and if you place your finger in the other, all you can hear is the river."
"Let's go." She answered.

God, she was totally free. It made me understand that though I thought that I was free, how caught up I had become over the last few months; burdened by the mundane and all the bullshit of this world and of life. She was a great reminder.

"Do you know why I love rivers so much Sandy?"
"Why?"
"Because in Mexico sometimes it doesn't rain for such a long time and sometimes there is almost no water. If you live in a house with no plumbing sometimes you get so thirsty and there is nothing to drink, nowhere to go, even though you really want to go. There is nowhere, and no way."

122

As she said that, I could see that she also had experienced her *hard-knocks*. Different *hard-knocks* than a city kid like me. But, we all have our deep pain. To some it's just worse than others. Some learn how to cover it up, some never can. Rosa, it seemed that hers had helped her to become freer. Maybe it was just the way I gaged it. I don't know?

After sitting for a while, Rosa began to kiss me. First on the neck then our lips met. The perfect moment, the first kiss, there can be nothing like it. That second of time that lasts a seeming eternity. That second of a perfect moment before the lips meet.

Post a little lip-action; we noticed that there was a cave type rock formation on the other side of the stream.

The stream, it looked to be only a few feet deep, so we elected to braze our way across the river; probably fifteen feet from bank-to-bank, to see what was on the other side.

So, hand-in-hand we jumped rock to rock and without falling in, though I am sure Rosa would not have minded, we made it.

Once there, we made our way to the cave, almost big enough for us to lay in. And, there in its truest sense, passion began. We lay there in each other's arms kissing and touching. She held me like it meant her life. A life, where nothing else can matter but the self-existence thereof and therefore. A passion that holds you tight, gives you a reason to hold on. ...Though one does not know the reason why. Simply that all else is unknown and, thus, the present is desirable to any further obscure realities.

As we continued, my hand found its way between her legs. There was no hesitation, no doubt. As I lifted her skirt and began removing her panties, her hand met mine to help. I looked down to see this beautiful black haired bushy beaver, full just the way I love 'em.

It's all so easy, came to my mind. Then, all the typical insecurities of the first-love, make-love session, chimed in. Will I be good enough? Will she like it? Will I blow my rocks too soon? Finally, I told my mind to just shut up and that there was no turning back now.

In the cave, as it turns out, the joke was on me. Just as I was about to pull down my pants, I heard these voices talking, coming in our direction. Rosa and I looked at each other and started to laugh. "Fuck," was all I could say.

Now Rosa being my new property, no one else was about to have the honor of seeing her beautiful clay colored brown skin except for me. Especially on this day. So, all I could do was hand her, her panties and help her to brush off.

Two guys were coming down to the stream from their car. Typical macho dudes: jeans, tee shirts, and a beer in their hands. They had obviously seen another car parked, and as mindless as most people are, seeking association, party, and the like, decided to come down and converse. We sat there as they approached. Finally, they noticed us upon the opposite side of the stream. I had hoped that they would not. They spoke,

"What's up dude?"
"Nothing man."
"Any good fish'n, we're looking for a spot."
"I don't know man, not fishing today."

Now I realize we must have looked funny, Rosa in her now quite dirty skirt and blouse. Me, the style jockey that I am, in my baggy, semi dirt covered city threads. I mean, at least they should have caught the vibes that we were *in-volved*. But no, they were obviously quite content to share our spot.

"Well Joe, what do you think, fish'n spot look good?"
"Good as any."

They went up to get their gear. Rosa and I took the opportunity to leave.
At the top of the hill,

"Oh, you guys leaving?"
"Yeah, got some things to do."
"Okay dude, take it easy."

Rosa and I back in the car, its motor started, we gave each other another hug and a final kiss for the adventure and we were off.

"Where to now?" I asked.
"The city, I guess."
"I know, there are too many people up here in the mountains," I jokingly exclaimed.

As we laughingly and lovingly drove down the hill, we decided to eat in the car, due to our appearance. So, we did the typical drive through *thAng* and once back deeper into civilization, Rosa suggested we head back for Melinda's house.

"Why?" I asked.

Now, that was the last place I was into going to. I did not wish to think of her and her apparent love stud, nor did I even care anymore. New love in hand, and all. I was quite content at the moment to spend the rest of my life with Rosa Isabel Del la Paz. Besides that, I was more than a bit horny, and the thought of that beautiful pussy did not want to leave my mind.

"I want to see if Christine is there. Why don't you want to go there? Come on, you're jealous."
"No way." I kept saying, "I just don't feel like going there."
"Come on, for me."

The typical chick *thAng,* "For me…"
Well, by hook or by crook, as the old saying goes, we ended up there. Surrounded by the awesome baroque quality of houses. Filled with Daddy's money and the promise that the majority of it was acquired at the expense of the average joe public.
As we pulled up, we noticed that, in fact, Christine's car was there.

"Oh good, she's there."

'Fuck, she's there,' I thought to myself. This is not a situation I was at all in the mood to deal with.
Asian lying eyes staring at me, blaming me for all that I was, everything that I was not. And, all that they, the Asian eyes, had led me to believe that they were and, in fact, were not. Once again, the cat was brought out of the proverbial bag, long before it

had its opportunity of enjoying it. I was not in the space for it.

I pulled up in front of the place just behind Christine's car. Rosa got out on her own, I didn't have the opportunity to open the door for her. Just then, Christine came out. She had obviously seen us drive up.

"You two look like a mess. Did you have fun?"

As she gives us this knowing look.

"How about it Sandy, did you have fun?"
"Fun is all what you make of it. And besides, I always have fun."
"Listen Sandy, I hope you're not going to be pissed, but Melinda is in there with another guy."
"Peter, I know, no problem. What do you think, I'm engaged to her something?"
"Oh well then, we should be on our way," says Christine, as she looks at Rosa.
"I guess so," says Rosa as she walks over and gives me a kiss.

I'm standing there in fucking disbelief. I mean, *what-the-fuck* is going on. Like is all that had gone down that afternoon nothing or what?

I was about to say something, but Christine and Rosa had already reached the car. And certainly, I am not one to go begging. Fuck that.

As they drove off, I was looking at Rosa; our eyes meet and for a second I wanted to cry, scream, do something... I see in her eyes all the love that I had touched for only a moment. I thought it would have been more.

As I stood there dumbfounded, out walks Melinda and Peter.

"Hey, how's it going Sandy?" shouts Peter in all his blue business suit want-a be-ness.
"Okay man."

Melinda looking at me rather funny asks,

"Did you have a nice day, Sandy?"

I start to walk to my car.

"Wait Sandy, I want to talk to you. This is not what you think."

I kept walking.

"Wait, I love you."
"I'm out-a-here."

I got into my 356 and drove off as Melinda stood there screaming for me to stop. I could see her in my mirror, standing in the middle of the street.

As I drove back Southward, heading for the South Bay, I try to fathom what had gone down. I mean come-on, was the whole thing a fucking set up. Was Rosa, beautiful Rosa, simply a *hoe* sent to test my true intentions towards Melinda? Hey, if Melinda wanted to know that, I would have been happy to tell her. I mean, fuck, the yuppie could have her. I didn't even care. He probably would give her a whole lot more stability than I ever would choose to.

As all the thoughts raced through my mind, I realized how mindless people were. Me too. ...To assume that just by the obvious implications of a given situation that one could think that they know what is going on with another individual or that they believed that they understand a person well enough to examine or predict their actions before they happened.

I didn't even really care all that much about Melinda. Rosa, on the other hand, well she was way more my speed. So, the joke, as it often turns out to be, was on me.

I decided the whole thing just wasn't fucking worth worrying about. I mean, hey, they have my phone number, at least Melinda did. And I was sure that she would give me a non-stop list of telephone pleas upon my telephone answering machine. I would probably have to change my telephone number again. It had gotten to be a habit. And if Rosa was more than a passion placed dream, then she too could probably get a hold of me.

I don't know, maybe I would see her some place/some time. Then, I realized, it was doubtful, for we hung in way different circles; their crowd and mine.

So, "Fuck it all," I said out loud, as I rolled down the other window and opened up the sunroof to let the wind blow through my long blonde hair. I turned up the radio, loud, and danced on.

But, as I drove home, I could not help but think of Rosa and that beautiful beaver which I almost had. And maybe, just maybe she would call.

CHAPTER 7
MOKSHA PRIYA

I had flow *Air India* up from Varanasi, landing in Delhi. As is generally the case, I waited the usual half hour to forty-five minutes when it should only take fifteen or twenty to get my luggage. But, remember this is India. I pushed my way right up to the edge of the luggage conveyor, as is the traditional custom in India; be as pushy as possible.

I stood waiting, holding tough onto my position as Indians pushed their way in, trying to move me out-a-the-way, and be as close as possible. How foolish, but in India one quickly learns that pushy and rude are the name-of-the-game.

I observed and listened to some French people discussing and describing, in their native tongue, this funny looking man with long blonde hair and earrings. 'He must be English.' I wanted to tell them, 'No, I'm American, asshole,' but I let it go...

The luggage finally arriving, after my having worked up a serious sweat, being so closely surrounded by people. I grabbed my bag and headed for the door. Naturally, I was assaulted by all the young boys, "Taxi, Taxi." To my response. "No!"

My bag was grabbed and pulled on by the boys who want to carry it for a westerner, with western tips in mind, in the general direction of their cousin the taxi driver. This also met my general response, "Jao Jao!" Basically, go away.

You see in any city in India, well for that matter in most cities of the developing world;

...Developing world... funny their societies were developed long before western one's ever were. Developed and destroyed, long before the industrial, machine, or information age ever came to be. My bro Saturday Jim likes to clump them all into the deserved category of *tres a mundos,* but anyway...

There are taxis that have meters, that wait in the lines and follow the general rules. Then, there are those that somehow, the meters always seem to be broken and they want to negotiate the fare and take you to a better hotel than you have reserved. The fares high, the hotel obviously a serious dive. Fuck all that shit.

I pushed my way out and made my way through the masses to the proper taxi service. The driver jumped out of his taxi, grabbed my bag, threw it rather roughly in the trunk and off we went.

He was a rather personable young man, early twenties, supposedly a college student. He told me of how his father owned three taxis, his uncle lived in Singapore and owned taxis there. He, Jaya, the driver was to go there, to Singapore, upon completion of college and work for his uncle. It seems all Indians desire to leave India and go someplace else. He was quite excited about the future prospect of his life

He asked had I ever been to Singapore.

"Yes, of course."
"Did you like it very much?"
"It's a beautiful country with beautiful women."
"Oh, you like the women?"
"Yes."
"Do you like Indian women?"

"Very much. They are very beautiful."

This is my typical answer, of course, to whenever this question is asked of me. Generally, I follow it up with the statement that I would like to marry a local woman, etc., etc. This time seemed sufficient to just keep it to the basics.

Jaya smiled and said, "I like American women."
I laughed, saying, "I didn't."
"Why?"
"They are too easy. Generally, by the time an American girl is twenty years old she has had sex with twenty men. I don't like that."
"I like easy," said Jaya smilingly.
"Yes, but would you want to marry easy?"

He began to think.
We arrived at the hotel in about twenty minutes. I paid him, threw him a tip, and walked into the hotel in all my bohemian style and glory. I walked up to the desk and was about to say that I had a reservation but was beat to the punch.
The lady working behind the desk, a very beautiful, fair skinned, longhaired, Indian lady said,

"Hello Dr. Shaman, I remember you. You have stayed with us before."
"Oh, you remember?"
"How could I forget? How long has it been now, several weeks I think."
"Yes, four or five."
"Where have you been, Dr. Shaman?"
"Oh, here and there."
"You must come to India often?"

I just laughed, for I would hate to count the amount of actual time I had spent in India. So many times, for so many reasons. Searching by whatever name it be called. Searching in the vast cave of mystery. Searching for truth, knowledge, and supreme union, in both physical and non-physical form. I continued to return, though I had long ago given up the quest—realizing how truly elementally easy experiencing enlightenment actually was—choosing instead to live the enlightenment rather than seek it out.

*   *   *

Enlightenment, it is easy. Most who seek it simply do not believe that it is so. They think it is colors and visions, but that is just insanity, that is not enlightenment. And in India, the crazier you are, the holier you are. So, don't seek it there. Find it inside.

Enlightenment is far emptier than all of those supposed experiences. Enlightenment is emptiness and you cannot know emptiness by thinking of emptiness, for then it becomes a form, thus not empty. Just feel it, just be it.

Be the wind—where does it come from, where does it go? Does it care? No, I don't think so.

But, no words can explain enlightenment and no person, no matter what pinnacle they may reach or claim to have reached, is any better or higher than you are right now. For they live and they will die, just like you. Thus, they are only human and what do all those proclaimed experiences prove anyway?

*　　*　　*

I had long ago realized India held nothing but myth and superstition. But how I loved to chase the illusion, how I loved to dance with the best of what South Asia had to offer: that myth, that ritual, that superstition. Its psychic realms are covered with the decaying ethereal bodies of many such as myself.

"We are glad to have you back, Dr. Shaman, we missed you."
"I missed you too, very much."

Our eyes met and looked deeply into the depths of one another's. My attention was, however, distracted by a Sikh who also worked at the hotel desk. He walked up close to his fellow employee. He must have overheard our last few words and perhaps was unhappy with their implications. I looked him square in the eyes, with a smile upon my face, and he walked away.

"Your room will be 617," she said as she handed me the key.
"How's the business here?" I asked.
"We are almost full."
"You must be working very hard."
"Yes."

I wanted to break the ice and make contact with small talk. I could see, I could feel, that she wanted the same.

"How many hours a day do you work?"
"Too many," she laughingly answered. "About ten."

"That's a lot. Then what do you do?"
"I like to go to the disco, when I am not too tired.
Do you like discos?"
"In Asia I like discos," I immediately added, "I love
to dance."
"Me too."

Well, I said to myself it was now or never.

"What time do you get off?"
"Six o'clock."

It was then 3:15 P.M.

"Want to do something when you get off?"

She looked at me, her eyes lighted up, just a
bit. But then I noticed her looking around to see if
anyone else had heard.

"Just come to my room when you're finished
working," I added.
"I am not supposed to. It is not allowed. If I get
caught…"
"Well, your choice."
"I will try."
"Hope to see you."

I smiled. I walked away.
We both gave that basic ending glance of
impending and desired lust. I knew of all that hotel
employee, customer relation, bullshit, for I had
fallen in love with a hotel employee once or thirty
times before. But, with the dice in play and only one
shot left in a game all too fast coming to a close,
well… You get the picture.

I went up to the room; nice enough. About as good as you can get in Delhi. And, though the promised passion of this five-star India style receptionist did tickle my fancy, and to just sit back and recoup for a few days in her arms came to mind, I had other inclinations; namely, get out of India. I had been there almost two months and was longing for the women of Bangkok, the pounding rhythm of Hong Kong, and the nights of Tokyo.

*   *   *

India is a country that takes it out of you, especially if you're continually traveling and not settling in one place. Even if you are settled: the dirt, the noise, the crowding, the pollution... It is everything everyone has heard, only it is a few hundred times worse. Yet, its essence is captivating.

While everyone from America wishes to travel to Europe, I find it culturally boring there; like America with a different language. But Asia hits you over the head and you either come out enlightened or with dysentery. In this particular case, I had been overcome by both.

*   *   *

Truth manifests itself in strange ways. The seer, the mystic, finds that gospel in the center of dysentery, in the whole of the moment. The intensity of abdominal pain, of riding shotgun on a bicycle rickshaw, dying inside with every bump that is encountered. Having to go to the bathroom, when there is none. Only a truck passing by blowing its horn so loud that it hurts your ears. Blowing the horn at the bicycle rickshaw driver. Then, it passes, accelerating and spraying you with unfiltered, uncontrolled petroleum exhaust. All this while a young boy throws a rock at you; strike the man with blond hair, in an obvious gesture of hate and despise of all your affluence. Affluence that in America would only be a soup-line ticket, but in India it would be a fortune.

*   *   *

My return air ticket was open. I pulled it together enough and went downstairs, keeping my key so the young lady hotel employee would not think that I had left the hotel, leaving her behind. I grabbed a taxi.

"Do you know where the *Pan Am* office is on Jain Road, near Connaught Place?"
"Yes."

Off we went.
Arriving there, I went in, took a number and was expecting a major wait and a major problem getting a flight out. Much to my surprise, my number was quickly called and I went up and spoke to an obviously well-traveled Indian man, with a graying beard and neatly trimmed hair.

"Can I help you?"
"Yes. I have this *Pan Am* ticket to Hong Kong via Bangkok and I know *Pan Am* doesn't have a flight out tomorrow but is there another airline I could change to?"
"No problem," he said.

I couldn't believe it.

"Would *Lufthansa* be alright?"

"Anything would be fine."

"It will leave tomorrow at three o'clock. It does not stop in Bangkok, it flies directly to Hong Kong taking three hours and forty-five minutes."

Though I had planned to pass back through the city of golden Buddha doom, golden dreams; Bangkok, the city I love, and go look up a few friends of the late-night persuasion of mine, my stomach had been hit pretty hard the previous few weeks: lomotil, vibra tabs, for the cure and all. And the night before in Varanasi I had some pretty intense psychic experiences, deep in the realms of the 3:00 A.M. pre-Brahmamurta witching hour. So, I knew it was best that I hit the trail and the hot spice of Bangkok, of and in the food and of and in the ladies, would probably not do me so much good at this present moment. Another time, another dream, hold my place in line.

"Sounds good to me."

So, I was booked upon the flight, First Class. I headed out of the office back into the blistering hot reality of urban India.

I purchased a few last-minute gifts in one of the shops of Connaught Place. Grabbed a three-wheeled taxi scooter and headed back for the hotel. Upon entering, the eyes of the receptionist met mine. Time moved to no time and eternity moved to no thought. In-action was achieved without being achieved.

My steps continued, as they often do. I walked out of eye contact range and into the elevator, maintaining only a memory of the brief union of no thought.

I went up to my room, showered, shaved, and counted my blessing of a plane ride out and onto Hong Kong tomorrow. Hong Kong, where I could heal my body, eat Big Macs, and fall in love every time I turned my head.

I put the clothing on that I intended to wear for my intended six o' clock sin meeting; straightened up the things in my room that had, by this point, been strategically thrown throughout the place. When I was completed, I found myself laying down in the air-conditioned comfort of the four-wall heaven or prison, whichever way one would chooses to look at it, and I zoned out.

Was it butterflies in my stomach, remembrances of painful amebic dysentery, or the reemergence of a psychic presence in the air; I don't know, but I woke up. Looking at my watch, it was 6:20. I was a bit saddened seeing the time and having all those thoughts that she would not arrive at all. Just as I was about to submerge myself in my own misery and write some longing poetry, there was a soft knock upon the door.

I open the door and there she stood before me. Her hair, now let down, it fell to about breast level. She was adorned in her hotel uniform sari; pure South Asian beauty.

"Namaste, Dr. Shaman."
"Please call me Sandy. By the way, what is your name?"
"Moksha Priya."
"Ah, what a beautiful name. Will you be my liberation?"

She entered. We sat down and began to discuss her life, my life, what kept me returning to India, and how she wanted to visit the United States someday.

"You can come and stay with me in California."
"I have seen pictures of California, and I listen to the Beach Boys music. It must be like heaven there."
"Better," I stated.

But that is not what I really meant. And besides, the Beach Boys suck.

"Where do you live in California?"
"I live at the beach."
"Oh, I love the beach," she said, "I have been there once. Someday I hope to see the whole world."
"All at one time?" I jokingly exclaim.

Our conversation continued as we drank the champagne and wine that had been price-fully situated in my hotel room refrigerator. It did wonders for my stomach. We finished all that had been strategically placed. And, as our intoxication grew, I began to pour mixed drinks from the little bottles atop the refrigerator. The thought did come to me of the kill hangover I knew I would have come morning, due to the mixing of all that *soma*. But, when the moment is dancing never let it be said that I would attempt to stop it.

We continued: the walls, the barriers falling down around us. I could hear them crash. The moment and India.

She spoke, I spoke. She sat in a chair. I eventually elected to sit on the floor leaning against the bed. The music of India played softly on the radio.

She smoked her cigarettes. Every time she brought another one out, she offered one to me.

"No thank you. I'm a healthy man. I don't smoke. I never have."

The intoxication continued. She moved herself down and began sitting on the floor, leaning against the chair.

Somehow intoxication in South Asia, or any foreign soil, seems so much better than simply getting drunk at home. I don't know what it is, perhaps a movement of space into space, removing the inhibitions. A flowing, a merging of culture to no culture. Is there any culture at all?

Obviously wabbly, she leaned over and kissed me. Actually, quite to my surprise, I tasted the cigarettes on her breath. Uck!

I thought how interesting the world is; everywhere, everywhere else that is, people are at the point where the smoking of cigarettes is *chic* and the oh so liberated thing to do. This was a point reached in the States and believed thereof, in and about the 1940s. Now, it is only a fool's sport in the States, but everywhere else, the market for smoking *chic* is cornered.

I mean, there I was India… How many Westerners go to India for spirituality, enlightenment? For health, salvation? And there, them, the East Indians, how many of them don't care. They only live the temporary-ness of their moment—of their momentary wants and need of their life. The desire for desire, cigarettes, and other things. Something for you, the spiritual, to think about...

I always found this to be a paradox. But then, my life too, it is a paradox....

*   *   *

I looked at her as she kissed me the second time, her tongue entered my mouth.

I laughed to myself, that there I was, India, driven by lust into lust. Lust merging with enlightenment, a true mystic's antidote.

I then began to contemplate what a low woman she must be, low among her people; to be there alone in the room with me. Then, the thought came to me, I wonder if she does this all the time?

I saw my mind working; low/high. Think this/think that. Stupid, I am stupid, laughing inside. If she is so low; good. Especially if she is low from a high family. The perfect paradox.

I love people of the streets, the people who leave it all behind. I mean, that is what India is all about: the *sadhu,* the holy man, Siddhartha Gautama, the Sakyamuni Buddha. Different name, different titles, different positions in a cast society. And, in the end, we are all the same.

I held her closer and kissed her deeply, letting all my love flow up from *anahata chakra,* the heart center. I let it all be stimulated. Momentary heaven, here I come.

I kissed her forgetting the taste of cigarettes. The taste I hate to kiss.

I touched her, she touched me. I began to remove her uniform.

I lay her bronze body upon the bed atop the golden-brown bead spread. I kissed and caressed her thin nude body. I took my clothing off.

I lay next to her; we moved closely together. I casually, as I always do, slid my hand between her legs and brought it back up so I could catch a wiff. Does she have a stinky pussy? No. Good. I move down between her legs and begin to give her a bit of the oral action.

As I move my tongue around, I look up at her body and saw the beautiful colors of her body fading into the bedspread, surrounded by the white walls. I caress her breasts as I move to her enjoyment.

She pulls me up and quickly her face is down by my legs, she begins to give me head. She is good. I was quite surprised. Most women are so boring when it comes to the wild wet lips of love. They just have no idea what they are doing.

She moves up, plants herself on top of me and goes to work. I kiss and suck on her firm beautiful breasts. Then, she begins to pump hard. I do know what is happening.

Our time to lose time, to merge as one, has come.

I move with her as her breathing sounds increase. She grabs me tight. I hold her and in a second, energy moves to the *ajna chakra,* the third eye; consciousness is focused there. The spectrum becomes darker, my eyes close; close tightly. Colors become black and dark gray. *Ajna* becomes radiant blue. For a second, a second that cannot be timed in the format of Greenwich time, I am her, she is me; we are neither this nor that. We are one. True enlightenment, *tantric nirvaculpa samadhi.* We merge to the nothingness of everything.

Our movements slow, the momentary enlightenment; pleasure is complete. We hold one another.

She soon rolls over, off me. And, as I watch her, she falls asleep.

I lay there seeing, witnessing *maya*. The illusion. I become a part of it. The time, I spent running from it: first when I was young and a monk. Now, that I am older, harder, far more tainted; I run towards it.

Lust and sexuality, it controls us all. Never let anyone tell you otherwise. I have never seen one person that this is not the case. Either they are controlled by the running from it or the running to it. And it means nothing, not anything at all.

What is, is. And acceptance or denial makes no difference to consciousness. The wind blows when it chooses to blow and the walls of this hotel that I am in only try to control it. Which in truth can never be accomplished. It, the wind, will forever be here; this hotel, it will not.

The India music continued to play on the radio. I lay staring at the almost spinning ceiling. I thought of all the stories of how Indian women had no real passion. I thought of all the times that this had been proven to me, too. An exception, I love the exceptions to the rule.

Maybe fifteen or twenty minutes later, Moksha Priya wakes and asks,

"What time is it?"
"9:42," I tell her.
"Oh, almost time for the disco. Do you want to go?"
"Are you crazy?"
"No, I'm not crazy. Do you want to go?"
"No," I said, "Think I'll just chill back this round."

144

"No?" She questioned.

"No," I answered.

She gets up and begins to dress. This was not quite the plan I had for the evening. Though in fact, I guess, I didn't really have any plan at all. But, there we were together and all, it seemed a shame to waste all the perfection of the moment on her leaving.

As she continued dressing, I began to feel a bit sad. Then, the thought came to me, as The Buddha had said, *'The cause of all suffering is desire.'* I laughed out loud.

"What are you laughing at? Are you laughing at me? Is there something funny?"

"No, I am laughing at me."

She brushed her hair a bit and said,

"Dr. Shaman, you should move to India. You have the mind for this place."

I just looked at her. If only she knew the whole story.

She walked to the door. I jumped out of bed and opened it for her, hiding my bad naked self behind it. I kissed her and said,

"Moksha Priya, I love you."

"Dr. Shaman…"

"Sandy, Sandy."

"I love you too."

She was gone.

I lay back down in bed, it was moving more than a bit. I lay there thinking of the last two months of travel, of Moksha Priya, and of her suggestion to stay. I pondered that if the situation had perhaps been different, I would, in fact, have probably remained in India forever. But, the situation was not different and Delhi discos were not my idea of enlightenment, but then again…

I fell asleep.

The next morning, I woke up, ten-ish more than a bit sick. I pulled myself together, took a shower, shaved, and packed. I worried of what I would say to her when she saw me checking out. I thought of all the lines, all the lies, nothing seemed appropriate. So, I decided to just wing it.

At about 12:00 I call a bellboy and had him get my stuff. I went down to the desk and Moksha Priya was nowhere in sight. I checked out.

"Thank you Dr. Shaman, please come again," said the Sikh who had laid the negatory vibes my direction the day previous.

I walked out to the taxi, wondering where she was, what was she doing, how she was feeling, or was it all simply another dream.

I got into the taxi, we headed out onto the street.

"Where to?"
"Airport, International terminal.

CHAPTER 8
THE LOFT

I had been living in this loft downtown.

Lofts, I was never quite sure why they called them lofts. Loft, being defined in the dictionary as a low space or attic elevated from the floor and directly under the roof. Lofts, why? Few even had lofts.

They simply were old brick manufacturing buildings that no one was using anymore. Industry had long ago moved to Japan, Korea, Taiwan, China, where standards were higher and the labor costs cheaper. Standards and labor, two things which America no longer possesses.

Once-upon-a-time these old unused buildings had become the haunts of the poor, the down-and-out, and the creative. The rent was cheap and the atmosphere abstractly aesthetic. That was long ago though.

The building investors, the property's owners, there lay the destroyers of this community that once thrived on the abstract nature of art. They began to rent space in these unused buildings. As is generally the tradition with commercial property, upon moving in, one must sign a contract which states, whatever improvements that one adds: be that painting, carpeting, heating, plumbing, even a loft, must remain once you check out. So, as these improvements moved in and the improvers moved out, the buildings being nicer, and the rents began to go up. This combined with the fact that the city finally got around to making these structures legal residences; it became time for the owners of these virtual tax write offs to shift into the money-making mode again and have another round of *danaro por nada.*

These refurbished ancient warehouses, industrial spaces, sweat shops; became known by the term, *"The resurgence of old L.A."* A lie in a lying industrial/material world where the information revolution had succeeded the industrial revolution leaving its mark by leaving spaces/places where artists could once live but now could barely afford unless they be mega successful in the commercial sense. But, the hip, the trendy, the affluent, the fashionable, well they could pay the rent just fine.

There is not much room for art in this world, thought the masses claim respect for the creators and wish to purchase a piece.

So anyway, enough of the history and philosophy lesson.

I was living in this big space, single level. It was on the third floor of this old building just a bit off of skid row.

I had moved in at a time when there was only one other person in the building, an old eccentric reasonably famous artist. He lived on the ground floor, I on the top, so our paths barely ever crossed.

Me, I had the opportunity to paint, play music, do just about anything I felt like doing with no interference from anyone. There was quite a feeling of freedom in all of this. A freedom known to only a few. A space where spacelessness was the essence. A sanctuary inside a prison; a prison of the city, of the streets. Yes, I had space.

Space, in the worst section of the industrial city where manufacturing had gone bad and all that was left were the remains of tired old buildings,

148

alone and lost old retirees who inhabited run down old hotels, and lost broken losers, by the standards of this world, who slept on the streets. In India, they would have all been holy men, *sadhus*. But here, they were just people who had nothing left to lose and nowhere else to go. Some of these people would kill you for a dollar, kill you for a bottle of the grape. I felt very much at home next to them. They surrounded me, they walked the streets with me. I walked, lived, drank with them.

Time as in all things, as it tends to do; yes, it does move along and things they do change. More and more of the, "Found," of the, "Into something," as opposed to the lost and the nowhere left to turn, came to live in the building, and in the area in general. There were parties and people always fucking saying, "Hello, what are you into?"

Time, it moved on. Time, it was close at hand. Time, it was almost the time to leave. The place had become a fucking yuppie apartment building.

On the whole, of course, the brick walls did give one a more clear sense of their own definition. Compared to that of a typical dry walled, plastered apartment building. But, the amount of movement in the structure, the amount of non-art action, and energy within the walls; well, the palace had entered into the same unnatural syndrome of all those upscale apartments or condominiums (condom-miniums) on the other side of the business class tracks downtown.

It was a Saturday night, one of those atypical ones when you feel like going out and doing something. One of those atypical ones when there is never anything to do or anyone that you would choose to do nothing with.

Saturday night is farmers' night out anyway; so my father told me.

I was kicking back, reading some, writing some, laying on my Japanese futon bed. I had just about drifted off to a nap of sleep, 10:00 P.M.-ish, when off in the distance I began to hear screaming, yelling, crying.

It took me a moment or three to focus my mind as to whether or not these were real or simply an alpha state vision or the beginning of a bad dream. It continued and I realized that it was a woman's voice and it seemed to be nearby. Sounded to be coming, upon closer examinations, from the next space over.

I knew that someone had moved into the space next to mine but me being my usual cynical, unfriendly, reclusive self had not ventured to see who or what it was inhabiting that space.

Now, the first thought to my mind was maybe her dude was tapping her up. In which case, I should just leave them alone, let their melodrama play on/play out. I know that I hate it when others chill on in and stick their nose in my scene.

Or maybe, it was just the chick having a temper tantrum. I mean, I once had this babe who used to scream and cry at the top of her lungs, obviously in the mode of let's get my own way, let's get attention, etc. Me, I would always try to get her to chill back but that never seemed to silence the situation.

Then, I thought, maybe it was murder, murder in my midst. I mean come-on, there has been more than a few murders in this area. So, the knight in shining armor came out in me and I had to go and check-this situation out.

I pulled on my clothing and shoes; walked quickly up to my big blue metal sliding door, noisily slid it open and walked down the corridor a bit. I listened at the door, the crying it was still going on.

Pound, I gave a pounding knock on the door. No response but the crying was silenced which set my mode of interest to the question, *'Exactly what was happening in there.'*

"Are you Okay in there?"

No answer.

"Hello, is everything alright? I am your next-door neighbor."

Nothing…

"Hello."

The door, rusty red, not pretty painted blue like mine; well, it slid open. There, standing before me was this more than halfway beautiful tall light brown-haired woman. I looked into her deep green eyes—eyes that whispered the pain of eternity. Eyes that had been crying way too long, way too often. Her eyes grabbed me; green surrounded by red. The crying as it does, had amplified their already clear intensity.

She says,

"Yeah, I'm Okay. Oh, you're the guy next door, I've seen you."

I thought that was funny, for I had never seen her.

She asked, "Did I disturb you?"
"No, not really. I was just concerned."

She wiped her face with the long sleeve white sweater which she was wearing. *'How artistic,'* I thought. She turned, began to walk, walk further deeper inside,

"Come in," she said.

For a moment, I was a bit stunned. *'Come in,'* I thought? What! I stood there for a moment contemplating. But, then never let it be me who turns down an invite from a lone lovely lady in the night. I slid on in.

"Close the door, please."

I closed it and strutted deeper into the realms of the great abyss.

Her place had almost nothing in it. There were two thousand square feet of Zen decorations, *nada*. Over to one side was a mattress with no sheets, simply an old flannel sleeping bag thrown atop it. Next to it was a suspended rope with some clothing handing on it, only a few. Over on the other side was a small red chest of drawers, an ice chest. And, except for a cheap stereo system and a few books and records, there was nothing. That was it. Nothing else in the whole place.

Chicks are funny, they are either full-on in to let's spend daddy's whole expense account or their inheritance on every type of household item imaginable and a few other things as well, or they live with zero. Someone should do a study on that, figure it out.

There were no lights on in the place. Illumination was provided by the reflection of the streetlight emanating from outside.

I said to myself that I could see why she was crying, this was a seriously fucking depressing atmosphere.

She walked over near the window, leaned against the wall, and sat down. I sliced my way on over, sat down in front of her; asked,

"So, are you really alright?"
Her answer was, "How long have you been here?"
"L.A. or this building?"
"Both."
"L.A., well I was born here. This building; a while."
"What do you do?"

So came the question out of her mouth. The question I hate. The question I never like to answer.

"Ah, this and that."
"Yeah, me too."

Her voice, it was soft, clear, educated. The way she sat reminded me of a ballerina I had once known—once, a long time ago. Her motions, they were soft as she occasionally whipped a tear from her face.

The moment it was heavy. It was like a mega fucking weight was placed on my shoulders. What could I say to a woman lost in her own soap opera, lost in her own dream? No council was asked, none could be given. Brought to tears for I knew not what. Brought to tears, no doubt, by the lies of the world. Sadly, I have known too many saddened women like her. I guess they say similar people attract one another. We all have cried our tears.

Just when I was about to say, *'Well if you are alright then I will bail,'* she said to me,

"Would you like something to drink?"
"Sure, what do you have?"
"Water."
"Water, it is then."

My mind instantly raced and hoped that it was not tap water from this building. I mean, the drinking of rust is not what I was particularly into. Living there, I personally even did my occasional dish washing sessions with bottled water. And, to drink that poison, *no gracias.*

She reached for her ice chest and pulled out two mineral waters. I was relieved. She popped the tops, handed me mine, and sat back with a smile.

I asked, "Do you live here alone?"
"Yeah, unfortunately. You?"
"Of course."

Well seeing how the ten or so words of conversation were flowing along so well, I decided to ask her,

"So, what're all these tears about?"
"For myself. For being alone, when I don't want to be alone."
"Yeah, I know that song. But you're not alone now."

She smiled at my comment and asked,

"Are you a musician? You look like a musician."
"I've been known to play a note or two."
"Oh, what do you play?"
"A little bit of everything."
"A man of many talents and I am living next to him."

I could feel the vibes of a move coming on.

"Just an artist in an artless world," I spoke.
"Do you paint?"
"Yes, I do that too."

The rap and what a way to lay it down into the eyes of green and red. Into the arms of a crying child in a reason that has no room for tears.

"How about you; are you a dancer? You look like a dancer."
"No, I am a runner. I run away from everything. I run away from myself."

Away from herself, away from something, into nothing. I know this scenario well. Away to nowhere. Isn't that where forever leads? Nowhere being everywhere.

She never realized, like so many others that she was something more than nothing. She never realized it, not unlike me. But isn't that the curse of the world, this world that holds us all down. It shows us promises of wealth, and fame. Gives us nothing, not a fucking way to reach whatever dream it is we dream. And those who have made it, they look down and criticize. They never understand what it is like to be nothing. What it feels like to feel the pain of nothingness.

So, she ran, one movement to the next. Ran away, like the hours of our lives.

We sat around and talked of the nothingness of life; laughed a little bit. Her tears, they were drying up.

We looked out of the window, the view of another old brick building and the occasional passing of a car on an occasionally used street.

It got to be pushing 2:00 A.M.

She took my hand and said, "I'm getting sleepy, would you like to stay with me?"

'Well," my mind said, *'Only two o'clock, a bit early to go to sleep for me but who knows, maybe we won't go to sleep at all. And come-on, what's a guy like me supposed to say, No?'*

So, I said, "Sure," and leaned over and gave her a kiss upon her cheek.

She stood up, pulled up her sweater, exposing this thin white skinned body. The light shown on her like an exquisite black and white photograph, full of depth and shadows. Shaded and created to perfection in the artist's eye. She reached down, as I now sat against her brick wall, below the window, watching a more than perfect mesmerizing view. She unfastened her white denim pants, slipped them off.

A woman with no underwear, an artist in the making.

I sat there popping a *hard-on* as she gently sat down on her bed awaiting my arrival. I kicked off my shoes and began to undress. My mind was turning and I wished I could get that bad boy down. I mean, a bit embarrassing, a bit awkward. What if she wasn't intending sex?

I stood up, turned, and faced the window: slipped off my pants, my shirt. Turned to her in the soft light of the downtown night. For a moment, I wished that it was darker, then maybe she wouldn't notice my bad hard pup. But, no luck, enough light to see.

Her eyes looked softly at my body in this night of obvious acceptance. I felt at ease. She lay down, pulled the sleeping bag over her. I crawled over the top of her and lay down next to her. She lifted her head. I placed my arm under her and she lay upon it; her arms around me, holding me tight.

We lay there on our sides. She took my dick and gently placed it between her thighs, slipping it slowly into herself.

An obvious motion to show that she was feeling the same as me. Shall we call it A-rousal?

We kissed and she said,

"I don't want to be alone anymore."

I understood her. We kissed again; we made love late into the night.

Her body was firm, thin; almost too thin. She moved gently yet directly; she did know what to do. A good quality in a woman, yes? She was no grinder but an artist in her movements. She left no stone untouched, unturned. Eventually we went to sleep.

The morning rolled around, well 11:30 or so. And, after a love making session or two. I said,

"Would you like to go and get some breakfast?"
"Sure."

She slipped out of the sheetless bed and slipped on into a brown sweater. She obviously was into sweaters. She pulled back on her white pants, put some sandals on and we went out.

We went to this little outdoor place I knew and had the proper European breakfast of *Cappuccino, croissant,* and some *torte.* We hung out until the early afternoon, not speaking a lot, just hanging. Back at the building, I was ready for my daily nap sessions. I mean, we had gotten up way too early by my standards. So, I slid into my skid crib. She headed, post a kiss, for hers.

The lights were still on, having left, last night, when it was dark. I flipped them off. I sat down on my couch for a few. Picked up a guitar, played a few notes and thought how for the first time I was glad one of those *'new people'* had moved in.

Ah love, and the moments of infatuation. How I do love that love. That love that maybe last an hour, a day, a week, but never a month. That feeling in the heart, like the feeling of the wind, which blows softly through my hair.

I thought of her and how nothing seemed permanent but then she was tired of being alone. I thought of her, someone to hang out with, at least until that feeling faded.

A cube of sugar in both of our teas. A momentary answer to an unasked question.

I walked on over to my bed, laid back. Enjoyed the alpha state and fell off to sleep for an hour or so.

Slowly, I woke up to the fading light of the day. A day that lasted long enough, just as it should have. Lasted long enough in the infatuation arms of love.

I went and took a shower, with my filtered shower water of course. Got dressed and decided 'Well, let's see where this relationship takes me.' So, I grabbed a bottle of *'the Dom,'* (Dom Perion). I wondered if she had ever tried it. And, I waltzed on over to her side of the wall.

As I approached from the right, I noticed her door slightly ajar and I looked in; nothing, not a goddamn thing. Clothing was gone, the records, the books, the sleeping bag, the ice chest, even the chest of drawers.

"Fuck!" I shouted out loud. I went in and looked around the nothing. Not even a note.

What the fuck happened here? What the fuck happened to her?

I sat down on the one remaining object, the sheetless mattress upon the floor. I cracked open the bottle of the Dom, sat back and killed it. Then, I got the great idea to call up the owner of the building to see what he knew of the chick. His answer, about the same as I, *nada,* just her name.

Well, I sat back that evening and dreamed of a momentary infatuation that didn't have its chance to run dry. A woman, who didn't want to be alone anymore and who, as she said, was a runner; she ran away from everything. I understood her. Damn, she reminded me of me.

Well life in a loft. A moment of people searching for their brand of pretense. Pretense in a pretentious world. All governed by the kind of car you drive, what you wear, where you live. They think it is all so fucking important. They all moved into an artist's world, my world. The world of the mystic, where pretense is only pretend and pretend is only another reason to dance.

So, they all move in, I moved out. As did most of the artists who could no longer afford this corporate infrastructure rent. All those that have remained, well they just wait for an earthquake to wipe out the buildings that are far below earthquake standards.

Everything always changes, nothing stays the same. And we all try to run...

CHAPTER 9
THE BUS RIDE

I had put together a few extra G's playing the crapshoot of the stock market and had decided to pick myself up either a yacht or a new Porsche. Now I had my bad '64 356 SC but for some foolish reason I had not yet come to the realization that they are the perfect car and that classic style was ninety percent of everything. I desired a new more modern Targa.

Desire is of course, as desire does. So, my cravings won out. Funny, how they often do. And how the mind makes itself up long before we ever realize or admit that it has. After looking at a few boats, I went into the market for a Targa full on.

In the paper, I came upon one. The price was right. It had a rebuilt engine and new paint. So, I mean, let's check it out. I drove on down to Long Beach where it was stationed and as it turned out it had been owned by a Thai. Now, this was a good sign, I thought; my long and passionate involvement with Siam and all. Funny though how Thais always seem to own fast cars, fixed up cars, and a lot of cars. Stereotypical of course, but stereotypes are always fun.

The ride was not parked at the guy's apartment but over in Belmont Shores. Obviously, to get maximum attention at minimal cost. I drove over there, the Thai dude rode shotgun. We pulled up to the car, a parking ticket placed neatly upon the window. The free advertising cost wasn't so low, huh?

It looked clean, drove clean. I checked it out and about it. The color of it was orange. Perhaps I should have taken the sign of orange more consciously to mind. I mean, my first motorcycle was orange, and it was nothing but problems. And I once upon a time, now a long time ago, was a Swami; orange, all I could wear was orange. And with me being a much subtler dresser, in regards at least to color, well anyway…

Being lost in the midst of desire, I didn't watch for the cosmic signs and besides, I thought, I could always get it painted.

It was about a day or so later and I was *en route* to Hollywood via Watts. A drive I sometimes make. The situation presented itself, so I put the proverbial pedal to the metal and I was out-a-there. That is, I was out-a-there until I hear a snap and there it goes, my clutch cable.

Fuck! I was mad. Mad at the car, mad at myself, mad at being in the middle of Watts with long blond hair and an orange Porsche that was not in any condition to run any farther.

Now, in actually, I have no problem with Watts and the South-central region of L.A. In fact, I spent my early years growing up there. Yes, the only white kid in an all black school. And yes, I was front-seat central to the Watts Riots of '65. It was just that, that/there was not where I wanted to be right then.

It was mid-day and the world being full of nine to fivers, I was left with virtually no one to call to get me out of my current predicament. Now even thought I could have called a tow truck, I really didn't want to deal with that for I had my main mechanics down by my abode in Hermosa and it would cost me probably a hundred spot to get it towed down there.

Money never being my main focal point in life, I probably would have had this done; towed it

162

that is. But money never being my main focal point, I had virtually none with me. The tow truck seemed out of the question.

I decided the best thing to do was to head up for Hollywood and wait for a buddy of mine to get off the nine to five shift, in his case like 6:00 A.M. to 9:00 P.M. and then we could either get the car together enough to drive it to the mechanic, or we could bumper tow it.

But now, how to get to Hollywood? That was the next dilemma. Walking crossed my mind but no-go to that, it was a million miles away. A taxi? Not enough *danero*. So, I guess it was going to have to be the worst of all forms of L.A. transportation, the fabled bus.

The bus, I hate the bus. A step into the reality of the nowhere nomad; nowhere fast. Mad perhaps best describing the situation, so being nowhere and a proverbial nomad seemed to ring true.

I headed on over, by foot that is, to the nearest main street. Leaving the newly purchased orange Targa to its own demise, favorable I hoped. Finding the bus bench, I planted myself in wait.

Waiting, what a horrible way to spend a life, oh too shortly lived. I sat there preferring to be somewhere else/anywhere else. I even thought how I wished I was awaiting a bus elsewhere, Cairo, Burma, Bombay, Bangkok; no not Bangkok, I never take the bus in Bangkok.

The time went slow, a few minutes seemed forever. Me, being the spiritual person that I am, tried to make the best of the time. I watched the traffic pass, smiled as the entirely black population drove past me. Some looking, at a white patty on their turf. Some even yelling, whitey or honky this or that—the young ones of course.

I laughed to myself, because if they only knew I had spent the first ten years of my life growing up not too far from this bus bench upon which I sat. Being the only honky in their school. Racial segregation, it does go both ways don't you know. That is, I was the only white boy there until I, meaning my mother and I, made the now infamous move to Hollywood after my father kicked in my tenth year. Better or worse, I am still not quite sure.

So, I sat thee trying to enjoy myself but not trying hard enough for I was still angry at the car, angry at my situation, and embarrassed to be sitting on a bus bench waiting for a bus. The lowest of all forms of transportation in this city, my city. And here I have one Porsche sitting a few blocks away, another one at home and one or two other forms vehicular transportation around my crib. I had a lot of cars. Big ego, huh?

Finally, here comes the bus. I get on with the two older black ladies who had joined my waiting vigil. I asked the bus driver, "How much?" He looks at me funny, 'Like what is this dude doing in this neighborhood, riding a bus and asking how much.' He probably thought I was a tourist or something. Embarrassment struck me again.

"Where you going?"
"Well, I guess I need a transfer because I am going to Hollywood."
"Seventy-five cents."

I get the money out, put it in the box and head for a seat. Planted, I watch the scenery go by, listen to the conversations, and reflect on how the average black bus rider doesn't know how to conjugate their verbs.

The bus headed North. It was almost amusing to watch how the shades of the clientele changed as the ride progressed. At first the passengers were entirely black, then some Latinos were added, then finally some *whities* came among us all.

'The bus riders of L.A ...' I thought to myself, *'Someday I would have to do a study of bus riding population demographics. But then, it had probably already been done.'*

The ride continued and as the bus became seemingly desegregated. The bus stops. Then/there in the sidewalk distance, out of my window, I see a lady, a beautiful vision, a goddess among the masses. My breath is taken away. Her hair is jet black, her skin a very fine caramel. My blood pressure rises. She walks onto the bus. She pays, puts her coins in the slot. She walks down the aisle.

The seat next to me is empty. Interestingly enough, none of the bus-riding locals would come and sit by this white boy. She continues her walk. My mind drifts. My mind focuses, "Please come and sit by be. Sit here, sit here." I throw the vibes in her direction. She, however, sits in the seat across the aisle and one in front of me.

My view is good. Sitting there, she looks like the goddess of all who ride the bus. A dream of the divine, placed in a world of mortals who have no car, no driver's license, too many drunk driving charges, or their Porsches have broken down.

Lust, desire, fool's pleasure in a fool's world. My interests are stirred. I embrace it.

I view her. She is dressed in designer jeans and a white tity scraper shirt or blouse as you prefer. Not particularly the clothing style I like on a woman, but society forms us all. Her shoes they are white patent leather, low cut exposing the white caramel skin of her legs. I wondered to myself, if my *Spirit Helper* had sent her to me to compensate for the breakdown of my car.

She sat. I sat. As the bus it moved slowly into Hollywood.

The stop where I was to get off, to transfer, came up and as fate would have it, she also was to exit at this point. Her pulling the cord to sound the bell to alert the driver put everything in my known direction.

We left the bus and I slowly followed behind her as she headed for the crosswalk and to the bus stop across the street. We were headed in the same *di-rec-tion.*

I sat on the bus bench, while she stood for a time. After a minute or three, she joined me on the bench. Time to make my move?

I sat there in all the anxiety that comes with the first word, in the first moment of impending passion, set in a public place. I mean, not being a forward person, what do you say? In a club, in a bar, it's all easy. But on a bus bench.

My heart pounded as my mind pondered my play. It is hard to be cool while waiting for a bus. At least, so I thought. I sat there lost in indecisive lust.

The bus was coming. She stood up. I stood up. We moved towards the triangular sign atop a metal pole, letting one know that this was quite and in fact a bus stop. Well, it was now or never.

"Do you ride this bus every day?"

166

She looks at me and smiles and in relatively poor English says,

"No, I was trying to get a job at McDonalds."

Now me being the *suave* dude that I am and picking up her obviously Mexican accent and being aware of her very light caramel sensuous skin, I ask her in my most proper Spanish,

"Are you from Spain?"
"No," she answers in English, "Mexico."
"Oh, where in Mexico?"
"Guadalajara."

At this point, a very crowded bus pulls up and on we board. I am very careful to stay tight with her so our conversation may continue.

"Did you get the job at McDonalds?" I inquire in Spanish.
"I will know in two days." She answers in English.
"Oh, that, good," I say in Spanish. "By the way, what is your name?"
"Lupe is my name." She says in English.

Well Lupe, form Guadalajara, dressed in designer jeans, seeking a job at McDonalds, and speaking to me in English at questions inquired in Spanish, time for me shift linguistic modes.

"Crowded bus, huh?"
"Yes, do you ride this bus every day?"

Ah, my chance to let her know my cool. My ego moves into full forward overdrive, fifth gear in a car whose clutch cable broke a little over an hour ago.

"No, I never ride the bus. My Porsche broke down."

She didn't seem to understand.

"My car stopped working, so I am taking the bus up to a friend's house."
"Porsche car, you have a Porsche car?"
"Actually, I have two."

As my ego parties.

Now, this young gay dude, whom I noticed had been listening to our *convo*. Gets a look of, *'Yeah right,'* on his face. I felt like telling him, *'Fuck you, faggot.'* But, as I thought about it, it did sound more than a bit like a bullshit pick up rap.

Lupe sat, well stood there, in seeming more or less belief and then she said,

"Oh, I get off at the next stop."
"Do you live near here?"
"No, I'm going to the YMCA to do aerobics."

Yes, her body did look tight all-right.

I hurried up and took a piece of paper out of the portable pocket notebook I always carry in my sport coat and wrote down my telephone number, telling her to call me and we could talk about Mexico or something. The gay dude looking on, once again I felt like telling him, "Fuck you."

Off the bus she got; the goddess of the carless. A dream of passion, lost to the hoards who flock to the bus line at dinner time. *En route* to their own fantasies, their own heaven, but more than

168

probably, their own hells. Imprisoned inside the walls of the city. A master who only takes hostages, leaving the rest to die slowly fending for themselves in the blazes of this aft-world.

There she went, the best part of my day. The bus continued on Sunset into the slums of East Hollywood where I had spent my younger years, post ten, and where I still felt so lost, while being so at home.

But my mind had found a new fantasy, something on which to dwell. A dream to dream.

Will she call? I hoped that she would.

My stop came up and I got off the bus, giving the gay guy a dirty look. I walked the block or so over to the apartment of a friend and knocked upon the door. No one was home. I knew where a key was stashed, so I let myself in and chilled down over a beer or three.

I put the call through to my main man Saturday Jim and talked to his wife for a few, well actually with her, it is quite a few. I told her to give her bad love lad the word that his bro, the big guy, was in need of *me-chan-i-cal* type assistance whenever he arrived at home. After the *convo*. And still no arrival at the stall of the main occupant, I had another brew laid out and caught me a few Z's.

I woke up about seven and still no one around and no call from Saturday Jim. So, I laid back caught some T.V. and once again waited.

Waiting, a destiny all too real, all so unnecessary but then, as we all sooner or later realize, life has no purpose anyway. So, what do we do with our time that doesn't really matter. The ultimate question.

Lost in the T.V., lost in my newly discovered fantasy of Lupe, my time passed. I got a call back at about 8:30 and Saturday Jim was *en route*. E.T.A., forty-five.

I left a thank you note for the unarrived homeowner and waited outside in the cool spring smoggy L.A. air. Saturday Jim pulled up at nine plus or so and said,

"Shit, aren't you glad that you don't live around here anymore?"

Saturday Jim being another Hollywood kid who chose to make the move.

"Yeah, this place is a hell hole of a ghetto anymore. But oh man, did I meet this babe of a chick today on the bus. Her name was Lupe. Oh Lupe, Lupe, Lupe."
"Hot, huh?"
"Fuck'n-A. Oh man, was she ever. Lupe, Lupe, Lupe."

And so, our conversation went in the vein of the general macho dude with his macho friend as we headed on down to Watts. We got there, the Porsche surprisingly still untouched.

This was Saturday Jim's first view of it, nice way to meet, huh? We did some basic mechanical maneuvering and got the pup running as long as I kept it in fourth gear. Thus, I drove it on down to Manhattan Beach, to my main mechanic's shop, burning the clutch all the way. Saturday Jim pulled up the rear just in case systems went down again.

We dropped it off, had a beer or thirty over at my place in Hermosa, and Saturday Jim bailed on, assuring me that Lupe would never call. Lupe, Lupe, Lupe.

*　　*　　*

A few days later, the Targa fixed, I cruised it and I out to Saturday Jim's on Saturday as is usual protocol.

"So, did you hear from your main bus babe yet?"
"No, not yet."
"I knew it."
"But hey, if worse comes to worse man, the chick said that she goes to the Y to work out and I can always cruise on by there."

We both laughed. But, in fact, the thought had crossed my mind. We spent the rest of the day, as our Saturdays often go, kicking back, pouring down a few, and taking a nap here or there. This Saturday had my continual reminder and that of Saturday Jim's, "Lupe, Lupe, Lupe."

I pulled it home about eight or so, my message machine was blinking away. As I listened, to my joy and amazement, my main *bus-rid'n* squeeze, Lupe had indeed called. Three times to be exact. She even left messages, which is always quite nice. Continual hang-ups always leave you wondering.

It not being too late, I immediately get on the phone line and am greeted with a busy signal. This goes on, to my growing antsy-ness, and repeated calls, for about forty-five, until finally the phone line rings and a voice, oh so softly answers, "Bueno." In my very proper Spanish,

"Puedo hav lar con Lupe."
"Sandy, is that you?"

171

Yes, indeed it was Lupe who had answered. No, she hadn't gone out with other dudes as my mind had feared. Yes, she remembered my voice. All was fine and perfect in all the universal realms of lust and suchness on the telephone lines of Saturday night.

We spoke a bit and though my intoxication from the day with Saturday Jim's was fading, I, in all my best forwardness asked, if she would like to go out tonight.

"Will we have to take the bus?" She asked.

Understandable so... But, I had to laugh.

"No, the car that was broken is now fixed and also I have other ones."
"Oh good, let's go out. Can you be here fast?"

Fast, ah, I liked her style. I liked what my mind thought she wanted, what I wanted. A night with no meaning—like to the max, lived fast. Nothing to lose for there is nothing to gain. Only placed pagan desire in a world so full of itself. Nothing to lose, for what is left to lose? A fantasy, oh yes, it was coming true. Lupe, Lupe, Lupe...

"How fast is fast?" I asked, but she didn't quite seem to understand.

You see, I tried to rap the *ingles,* beings as that seemed to be her *pre-fer-ance.*
It went on for a bit, and she told me of her location over in East Hollywood and I explained that I lived at the beach and it would take me a little

while to get there. It was agreed that I could be there in an hour, though it would be a rush.

Into the shower I got, and into a change of clothes, and *on the road*. This time, in my bad '64 Porsche 356 SC, so as to knowingly not encounter any mechanical mishaps.

I was slowing down a bit, on my way there. It had been a rough day of drinking, napping, and conversations of, 'Lupe, Lupe, Lupe.' You know how it goes? I grabbed me two large cups of the *java* at the McDonalds drive-through on my way as I wondered if she got the job. I had forgotten to ask.

I pulled onto her street and looked for the address in the *lat-en-ing* hours of the darkened streets of East Hollywood. I knew the area: the neighborhood of refugees, of lost Catholic's souls praying only for empowerment, for employment, in a world that uses them up, spits them out, and is none the better or wiser for it. I saw her address and I thought to myself, this is not where I want to be.

True to my nature, I, none-the-less, found a scarce parking spot and parallel parked into it. On the old apartment house wall, in front of where I parked, sat three *vatos*. I thought, *'A great place to park my baby, my 356, my Porsche that almost never breaks down on me.'*

Out of the car I got, the *cholos* said,

"Kapaso Weto, (What's happening, blondie)" as I walked by.
"Nada," I answered.

Though I was worried about my coupe, up to Lupe's apartment I went. It was on the second floor of a two-story old wooden building that probably was once a large house. The walls were filled with graffiti: names, a trophy, and claimed allegiance of boys becoming men within a world where all that matters is how bad you are. And bad, is the only way to stay alive.

All the self-serving bureaucrats talk, all this shit about how these kids don't need to be in gangs is bullshit. If you live in these areas, and if you want to stay alive, you are in a gang.

I could understand, I was once a *gringo cholo* in a *vato* gang, *es-say*. But it did not stop me from feeling for them and for Lupe. I wouldn't want to live there, be there again, do that again. But then/they, all those who do, probably don't want to be there/do that either.

I knocked on the door and quickly it was opened by a smiling Lupe. Ah, Lupe, Lupe, Lupe, complete in herself and dressed precisely in her designer jeans and this time a blue tity scraper top. Fashion?

She brought me into the apartment. Funky, would be a gracious description. There was a couch with some kind of cover over it, three beds made up on the floor of the living room, another army cot style bed in the very small kitchen; (who knows what was in the bedroom), and a very large cockroach that I could not help but notice walking casually upon the wall. Uck, I wanted out.

There were introductions all around. *"Mucho guesto, Mucho guesto,"* to her parents and two other adults, and, *"Kapaso,"* to the four or five children that were there playing and laughing at my being there. I made the excuses and suggested we go out; it was getting late and all. Out we went.

We walked to my car, which was still quite luckily intact. I opened the door for her, to the

174

expected comments of the *vatos* sitting upon the wall. I fired it up and off we drove.

Normally, I would have sat in the car, made small talk, and decided where to go. But the area and situations would have depressed me if I had let myself sit in them too long. Too many reminders of a forced down my throat youth, that I never had any choice in.

Off and on the road,

"So, what would you like to do tonight? Maybe go dancing, go to dinner?"
"You say you live at the *playa?*"
"Yes."
"I love the *playa,* let's go there."

She must not have known the word for beach.

Now, could I believe this whole situation? I mean like, that is usually my suggestion after the babe has been wined and dined. Like, *'Hey, would you like to take a walk on the beach? It's so natural and refreshing. I love to be in touch with nature. That's why I live there.'* You know, something along those bullshit lines, as the rap generally goes. Then, once we are in the vicinity, *'Well parking is always a problem at the beach, let's just park at my place, then we can go take a walk, etc. etc. etc.'* And the rest is generally history. But her, this babe of a *Mexicana* is inviting ME, to the beach.

Almost stunned by the situation, I headed out for the waves but instead of heading down by my crib, I don't know, I just had this feeling not to show her where I live. I drove to Playa Del Rey.

The drive was nice enough. We discussed Mexico and the fact that she has been here, in the

U.S., only three months. We talked of her new job coming up at the Mexican food restaurant, not McDonalds. My mind screams, 'Oh no not another waitress, Uck!' We also spoke of the fact that this is not the Porsche which broke down but this is, in fact, another one. Overall, she seemed intelligent enough and my infatuation had more than deepened.

We drove down to the ocean. It was pushing 10:30 P.M. as I looked at my watch. She mentioned that she should be home about twelve or so. I jokingly ask, *'A.M. or P.M.'*

Well, there goes love rolled up in a *tortilla* along the *playa* tonight. For I know full well that it takes time to put the total move on a babe, if you know what I mean? At least a good Catholic girl from Guadalajara.

Though I initially was let down, I kept my eyes on her movement, her form, and I hoped at least for a future bout with a few more hours involved.

We walked down by the shore, talked a bit, listened to the ocean, in all its suchness, and I have to admit, I was more than a bit lost in infatuation and the lust of the moment.

I love infatuation. It is what love is all about. That feeling of just desire-full awe. That place in the heart that is just exploding for the person, for the moment, for the only reason of no reason. Its only fault is that it lasts so short a time. But the up-side, it reinstates itself by happening again and again and again, for the next person and the next and the next, on down that line.

Nothing is like it, nothing. I always wondered why people bothered to get married for at best this feeling could lay the foundation for boredom and attachment but nothing could ever compare to it; that initial and intense feeling of what the poets have called love.

With some women I felt it, with some I do not. Perhaps it is my choice, some say that to be true. But there I was, the ocean and Lupe. Ah Lupe, Lupe, Lupe.

And textbook love, I don't believe in it anyway. At least not in the way it has been defined by philosophers, scholars, and the like. Infatuation, yes. Lust, yes. Desire, definitely. Even attachment, yes. But forever love, no way.

We walked on a bit more, then she took my hand. My heart soared as she did. In fact, I believe I even got hard.

She asked me, "Sandy, do you like me?"
"I think love is a better word."
"You love me?"
"Yes. Why, don't you love me yet," I quickly respond.
"Yes, I do."

Things were definitely looking up.

"And it is all so fast," Lupe said.
"Life is lived in seconds." I answered.

She didn't seem to quite get the point. She seemed never to understand whenever I got a bit philosophical in the English language.

She then leaned in, and being nearly a foot shorter than I, stood on her tiptoes, and planted a kiss upon my neck. A chill went up my spine.

The pieces were placed, the moment of motion was upon us, and it was set for me to move. Or, should I spell that with a capital "M," Move.

I suggested that we sit down, which we did. And the rest, well it was almost like a movie script. Not of a porno nature, though they definitely have their appeal and placement. But, more like that of a B-grade, low budget movie. But hey, I wasn't complaining.

As we sat down, it/we got right down to business. We kissed and I do mean kissed. Lupe could lay some serious slobs. After our initial exchange, I went for the boobies. They were not too big, just the way I like 'em.

Things seemed to be going along so well, why hesitate. So, under the blue shirt I went. Skin against skin, it felt good. She felt good. Her tongue in my mouth felt way good.

The boobies were easy enough, so at the designer jeans I preceded, no defense. I tried to get my hand inside, but tight as they were, that was no-go. So, as our mouths are lost in serious kisses, I try to unbutton them. After having a little problem with that too, her arms free from around my body, they lent assistance. We laughed as we kissed.

Once inside, my hand finds its way underneath the panties. A route well known, and for the beaver I go. It is wet, very wet. No problem with this one. I am up and more than ready for action.

That feeling when all systems are go and you want to plant the puppy deep. That feeling where just from the excitement you know you will cum in your pants if you don't get down to business soon. Hot…

I sit up a little and begin to pull off her jeans, we are still laying serious slobs. Her pants are tight, very tight. She reaches down and lends a secondary helping hand. The thought comes to my mind, and I would have laughed had it not been so intense, that I had never taken designer jeans off a chick before. Levis yes, but designer jeans, never. The type of chick who wore them was never my thing. I mean, I'm into the classic look of long skirts and so on. But there I was. There she was. We were on the sand. The air was cool, but we were hot—as the ocean, the divine ocean laid waste to the seaside with its ever-churning waves. And yes, she moved on down in the direction of our feet, just like a fucking movie.

Once her pants were off, I slipped mine down and my rod found no trouble finding its mark. No time for playing games, in it went, so easy, oh yes. She was ready for it. Her pussy was not so tight, but then under used ones seldom are; Latina ones, rarely are. I put it in there deep and found the top and it definitely caused her to squirm.

Laying there on top of her I raised her shirt up so I could change from the lips and nibble on a nipple in the process of the love making. Our size differences became a bit of a problem, so I rolled her over on top to have a better angle on the boobies.

I lay on the bottom and Lupe, oh Lupe, Lupe, Lupe didn't have many moves from atop. But I was there pumping myself away from below. Enjoying every minute of it.

Finally, thinking she probably hadn't had much experience, I rolled her back over, pulled out, came in from the side, legs intertwined, so I could have a good finger shot at the clit and went back to work. I put the power pile drive to her. As I was banging away, I just couldn't help myself from saying, "Oh Lupe, Lupe, Lupe."

From my maximum position of *erot-a-fica-tion* and manipulation I had her cuming pronto. And though I wasn't quite there yet, when she did, I blew the cookies off in a few. I had to admit, it was a good one.

We lay there kissing, laughing. "Another night in the big city," I told her. Finally, I pulled the wild *thAng* out.

This chick was soup city. I like them that way. There was really nothing to clean her or me up with, so I just pulled on my pants and helped her pull on her designer jeans. Just about this time, I see, not too far off in the nighttime distance, the lifeguard, beach ranger, a man in a uniform, cruising the beach in his 4X4 to get his cheap glimpses of nighttime beach love makers; passion wrapped in a garment of sand. He patrolled his dutiful beat in search of the culprits of the night, in order that he could issue cheap-shot parking tickets, for indecent exposure and all of that bullshit. I pointed the oncoming beach night stalker out to Lupe, we both laughed and agreed it had all been perfect and meant to happen, as we walked from the beach.

Never receiving our souvenir love making ticket from the man on patrol, we piled back into my 356 and headed for Hollywood. It was already a bit past midnight, and Lupe was anxious to return home. She sat close to me caressing my leg, kissing my neck, and basically getting me hard all over again.

We cruised up Santa Monica Blvd. The get dicked in the butt love punks were out in full force. All after a dollar and a case of AIDS. But, then most of them have little to live for and there are too many people in this world anyway.

We paralleled some old fags looking for booty and a young and still capable of getting fully hard dick. I had to explain the whole *maricone* thing to Lupe. She never knew anything about this scene. To her, Hollywood was a more than nice place and assuredly it must have been better than where she came from if she felt that way.

Aside from a few youngsters still looking for the life of the night, Lupe's street was fairly quiet. I found no place to park, so double parked, New York style, and walked her up to her apartment. She laid a serious good night slob on me and made me promise that I would come and see her tomorrow. She wanted me to arrive at 9:00 A.M., but fuck, that it was far too early for me so we agreed on eleven o'clock.

I drove off, off onto a Saturday night; farmers' night out. There was still a certain amount of cruisers out but that was nothing to me. I was hot, I wanted more pussy. Lupe had definitely struck a note in me and it was a note of fire.

I could not think of any of my on-the-line-babes that I could go to and relieve my LOVE notions upon, and I didn't feel like partying with a whore. So, since I was in the area, I hit an old haunt late night burger stand and ate a chiliburger and talked with some of the nighttime Mexican immigrants. *Wetbacks* by any other name.

Since there was no other available princesses for the evening, I pulled it home two-ish and kicked back, wrote a poem or two of the night; ah Lupe, Lupe, Lupe. My sights they were set on our next meeting. If things had gone so well on our first date, who knows what tomorrow would bring.

I eventually cribbed at my usual four or five in the A.M. with dreams of what was to come: *come/cum*. I fell asleep with a hard-on, as my mind counted the hours until our next meet.

A touch, a dream, what else is there to live for. We walk the streets in search of something to fill our time, when in most cases, it is a waste of time. But then killing-time is not as bad living no-time.

And the promise of the perfect kiss, of perfect passion keeps me searching these palaces in the realms of the night.

Ring, Ring, my telephone woke me. As it did, I noticed the clock 7:00 A.M. "Who the fuck can be calling this early?"

As it turned out it was my mother telling me that my uncle had arrived the night before and she wondered if I would like to come to see him. Sure.

Now my uncle is a basically mellow cat. He is pushing seventy and has a more than *bitch'n* flat top, rides around on a Harley, spends most of his time living on the positive side of Viva Las Vegas, and overall, chills rather seriously. What impresses me even more, is that he never fell under the illusion of the promise of love forever after. You know, the white picket fence, kids, and all that bullshit. Now that is not to say that he didn't crib down with a wench from time-to-time. In fact, I think he is cohabitating with one now, but like any cool womanizer, he keeps his distance from that wedding ring, keeps the illusion at bay.

Even though I had only two hours of sleep, I pulled myself out of the sack jack, kicked in a few wake me ups, if you catch what I mean, and went out and fired up my new toy, the Targa; to show my uncle and all. I headed, once again, for the city of the stars, Hollywood. Yeah right...

Once there, I gave the call of consideration to Lupe, Oh Lupe, Lupe, Lupe, and explained that my uncle was in town and could we hook-up the next day, instead making our meet of day—today. At this, she mega freaked. She went on how much she loved me and needed to see me, and how she thought I only used her the night before. Well...

But I consented and said I would come by at about two or so. Though she obviously was not happy with this; I mean hey, she was lucky that I would come by at all. But me being the nice guy that I am...

My uncle and I kicked it around for a while; went out and had breakfast and decided to head on down to the Harbor.

During the big one, W.W. II, my uncle had done his time as a sailor and had never lost his love for the ocean and sea going vessels. So, we walked around some old docks, talked with a Portuguese fisherman or two, strolled and stared at the old ships, wondering how they ever stayed afloat. Looked at the L.A. Harbor water. Lost, unsaveable long ago due to the dumping pollution of man and his ventures into the realms of other life forms to capture, take control, and attempt mastery of the unknown reaches of Mother Nature and the sea. Attempted, for no better reason than for the pursuit of the dollar, pursuit of adventure, leading by all roads to desired fame, fortune, and power.

The air was bad at the Harbor, as the air generally was. I always wondered how people could ever live in San Pedro or Wilmington and have to, on a daily basis, consume that quality of polluted oxygen and view the beautiful ocean lost and changed to a dark murky green/brown color, inhabited by ships the size of apartment buildings, nuclear submarines, and fishing boats that just don't seem to care anymore. *Life on the fringes of the big city.*

As we were walking around my uncle asked, as he always does, was I seeing any girls. "Nothing serious, of course," I told him. "But, I did just meet this nice little girl from across the border."

"Now Sandy, you know I have never told you what to do. But it has been my experience; don't get mixed up with those Mexican girls who have just come here. You just cannot trust them. I don't know why, but they are always after something. They will go out of their way to mix up your life. When I have gone out with them, they would call my other girlfriends and tell them things like I didn't want to see them anymore and they would try everything just to get me to marry them. Any kind of a woman is alright with me, but just be careful of those Mexican girls."

Knowing my uncle, the way I do, and respecting his knowledge of women, if nothing else, I took what he had to say to heart. I thought about not going back to the *senorita* Lupe's apartment at all. But as the day wore on and my lusting remained unfulfilled, it was flesh I craved and desire is a terrible master. As Siddhartha Gautama, the Sakyamuni Buddha put it so eloquently, *"The cause of suffering is desire."* But me, I wanted to party.

We had a good day, my uncle and I. The car seemed to be running fine, and we drove back with the top off. He enjoyed the ride, I could tell. And I always enjoy our conversations and hearing of his life.

We pulled up to the doorstep at about three. I was conscious that I was already an hour late for Lupe. So we bid our farewells and I hit over a few blocks; kicked in a few more wake me ups, for I

184

was slowing down again, and drove onto Lupe's street.

As I drove down the avenue, I immediately noticed her form gracing the steps of her apartment building. She didn't particularly notice my arrival for she had never seen this car before. I pulled up in front, across the street, and sat there watching her stare down at the sidewalk as a few children played around her.

I looked at her deeply and any doubt I had for making the return visit vanished. She was beautiful, her skin fair, her hair long, and her body small. Even though she was once again wearing designer jeans, I was attracted to her all over again.

After maybe a minute or so, which seemed like ten, she noticed me, said something to the children, and came running up.

"Where were you, I was so worried."
"Worried about what?"
"That you would not come."
"I told you that my uncle was in town."
"I didn't know if I should believe you or not."
"Who me? I never lie."

So, into the car she got.

"Is this your car, too?"
"Yes, this is the one I had problems with the other day."

She patted the leather dashboard of the car and said,

"Oh, I like you, you brought Mr. Sandy and I together."

I looked at her. After a moment of disgust, I ask,

"So, what do you want to do today?"
"Anything," she said.

Now I was beginning to wake up, widen my consciousness again. In other words, I was ON. My energy was flowing in all the right directions, so a little drive sounded good to me. (You remember the pick-me-ups, don't you?)

"You want to go and watch the sunset?"
"Sure," she said.

It was getting close at hand, so I decided instead of rushing for the seashore, even though the rush was on, we could easily head up to the Hollywood Hills.

We cruised out of the ghetto and within a few blocks were surrounded by the homes of the rich, famous, and the fools. These hills, I knew them; oh so well. Well, at least I knew how to drive in them.

It was back in high school, my days at Hollywood High; each lunchtime my buddy Saturday Jim and I would hit Mulholland at full speed. Drive the curves looking for instantaneous death from the slightest false move. At night we would cruise the cribs of our classmates. All well out of our financial bracket, as it were. For we lived on the wrong side of town, the ghetto side of the tracks, if you know what I mean. Yet, back then, the hills seemed to offer us something: a place to hide from the streets that we lived upon.

There was this little place I knew of up at the top of this one little road. It seemed as good a spot as any to sit back and enjoy the sun as he fell slowly to sleep. We reached the location with little incident. Lupe's body leaned close to mine. We pulled off the pavement and on to the dirt road that led behind a small hill.

As I stopped the car, Lupe began kissing my neck, our lips soon met. Eventually, I instigated getting out to watch the setting sun. Which we did. We walked up to the top of the small hill and to my amazement with the season, direction, and geographical placement of the sun setting, we would not have a view of it. So me, being the naturalist that I am, suggested that we drive a short distance to this other location, in which we would be sure of witnessing the sunset.

Though Lupe didn't seem too much into it, she agreed. Down to the Porsche we walked. I open the door for her, close it behind her. Walked myself over to the driver side; in I get. Insert the key and attempt to turn the car's engine over. Attempt is an excellent word. For though the starter ignited, it kept on-and-on for several minutes with no luck of ignition and even with the key removed, it kept *rock n' roll'n*. This continued until the battery seemed to be dying.

I was unhappy to say the least. And being wired didn't help my emotions.

Lupe, however, was undisturbed and got out of the car and sat on the hood. I realized that trying to start the car would only result in further battery drain, so I joined her.

She was sitting and as I walked over, she pulled me close in between her designer jean covered legs and laid a more than passionate kiss upon my lips. The moment was set into the motion of a movement.

She asked, "Sandy, will you marry me?"

I laughed to myself, for she was doing all the rap'n for me. For that was usually my line to the babes. You know, tell them what they want to hear.

"Of course, I mean we are talking serious matrimony here."
"What?"

She obviously didn't understand what I said.

"Yes, of course," I said.
"Oh good. I love you, Sandy."
"Yeah, that's what they all say."
"What?"
"Never mind."

But with that, we were off and running. The kissed began to flow like the sweet honey from a glass jar inadvertently turned over in a moment of unconsciousness. Conscious unconsciousness: I needed these endeavors into lost lustful moments.

Though my pony is not usually so willing under the influence of the wake me ups, it flung into full-on form in no time at all. I slowly began to touch her breasts, lift her shirt, and undo her jeans. She had her hand quickly on my rod and was massaging it into readiness.

This time, I opened her shirt and properly unfastened her bra. It was still light outside, so I had a good view of what my prey had to offer. Her boobs were small, yet firm. Nipples were also small and they did come to life as my tongue began its devouring.

As I slipped her designer jeans off, my lips and my tongue found their way to her black-haired beaver. Her soup kitchen was full-on and flowing. It was of the preferred flavor and variety; that of no stink. I wouldn't have been there if it was of the non-preferred distinction. I licked and she moved. I got her close but wanted to save the moment for my dick to master.

I rose from my kneeing position, salutation to the lords of lust. As I did, I immediately, as I always do, laid a serious kiss upon her lips. Just to let them know what I have been a-tasting.

I turned her around and let her lay her breast on my orange Targa. You know the one that isn't running. And I powered it to her from the backside. Put the pedal to the metal.

This time, I think was better than the night before. We went at-it. In one hand I had a breast, in the other I held tight to the hip, with the occasional clitoral massage. She came in maybe two. My mind wanted to join her, but the induced condition of my body held me back. I remained there pumping my piston for more than a little while. It was almost like when you wear a rubber and you stroke it until you choke it—pump too long and the rubber gets too tight and your dick almost feels numb and you got to work and work and work to cum.

Finally, I got it off. Her huffing and puffing slowed until it stopped and I pulled out and we stood there kissing. It was getting dark and the sun had obviously gone down. I was way covered with sweat.

Lupe said to me, "Oh, you are so good. When we are married, can we do this everyday?"
"Do you think you can handle it everyday?" I asked.

From my experience with her, I knew that she could.

"Oh yes. You are so good Sandy, you must have had many lovers."
"Who me… I was a virgin when I met you."
"No?"
"Yes, really. And how about you, have you had many lovers?"
"No, only three or four."
"That's a lot," I said, "I was a virgin."

She stared at me, wondering if I was telling her the truth.
She got her clothes together. I pulled up my pants.

"Well, let's try to start this bad pup again, Okay?"
"Okay."

We got in and she immediately began to kiss me. I have to admit, I was a bit out of the mood after just getting my rocks off and thinking about the car.

"When can we get married?" Lupe asked.
"Soon."
"How soon?"
"Very soon."
"You know Sandy, I need to get married soon because I am here with no visa."

190

"No shit," I said, like I didn't know why she was so interested in getting married *pronto*.

It was so reminiscent of the green cards and dollar signs I see in all the women's eyes in Asia who have so hastily proposed to me. I mean, if I didn't know that I was such a catch, my ego might be hurt.

"Why should you worry, many people from Mexico don't have green cards."
"I want to be a good American girl and a good wife with lots of children."

Oh fuck, here comes the part about children.

"So when can we get married?"
"What's the hurry, you're not dead yet."
"But my mother had me when she was my age."
"Yeah, but you're not pregnant."

She thinks for a moment. Looks away. Looks at me.

"Yes, I am."
"What!"
"But, it must be yours. We had sex."
I mean, come-the-fuck-on! Pregnant! Mine! In been like two days. How the fuck stupid did she think I was?

I couldn't believe it, couldn't believe her, *lay'n* this kind of bullshit on me.
To keep the situation cool, being the gentleman that I am, I kept my comments to myself and was just casual, in the truest sense of the word.

Not wanting to draw suspicion to my plans of *asta luaga* on the flamenco guitar.

The car, luckily it started. I guess it had been flooded. We drove off into the already set, sunset, and on to the city, Hollywood. I explained to her that I was quite tired and that we could meet tomorrow to set wedding plans.

I pulled down her street, pulled up in front of her apartment, and she laid some serious lips upon me. Though I had to play along, my heart, well better put, my lust, was not into it at all.

So, I drove off, saying once again to myself, *'See what your lust has gotten you into.'*

After hitting my usual haunts on the street, I got home, it was close to midnight and though I tried to go to sleep, my body was still too artificially pumped. So, I lay there, thinking that I should have listened to my uncle, a very wise dude, and laughing because did Lupe really think she could find a dude that stupid.

I even sat there entertaining the idea for a moment or three; you know, due to the drugs and all, of the what if I were to hitch up with her. But *naw,* no way, Mexican chicks are always babes when they are young, then hit twenty or so and they plump out.

I didn't want to deal with the thoughts anymore, so I got up, took an opposite capsule of what I had taken earlier, to take me down. And, just as I was dosing, the telephone rings. It was Lupe calling to say that she loved me and asking to set the date. I told her how tired I was, and we could speak the next day.

As I dozed, I realized that I had broken one of uncle's golden rules, one that he had told me since childhood: *"Love 'em and leave 'em and don't give 'em your phone number."*

The next day, I left my phone machine on and was bombarded by calls from Lupe. My message machine got to listen to the love, the loss, and the anger of sweet young Lupe. Ah Lupe, Lupe, Lupe.

She talked to the machine for almost a week. Then one day, I came home late, hit the play button on my answering machine. It was Lupe telling me that she had found someone else—someone better than me. *'Well, that wouldn't have been hard to do,'* I thought. She finished by telling me, "I could go to hell," (in very accented English). I smiled, *'I've been there, baby.'*

The Targa, I eventually sold it. Leave it to someone else to deal with.

Women, desire, and the there abouts, well...

Desire, it is the demon. It is obviously the cause of suffering. And in the middle of it or at the end of it I always wonder, is it/was it ever worth all the problems and pain? Maybe, someday I will learn.

Ah, Lupe, Lupe, Lupe.

CHAPTER 10
THE SINGLE BARS OF THE 80S

They have titled health spas, *'The single bars of the eighties.'* Personally, I never found that to be true. But then, who am I to argue with, *'They.'*

Other than the serious power-lifters and the too busy for any other type of fitness yuppies, what one basically finds in the health spas is a jacuzzi full of bar bell boys and overweight middle aged men whose eyes light up and their heads turn the moment a girl's presence is noticed: be they beautiful, ugly, fat, skinny, or anywhere in between. Well, the power lifters, if they can still get it up, and the yuppies, I am sure are after pussy too.

The good girls, the kind one would take home to meet mom, never seem to go into the public areas of the spa; preferring to remain suitably secluded in the *'Women's only'* section. That's A.O.K. with me, I rarely hit the public/pubic jacuzzi myself. And, I never really wanted to bother with the type of woman who were out for the hunt into the realm of the wolves, the boys, and the semi-men anyway.

I mean, every now and then, I have forced myself out of my reclusive state and go public/pubic and have seen one or two felines that had the look. But, that was generally accompanied by the, "Hey check me out," syndrome. Fuck that.

At the public/pubic *ja-cuz-say,* I have caught, more than once, a good beaver shot or a decent boobie glance through those almost see-through bathing suits that some women either knowingly or unknowingly wear. But, there is always too much chlorine in those jacuzzis and it

194

turns my hair green, so it is infrequent that I pose along with the other wan-a-be laid macho dudes that inhabit that underworld.

At any rate, I had been working-out one part of my body or another. It was late on a Thursday night, and I had finished up and bailed about 11:30 in the P.M. or so. I was walking out toward the spa's main door and about the same time came along this little *thAng* of an Asian lady. She wore blue jeans, a tee shirt, and wasn't at all that pretty. Not exactly my type, but somewhere cast to the realms of destiny, and the movement of nature, our moment was set.

I opened the door for her, she smiled and out the door we went, walking through the parking lot to our respective *au-to-mo-biles.*

As I walked to my car, the L.A.P.D., the proud boys in blue, pulled up tight behind me obviously checking out the parking lot scene and the security thereof. *"To Protect and Serve,"* yeah right. They moved slowly, cautiously through the lot like a cat ready to pounce upon its prey.

The lady walked gently a few feet in front of me. I watched her movement as she walked; her steps were a bit too hard, her sway a bit too much. Definitely no poetry in her strut. Obviously, a girl, born in L.A., of Japanese descent, who tries so hard, like so many others, to assimilate America. Tried too hard to be accepted and in doing so lost all her native soul and replaced it with a heart stocked full of pagan American dreams and lies; the great American wet dream.

My interest was somehow aroused though, none-the-less... Well, pussy by any other name.

*　　*　　*

I had been spending the last few weeks alone; too alone.

At times, alone is a longed for retreat, at other times it is a dreaded enemy. My life had spun both sides recently, and I was longing for either new travel or new love; well at least new infatuation. In times like these, any fool knows that you take whatever you can get. And there she was, whatever I could get.

She walked through the cars, over to the other aisle; I walked to my 356 and opened the door. The cops, they drove on by. As I began to get in, I saw her opening her door; the car door of a mid-seventies Toyota, or Datsun, or something; something faded brown, faded into the night. Suddenly, as suddenly always is; she looked, I looked; eye contact.

Eye contact, ah the all pervasiveness of it. The meeting of four lost eyes in a lost late night where there is nothing left to lose and no reason to lose it.

She got in, I got in. I sat there for a minute or three listening to her car trying to start, finally it fired up. So, I started up my ride, put the pup in gear, and began to back out of my spot.

For a moment I lost sight of the illusion in the night; thinking, *'Oh well another time another place, another dream, another moment.'* Out of the driveway though, we both went; meeting again, a second chance at the dance; first her, then I. I came to the conclusion that this time I would not give up so easily.

Down the street we both drove. Now normally, I would have turned left on Olympic, to pick up Sepulveda, and head on down South to my crib in a South Bay beach city, but the moment it was fresh and I followed it on through.

We, she and I, kind of danced around: passing each other, speeding up, slowing down. A game, a movement, going nowhere fast.

As we reached Culver Boulevard she pulled in the right turn lane, I next to her one lane over; eyes meeting, the outcome was sealed. I smiled, she smiled and with a nod of her head she motioned me to follow in her direction.

The fantasies that can be placed in one's mind in oh so short of a time. I changed lanes, turned right, and followed her.

She was obviously an Ocean Park kid.

We cruised a bit and over pulls her car. I pulled up behind. She sat there, her car still running. I wondered what game she was playing. Finally, I got out and walked up to her car.

Filled with a face full of false smiles she says to me,

"Hi, what's going on? I notice you are following me."
"Who me?"

We gave the usual false laughter.

"Well maybe. Anyway, I was wondering if you would like to go have some coffee or something?"
"Sure," she says, "I know just the place, follow me."

So off we go. A mile or so further she pulls up in front of this very West L.A., Ocean Park kind of apartment structure. The square gray 1950's ten-unit type. I pull up and in behind her.

Her car still running and no movement. I once again assume it is I who is supposed to get out and check the situation.

She says, "Wait here, I will be back in a few minutes."

So, I go back to my car: turn it off, close the door, and stood coolly, casually leaning against it, looking as nonchalantly vogue as possible in the cold evening air. My mind basically going to all possible points of reference. Is she parking her car? Will we then drive somewhere together? Or, did she just chump-me-out and leave me standing here *oh so bitch-n-ly* leaning against my ride, like a fool?

Maybe five minutes went by, and no sweet young babe arrived. I began to wonder if it was really a chump session or perhaps she had gone to get her dude. In which case, I would have to fist-a-cuff with him, tap him up, take his number out of the yellow pages, knock him out. Or maybe, she was calling the police? A few minutes can turn into an awfully long time...

As the seconds spin into the dream waiting to be lured into a world not quite ready for love. In a hopeful illusion of times lost to fulfillment in lives, cast to nothingness, it is all so meaningless.

"Hi, I'm Terry," she says.

She comes up from the side, in the dark night. She startles me. I jump. I smile. I say,

"Oh ma nee cockaret ta ur da she des."
"What?"
"Oh, you don't speak Japanese?"
"No, you do?"
"Yeah, a bit."
"Oh, that's so neat you speak Japanese," she said. "My grandmother does too. Where did you learn it?"
"Here and there."
"Have you ever been to Japan?"
"More than a few times."
"Wow."

Obviously, a lost soul in a lost country, seeking identity in something that she is not. Sad, I thought. But, me too, me too...

"Anyway, nice to meet you. That is what I said in Japanese."
"Oh, nice to meet you, too."
"I offered to take you to some coffee, would you like to go?"
"Yeah," she says, "I know just the place. Can I trust you?"
"If you can't trust me, there's no one you can trust," the answer I give to all the women...
"Come on then."

She leads on—on into a dream. She leads on, towards the inward realms of her abode, her apartment.

My inner-city kid upbringing rushes to my memory banks of stored up paranoias and I wonder why she would bring me to her place. I mean, she doesn't even know who the *'F'* I am.

But, up the stairs we go and enter I do. The place was a single, painted a pale green. There was an old couch, which obviously made into a bed, a coffee table with a small T.V. on it. In the corner was a stereo placed upon bricks and a board, with twenty or twenty-five albums leaning underneath. There was an old funky kitchen table in the room as well, with two plastic chairs. Obviously, a furnished crib.

"Have a seat. Oh, by the way what's your name?"

I was wondered when she was going to get to that.

"Sandy. Sandy Shaman"
"Decaf or regular?"
"De-caf puts me to sleep what's the point of it?" I said.

She walked in the small kitchen. I kicked back on the sofa.
A bed, huh? Instantaneous love in the making. I am sitting on her bed.
'Stupid thought,' I said to myself, as she walked out with two cups; *java* in them.
Instant *java* for instant love.
She hands one to me. My paranoia races again, is *java* the only thing in this cup? She sits down, joining me on the couch.

"So, what are you into Sandy?"
"Oh, this and that."
"What do you do, what's your job?"

"Job! Jobs are against my religion."
"So, what do you do for money?"
"If you believe; it is always there. As long as you don't chase it…"
"Oh really. How neat," she says.

A *'how neat'* person. God, what had I gotten myself into? I wondered if she grew up in the Val.

"So, what do you do with your time?"
"I dream. Someone has to do it."
"Wow, how neat…"

I wanted to scream.

"So Terry, what do you do?"
"Me, I am kinda a secretary. I work in this office."
"Aren't you up kinda late then?"
"Well, I don't think I'm going to work tomorrow."

My passion rose as her statement reached my ears.

Thoughts of a woman, though not so beautiful, and a bit of a *teenybopper*. Yet, there was possibilities for I was invited over in the night; a night, where there was no work for her tomorrow. Hum…

We kicked back. We conversed. I began to feel more at east that there was only *java* in my *java* cup and the moments of wonder spread to minutes of desire.

She came close to me, sliding over on the couch. And, being no fool to desire, I knew what was coming. What path it would take, *be* the only question remaining.

I remained passive, semi-disinterested. You know, you *gotta* stay cool for when there are no moves to make. Why make any? Let it come to you, when it is moving in your direction and all.

Her knee touched mine. Her leg came close; leg-to-leg, side-to-side. She leans over, her eyes close as she does. I watch them close.

In her movement of anticipated action. Action within action; movements that lead to an end. The perfect moment, as she begins to touch my lips. I watch that moment. First kiss; it is only lived once. It is the only one that truly matters.

Sure, enough she does lay some serious lips upon me. A not so practiced kisser but she does have her appeal.

For a moment or so, I let it take me and then I pull back to see the feeling in her eyes. Closely our heads remain. We stare deeply eye-to-eye. Ah, how I love Asian eyes: dark, hidden, leading one into the mysteries of life, mysteries of the moment. A movement spent in pagan passion.

She smiles and says,

"You probably think I'm a bad girl."
"You probably think that I'm a bad boy."
"You know, I have never done this before..."

Now there is a line I have heard more than once.

"No really," she says. "Do you know why I am doing this?"
"What? You mean that you are not totally in love with me?"
"No," she says, "It's for a reason."

'Reason' I thought. Life has no reason. Simply a ridiculous moment, lived and lost. And no matter what the gain, it all remains meaningless.

"I have this boyfriend," she went on to say.

'Oh shit,' I thought, here it comes.

"He really loves me but he's been going out with this other girl. He says he needs to experience more women before he and I settle down. You know, I have seen a picture of her, she has long blond hair just like you. So, there is something symbolic about all of this."

I look at her,

"You know, this is a bunch of bullshit. I really don't need it. I only make love when I am in love with the person and the person with me. As temporary as that feeling may be, of course."
"But no, no, you don't understand. I really like you. You have good energy."

Good energy. What the fuck would she know about good energy? Would she know it or understand it if she felt it?
So, the con went on a bit, going paths/places to nowhere. I explained the metaphysics of lovemaking, she explained how she wanted three kids and a house in Torrance someday.
Lost in a reason of no reason, a lie of no lie. Choosing a life for all the wrong reasons. The reasons that make up no reason at all. And believing and accepting that kind of bullshit, from a bullshit

dude that just wants to keep her on the line. I know, for it sounds like a rap that I would give.

She got up to go to the bathroom, at least so she said. I sat there pondering whether or not to just leave while she was behind closed doors.

Most men, of the health spa breed, in fact, most men in general, would have jumped at the chance/jumped in her pants. Those chances that were being laid out before me. Most men, but not I. Somehow, I, this situation; her, one and one did not add to my two.

*   *   *

Soon I heard the bathroom door open, as I was sitting there remembering India and the dreams of eternal monk-hood that I had long ago.

"Sandy, come here."

I got up and walked to the bathroom. There she was sitting on the yellow bathroom sink counter. She was quite naked and had the look of conquest in her eyes.

Her body, thin and more than partially tan. The tan etched lines of distinction upon where her unexposed bathing suit had protected her from the rays of *Surya,* the god of the sun. Her breasts small, firm. Her beaver, black haired and full; more than an incentive. But I, I held my ground.

"I don't need this."
"But I do."

Well, now here came into play a whole new idea: '*Need, hers. Not mine.*' An excuse in search of a home.

"Nice tan," I said. "But you know it is really bad for your skin."
"Yeah, but it looks good, doesn't it?"

Here I was with another external person. Modern society is full of them. Everything for the outside, no time spent knowing the inside, how sad.

"You know, in America it's funny, beauty is rated by how tan one is; how dark the skin is. In just about every other country in the world, with the exception of a few European ones, beauty is rated by how light the skin is. Your Japan included."
"It's what is inside that worries me."
"I'm clean. I have no diseases."
"That's not what I meant."

Off the sink she slid her body, pushing me up against the door. Her hand, a bit cold, holds my face and she begins to kiss me.

"I really don't need this," I repeat.
"I really do."

Now, in my life I have walked away from far more intensive situations than this and often times they were situations that I wanted to leave far less. Maybe it was the earlier anticipation of love, lust, and desire. Maybe it was that I had been alone so much of the recent past and needed some interaction of affection. Maybe it was my weakness.

But I let her lure me into her web and take advantage of me.

She pulled down from my shoulders my long, knee length, light brown overcoat. For I had left it on upon entering her zone of inequity. She removed my sport coat. She unzipped my pants, slipping her hand inside. My dick was already hard. She began to undress me.

As she pulled down my pants, she lowered herself on her knees and began a little lip action upon my love pup. She was no expert by any means, but it was a cheap caviar appetizer to a moderately priced dinner.

After a few, I decided to go for it full on. So, I laid her down halfway between the bathroom and the hall; why bother with all the preludes of pulling out her couch bed, as desirous as she was, and I *wang-ed* it on in.

She had a nice tight pussy, obviously from working out. Not too deep. The kind when you put it in straight, you touch the top and give the woman a bit of a chill. It was soup city, just the way I like 'em.

We went at it for a time, mostly she lay there not doing much of anything, simply absorbing the pleasure.

Absorbing an impact of measured strength, a movement in a measured night. A night which promised her, trouble in the future. More than she probably anticipated. Trouble in the future with her boyfriend/husband-to-be. I mean come-on, with most men what they do is fine but let the chick do it and it's *sayonara* on the bamboo flute. But, when you but the ticket, you have got to take that ride and she bought the ticket tonight. Me, I was just the conductor on the train. A train that meant little more to me than added spiritual awareness and a story to write.

"This is it," she whispered, "This is what you men like; good sex."

I would have said something, but she probably would have felt put down. The sex wasn't that great, nor was I one of those men. But, she began to cum so maybe it was what women like her liked, a good power thumping.

She came kinda nice. Her legs shaking as she held on tighter and tighter. She was no screamer, which was good in the modern-day apartment complex era and all. But, she did make these heavy breathing noises, which sounded like the sweet winds of Kyoto.

As she held me tight and I put the moves on to intensify her cuming, my mind drifted to the thought, *'How it may had been nice if we had met at another time and another place, sometime earlier, somewhere younger.'* But, then I realized that her mind was never turned to the other side of reality; mysticism, just three kids and a house in Torrance.

I could have pumped it off and came in her, for I was close, but I decided, let's play it a little bit. So, when she was done, I pulled it out and rolled her over.

I had a discussion with one of my main L.A. squeeze kittens a while ago, about the best way to give a babe the first backside. The best technique, especially in a lust situation, was to just do it. So, here I was, *just doing it.*

"What are you doing?"
"Just relax," I said.

As I quickly shoved the love pupster in the backdoor. She didn't even jump, just kept breathing heavy as she said,

"I have never done this before."
"I have."

Her poop shoot was more than willing, some babes do not have the physical construction to claim the same, but hers was fine. I sat there tailgating for a time, power pumping it until I finally blew off the cookies.

I pulled out and she rolled back over and said,

"I don't think my boyfriend is as good as you."
"That goes without saying baby."

We lay around on the floor for a few. The feeling was kind of strange. It was not so much the typical after sex emotions but more of a far-off distant feeling, like the kind I have felt with sluts or whores, like there must be something more to this process than just this. Time slipped on.

She eventually got up and went and began to prepare her couch bed. I walked into her bathroom. I closed the door behind me: washed up a bit, pulled on my clothes, combed the 'do,' and came out.

"I want you to stay," she said.
"Sorry baby. It was beautiful, you are beautiful, and I would love to love you, but I am going to go. I hope this answered your needs."
"But we can have all day tomorrow."
"For what?"

208

"I don't know… To hang out."

"Why, you have your boyfriend."

"Yeah, but he works."

A moment passed. I thought, I smiled; I embraced the perfect imperfection of this moment lost to no-where, no-thing, nothing but the realms of literature.

"You know it's all bullshit. What he's telling you about needing to experience other women before you marry. He's just stoking the fire at both ends. If he doesn't get lucky out there some night, he always has you. If he loved you, he would only need you."

"But, he explained it all to me and I understand."

"Whatever… I hope he's as understanding as you. But I don't think he will be."

"Don't' go, we can make love again tomorrow."

"Ah, I would love to, but I've gotta bolt."

I gave her a kiss, and she held on, but I pulled away and went for the door. On my way out, I flipped the light switch off and said,

"I hope you have a nice house in Torrance and nice kids. *Matana,"* (Japanese for see you again.)

I was out-a-there. Like so many times before, planned and not planned, wanted and unwanted. I was gone, out there in the wasteland, alone again. But, the cool breeze of the evening blew into my hair—the night had been right, the time was right.

Once again, I had been cast into desire. Desire for love, desire to need, desire to be needed, desire-to-desire. Desire, as said before, unfortunately the cause of all suffering.

Some might say I made a conquest; a real man would. Perhaps I was the conquest. A fool in a fool's game, the outcome, it's all the same. It can only be that way.

I got into my ride and headed on home in the direction I usually go. I stopped at the donut shop I generally hit *en route* from my health spa sessions and pulled in. Behind the glass counter was this more than beautiful post-midnight Mexican babe who gave me the smile of desire, but another dream, another time. I picked up *tres* donuts and a large cup of the Joe. I put a top on it, grabbed a straw. Went out to the 356 and drove on home thinking of Terry, thinking of the Mexican girl at the donut shop, eating my poison, and drinking the coffee as I do, when I drive, through a straw.

CHAPTER 11
THE ALONE LINE

Lost in the aloneness. Have you ever felt it? Most people never have. They claim, "Oh, I've been alone," but they have not. Most have their AOK well-adjusted family, their AOK well-adjusted friends, an AOK lover here or there, or an AOK date somewhere in the distance. Few ever really walk the alone line.

Believe me, it is not fun. Go get married, it's easier. Go get divorced, it's far more enjoyable. Have a family. Have some children. Then, you will always have blood on this planet; the family tree will move on.

Some of us out here on the extremities though, our path lies in a different fold: be we ugly, be we pretty, it doesn't really matter. Fate, destiny, lack of logic take hold and we spend our days searching, our nights loving, and when there is no new current fantasy, we go casually insane.

Alone, it is not for the weak of heart. Just as pure passion is not for the family man. So, I/we, those of us out here on the boundaries, out on the outskirts, we live life for that momentary fulfillment, however short it may be. And, we hold onto it like eighty-year long lovers hold one another; for in this space is also held the truth.

Truth; *nothing lasts forever, certainly not you or I.* No matter how tight you hold on, it will pass away. So, it is better to love it, leave it, no further contact in contract or in mind. Hold onto the moment. Go insane in the alone. Leave the feelings for the poetry and leave the families for the sedentary, and leave the mundane for the attached. Me, I live with the fools.

I was way alone one of those nights where nothing seems to matter, only to get away from the aforementioned pain. I cruised over to late night Jay's, (a burger-joint deep in East Hollywood), listened to the new Mick Jaggar tune, as it played on the radio. Put myself down a double chili cheese. Still lost, still alone, I drove on into the central city autumn night.

I was driving down Pico, over by Hoover, a chance in any dance would do. The urban geographer coming out in me, just witnessing the shapes and forms of the inner-city night. Crossing the street up in front of me was this semi sweet little Latin number, hot in true Latina form.

I drove up, I stopped, let her pass in front of my *ve-hi-cle*. I studied her movement. I studied her form; as any good researcher would do. Hard and hot, like the juices that flow from a blood rare steak; kiss me midnight.

She passes. I move on. But, a thought or two had indeed come to mind. As I studied the fading form in my rear-view mirror, a yellow El Camino pulls up and to the window she does walk to talk.

More than a little pissed at myself for letting it all pass me by, I turned and went down Hoover, figuring on catching the freeway in the direction of home. Home, such as home is.

I began thinking maybe, well maybe... And, I can't let it go without a second try. "Fuck it," I said out loud and hung a *U-ie* in the middle of the street.

Now, it was maybe twelve, one A.M or so and though I guess that you still can't do those kind of things, but for whatever it was worth and whatever California Traffic Code enforceable law that may be put into effect, I did it anyway.

I headed back with a hope, a hope and a hard-on. The thoughts they do sometimes take control. I hang it down Pico, and there she was still walking, a perfect Latina princess, caressing a pagan night.

I was perhaps just enough tiled, though it had been a while since the last wetting of my lips; just enough wasted that I drove right up next to her. Her body poured tightly into her jeans and a red polyester shirt, "You need a ride?" She walks towards the car, looks at me and says, "Okay."

Oh, I wish it was always that easy. Sadly, it seldom is. Oh, I wish all we ever needed was the wish. A wish that would be granted, then there would never be the predestine ritual and the need to *stroke-it till you chock-it.*

"What's your name?"
"Esperanza."
"Hello, Esperanza."

Hope, hoped for in a seemingly hopeless night.

She in. The car door closed, as I moved the motor car forward and on into the night.

"Where you going?"

She answers in her very thick Mexican accent, "I don't know, where are you going?"

Here I was, it was handed to me on a platinum platter, a pastry of earthly delights. An easy woman, with no place to be. Just like me. *You know me, I have no place to be.*

"I'm not going anywhere, nowhere that you have not been before," I exclaim.

In alter consciousness, a rapidly sobering state. You know how they are, that fine high, just where you want it to be, but food and time and the space and the mind—*fuck I hate it when I am coming down and I do not want to come down.*

I could waste no time. I put my hand on her blue jeaned leg, high on the thigh. I mean, you know, I just wanted there to be an understanding between us/in between us. There was...

Reactions, there were none. Forward motion was at hand. In hand, of hand, another lost traveler in the city's lonely night.

"Do you live around here," I inquired.

A question foolishly asked. I realized it as the words sprung from my foolish mouth. I would not have gone to a love shack in this neighborhood at this time of night anyway.

"That's not good," was the answer. Obviously meaning it was no-go at her *palacio de amor.*

She reached over, kissed me on the neck. My driving slowed down. Her hand gently moved onto and caressed my shoulder as I was shifting the gears.

Now, I could have taken her to a hotel but fuck that. That was for the movies on the television set. Movies and whores that you had to bargain with.

Here I was with a Latina love, who for one reason or another, had turned down a yellow El Camino and gotten into a black Porsche 356 SC.

I pondered in my mind for a few what was the best thing for me to do. It passed through my mind, *'My place'* but fuck that, as well. Her hand had moved onto my leg; kisses still caressed my *gringo* neck.

I saw a street, rather dark; nice and dark. I hung a left and pulled down into darkened realms. I pulled up. I parked. Shut down the engine. Leaned over and kissed her red *lip-sticked* lips. *Lipstick kisses.*

We got down to business.

I have always loved my 356. Though it looks small from the outside, there is a lot of legroom. And the seats, they do fold back. Designed for passenger comfort and...

Some slobs were laid, some boobies grabbed. I had to pull awhile to get her fucking jeans off—an explosion of hips once they were down. Why is it that Mexican chicks always wear jeans?

A nice wet pussy greeted me. We played awhile as I slipped my pants down.

I climbed on top of her, dunked my cookie. I sunk it in deep into her typical loose Latina cunt. Due to the wide hips and all... No time to play around, no time for the magic. We both knew what we were after.

Lust, the opposite of alone, was the name of the game.

I pumped for a while, trading slobs the whole time. She started to cum. Finally, I blew my rocks. She held me tightly biting my neck.

I looked out the rear window. I looked out onto the street, out onto the night. The city streets that breed this kind of passion, this passion and this morality. Morality where there is none. Only *frijoles,* only *tortillas,* only poverty; poverty and *La Megra.*

I rolled off; off and over on to my seat. I was still clawing at her breasts. I asked, "How much do you want?"

"What?" she asked.
"Quantos para. Que precio?'
"Nada."

I looked at her, "Nothing?"
"Nada, nada," was her answer.

I hate sluts; whores are just doing their job, but sluts have no reason at all.

I reached up, leaned back over her, still lying upon my reclined seat. I slapped her,

"I hate sluts," I exclaimed.

I see in her eyes, the feeling of the slap and how she had felt it before. I saw how she knew its meaning. She learned it, liked it, lived in a space somewhere lost in the fields of her mind, learned in Old Mexico. It made her feel disciplined, loved, wanted, and secure.

The world is full of fools, psychological basket cases, who like myself seek pleasure in their own form; pleasure in the depths of the night. Pleasure from things/passion in forms that the average, the non-alone, the non-mystic, man or woman; functional servant of the masses that they

216

are, would have nothing to do with, could never understand.

As I looked at her, she at me, my dick again began to get hard. Over I pull myself for another round, of the purpose of the passion. She liked what I had given her in the first-round. She held me tight, pulled me close, and had the piston-pumping pedal to the metal for the second-round.

Her breathing picked up rhythm as the pup moved into gear, and the emotion were in motion. We went at it, she started to cum. I hear some words, something about, *'Weto'* and *'Amour.'* Then, she really starts to make some noise.

Now actually, I could really care less if she came or not, but it was no problem that she did. And, it is kind of nice when a chick makes a lot of noise at these times. But, here we are, in a Porsche, on a side dark, dirty street, on the wrong side of the tracks. Me, a *gringo,* humping on this local chick that I do not even know her name, in the depths and darkness of the inner-city night. With the screaming and all, I did keep my head up, looking out of the fogging windows to keep my vision on what may be coming up.

She came, I pumped for a while as the juice began to dry and her pussy tightened up. I got it off again and hit on over to the driver seat. Pulled up my pants. Watched as she struggled pulling on her jeans. As my zipper went up, I realized that I should have worn a rubber, but too late now.

She leaned over and kissed me and then almost immediately opened the door.

"You don't need a ride?"
"No."
    She got out.

"Di amos," she said.

She walked back up towards Pico. I headed on down the side street in the direction of a South Bay beach city, which held my apartment and/or home.

Where she was going, I guess it didn't matter. Where I am going well, I guess it matters less.

We lived; I knew it, she knew it. The perfect meeting. The perfect parting. It had all of the qualities that make up any relationship, loving and long-term as they may be: the possibility, the meeting, the loving, the making love, the violence, the cuming, the end. All so orchestrated, all so perfect.

Art and poetry it be cast, there it be lived. Lived by her, loved by me. For a second, we were together, thus not alone. The kiss of passion, the kiss that is the making of a dreamer, the prerequisite for the fool. The kiss of forever, like the sex of never and may it all go on and on and on.

Fuck the suburbs. Fuck the families. Give me the dreams that only last a moment in a night; any night/any dream will do. Fuck it all for it all adds to nothing. And nothing ever, no not ever, lasts forever.

I love the children of the night. I think I will go out now, as these pages are finished, this story complete. In the raining late night of this autumn evening, a year or two post the experience, previously detailed. Let's see what else that there may be to live...

CHAPTER 12
CURRENCY EXCHANGE

'84 wasn't a bad year for me. I had some bucks and spent more time out of the country that in it. That is to say I had some bucks until I spent more time out of the country than in it.

When *en route* to distant illusions, I would generally pick up some of the currency, if it was available, for the ports to which I was bound at the LAX currency exchange booth.

It was October, and I had headed in from Indochina by way of my second favorite country in the whole world, Japan. That is, second favorite in terms of promised illusion(s), of course. I was burned out, jet-lagged and there was no one to meet me, my luggage, or newly acquired possessions at the airport.

Now U.S. Customs always seems to have a need to fuck with me. They look at my long hair, seven earrings in my ears, my passport full of international stamps, plus, the official government pages added to the original passport to facilitate the newly arrived ones. My occupation listed as artist. I used to leave it blank but in this modern society a Zen statement of zero just doesn't sit very well with government officials and they are apparently driven mad about how I get my *danaro*. They always make me tell them something. Thus, "Artist." This arrival was no different from others and they, the Border Guards, the Customs Agents, sent me into the baggage claim with the official paper that I am to be, *'Checked Out.'*

So, I kicked back, waited for my luggage. It arrived amazingly slowly on this day. I assumed it was probably due to the L.A. rain that was a-coming down. My suitcase and newly acquired guitars, to add to my collection, arrived among the last load. I had flown First Class, so this was unusual. Generally, First Class luggage is among the first to arrive. Get it FIRST class, right? I had stood there beaming with paranoia that my possessions would not come at all and had been lost into the air stream of the mainstream in the jet stream for all eternity.

When they finally came meandering around the corner, I realized that to my amazement the airlines had probably taken special care not to damage the guitars and had placed them, oh so carefully, in some special sacred compartment space so as no harm may befall them. Amazing, yes? Thank you, Japan, that would never happen here in the States.

With my suitcase and acquisitions placed neatly upon an airport luggage cart, I headed for the *Check-out, Check-up, Check-me Out Line.* I had hoped that due to the fact I was following in the rear of this flight's massive passenger profile that they would just slide me on through; though I knew, this would probably not be the case.

Finally, up to the teller of customs, the decider of *Duty Free* or *Duty Paid* lives, I go. She was a lady, maybe thirty or so. She looked at me, my long hair, my expensive clothing, my First Class tags on my bags and I saw the suspicion in her eyes. She took my passport and disembarkment card and read my profession, artist.

If there is one thing that I always dislike is the need this world seems to have of knowing the occupation of a person. I mean, what-the-fuck difference does it make? There are so many more important things in life than what a person supports themselves with or where they went to school. I mean, what bullshit. They should ask a person what they feel, what they observed, what they think. Well, as few people ever think, I guess that is why they ask only about their occupation.

I have often toyed with the idea of entering, *'Mystic'* in the appropriate spot for occupation. But then few understand the meaning of the word, let alone its connotations. So, I have elected just to play along in a world, where there is no room for the mystic and only a small arena for the artist. At least the word, by definition, is understood.

The lady asks, "You're an artist?"
"Yes."
"Oh, and you have traveled a lot."
"Yes."
"What countries are you coming from this time?"
"Hong Kong, Macao, Japan, Malaysia, Burma, and Thailand."

Now I always try not to completely enumerate the countries I have been to, for it just adds to the Customs Officers' suspicions. They generally check all the dates of the visas and stamps anyway, so at least in my case, it doesn't do much good to cover things up.

"Oh, you've been to Thailand several times, I see."

As she looks in my passport. I mean, the minute you mention Thailand to one of these vultures, their eyes open up and suspicion etches itself across their face. Drugs, they know there must be drugs.

"Yes, I have been to Thailand."
"How long have you been gone?" She asks.
"A few months."
"What was the purpose of your journey?"
"Experience."

She now asks me to place my bags on the counter and to unlock them. As she begins her study in oblivion she continues,

"So, you're an artist?"
"Yes."
"What type of art?"
"Life is an art," I tell her. "But if you want specifics; I paint, among other things."
"What type of paintings?"
"Big ones. Very big ones."
"What type, you know, what style do you paint?"

'Like she really gave a fuck,' I thought to myself.

"I paint my feelings."
"What does that mean? Is that like abstract art?"
"You may call it that."
"Do you sell your paintings?"
"No, that would make me a businessman."
"Then where do you get your money?"
"Why, do you work for the Internal Revenue Service, as well?" I bluntly asked her.

At this point she finds some prayer beads, which I had purchased in Thailand. Now, I had maybe fifteen or so strands of them and they were in a camping stuff bag. Her eyes light up as she opened it thinking that now her life had become complete for she had found elicit, illegal drugs on a not so normal looking artistic individual.

She raised them from the bag and begun sniffing them. She was sure they were hashish or some distant, foreign, and undesirable substance.

It's almost a bit funny; international travel in the remote regions of Asia. For those dreadful, horrible, mind-altering substances are generally readily at hand. Now, I am certainly not one who, *'Just says no,'* to these controlled substances. But, I am certainly not one who is fool enough to try to bring any of them into this country or any other country for that matter. Yet, I always find that there is just a hint of paranoia in the back of my mind as I pass through customs. Did someone stash something on me for fun, profit, or just to fuck up an American? You never know… And that's where the paranoia rises.

"Prayer beads." I told her.
"Are you a Buddhist?" She asks.
"Are you?" I answer.
"No!" She says, with an expression of disgust upon her face.

I mean, *'Come-on,'* what bullshit. This American continent filled with self-righteous Judeo-Christians who damn the idol worshipers of the world. *Idol Worshipers,* as they call them. Feeling themselves to be oh so fucking holy as they worship their visualization(s), their pictures, their crosses of God.

She goes over to another customs inspector and returns with a disappointed look on her face, after finding out that they indeed were not drugs at all, but simply and, in fact, prayer beads from Thailand. Her search continued.

Finally, as she was getting so knit-picky as to be taking my cameras apart I told her,

"Look, if I was going to be a drug smuggler or be doing anything illegal, I certainly would not look like this. I would appear as your average Joe businessman."

I could see she finally realized her folly. Though she questioned the origin of the two guitars I had brought back. I convinced her that they had been taken along with me. I told her that I could not travel without music. Actually, I travel, well at least leave traveling, as light as possible.

She let me go. I was relieved that they had not taken me into a *Private Custom's Room,* completely with an armed guard to search through my stuff as had happened to me before. As well as, I was content to not have my stomach X-rayed for swallowed balloons full of opiates as has also been done before. I was just happy to get the fuck out-a-there. I mean, in the South and Southeast Asian countries where there are drugs, I just walk right through customs. But here, the U.S., everybody wants to be a power-tripping somebody, when they are a no-body...

Though I had a considerable amount of foreign currency to be exchanged, I was far too burned out to deal with it. So, I just went out into the reception area of no reception for me this time and out to the street and grabbed a Taxi.

*　　*　　*

L.A., I was back home again. Home, such as home was. It was raining and cool, my kind of California weather—the was winter coming on. The driver and I, well we headed for the beach and *me casa.*

It was a few days later and my jetlag was residing a bit. I pulled myself out of bed at the crack of noon or so, caught a shower, looked at my face that needed a shave. *'Fuck that,'* I thought. I always needed a shave. I put my clothes on and headed for the airport currency exchange. The closest to me, but by far the worst exchange rate.

En route, I chilled into one of my favorite *cappuccino* haunts in Manhattan Beach, had a cup and a *croissant* or two, then back on Sepulveda, LAX next stop.

*　　*　　*

There she stood behind the glass: black hair pulled back, golden skin, Asian eyes hidden behind her glasses, that gave to me that look of willingness; willingness/desire for the moment, that glance of a chance at love. Love, whatever that may mean. She exchanged my money.

Back in the direction of my abode, well kind of, out of the way, but in that general vicinity; I stopped on by my buddy's guitar shop. He, *my main guitar making man,* who has the revered task of making guitars for me, doing the modifications, *et cetera* and so on. Anyway, I mention the love in the eyes of this babe at the LAX currency exchange to him. It was one of those pure dreams, the dreams of waiting for it to happen. You know the kind, that passing glance that stabs a knife in the soul of your desire, and you want her; she wants you. Wanted and passed in the tides of life.

That was October. I sat back, felt some jetlag, played some music, painted some paintings, wrote some poetry, had an affair, and then three weeks later, I was back on the *hard road* again.

I was about to do a little around the world *thAng,* finish 1984 off right journey: East to West. First stop to be Madrid, where my main L.A. Babe, (though she was Spanish), was cribbed up, doing her time in art school. From there to Paris, to Venice, then we would separate; she back to school, me, back to India, and onto the there and the there-abouts.

Exchange booth, there was that babe again; obviously Vietnamese.

"Where are you going this time?" She inquired. "I see you here so much."
"Asia, I always go to Asia."

The *convo* was short and sweet. But, the dream, it was again set in motion—waiting to be lived, known, experienced, loved, and then lost.

I left with just the basic amounts of currency, for the lands far unknown, and her telephone number and the invitation to call her upon my return to the States at the end of the year. Life, sometimes it does all feel in motion...

I flew on and out. Europe, momentarily romantic. Asia, well oh yes Asia, but that is another story, many other stories, in fact, to be told another time.

I hit back into the city, L.A. the day before Christmas. A week or so earlier than planned. But,

226

then, what are plans? They and I never seem to work out.

I did the good son, go and visit my mother up Hollywood way for Christmas. My uncle, one of the early and original bad Harley guys that he was/is, in town so we hung out. But, *nada* in a *nada* world.

I sat for a few days in the extremes of jetlag. In the dilemma of the, *'Should I, Shouldn't I,'* give the babe a call. You know, the one at the exchange booth. Finally, well what else could I do? The dude was back in action. I gave her the call a day or three past *X-mas*.

Our fist conversation was as bit of a let-down, she didn't immediately want to come over and have a passionate momentary mean nothing love affair with me that we would both forget the next day. We just talked a bit. I listen to her story; 'Saigon, father some government official, came to the U.S. '75, lived in Illinois, did the University of Illinois, etc. Now was out here, family and all. Nothing too exciting, to say the least.' She wanted to know what I did, "I do nothing," so that was that.

I wrote it off as a lost cause. So, my mind just moved on to whatever new fantasy may come up and come on.

That was two days before, two days before she gave me that oh so interesting call back-jack. Did I want to go to a New Year's Eve party with her? Well, parties not really being my thing, but sure why not…

I arrived the night in question, a dozen red roses in my hand. I go to the door of the house that had been described to me, to be far greater, far more, far better than it was in actuality; in this rather borderline funky area of borderline central city L.A. But then, I guess their judgments, their standards, Vietnamese/Asian and all, are way different than us locals.

I knock; a honky, clean-cut, and smelling of the Mid-West dude answers he door. I did-not-like-it.

He looks me up and down. He was obviously less than pleased: my very baggy clothing, sport coat and pants, my tennis shoes, my long hair. *'Fuck him, white trash,'* I thought. He leads me in, tries to make nothing conversation. I see an Asian figure passing: Asian, female, and older. She looks at me. I heard the raised voice in Vietnamese began to shriek. She obviously did not dig my scene.

The main babe of prey struts in for a second, accepts the roses, rather non-graciously, and then was out-a-there. Homeboy/white boy, the W.T., *'White Trash,'* was in there, *rap'n* to me; mentioning that he was going to the party, as well. I was thinking, *'Well fuck me, if I'm not going solo with this babe, then I'm not going.'*

He told me the story of how he was, as he put it, the *X-fiancé* of this babe, my babe's, older sister, who was now shacked up with a dink. Like a fucking trophy on the shelf, an *X-fiancé,* I could not fucking believe it.

She, the *X,* was way pregnant and way married. I thought how fucking weird he and this family was. I mean, all *crib'n* down and hanging tough to-get-her. I mean, call me old fashion, but you just do not have the old love stud in the vicinity of love central when there is a new dick in motion, even if it is a dink dick.

Finally, he sensed my disinterest and bailed the room. I sat there scooping the scene, listening to

228

the vague rumbles of Vietnamese in this old and almost Victorian house. I mean, this was pure Mid-West. I know, because my aunt lives back there. I mean, the furniture, the uck floral patterns, the old woods, *et cetera* and so on.

This was not going according to plan.

A few later, actually more than a few, out pops the babe in question: roses in a vase, and a white dress adorning her golden body. She sat, we spoke, for a moment or two. I asked as to the presence of all the others: mothers, fathers, sisters, brother-in-laws, and *X-fiancées* in preparation to go. I was told as to their attendance, but travel plans dissimilar with ours.

AOK then. This little indulgence, it was still ON. We were to be headed to this Vietnamese nightclub over Monterey Park way.

*   *   *

We were finally out-a-there and into my '64 Porsche 356 SC, my bad black Bat Mobile. The time inside her house, it had been uncomfortable. The ride, well perhaps a bit on the improvement side, but...

She told me of her mother's immediate disapproval of my hair. I laughed and went into a discourse as to the small mindedness of people. But basically, I was thinking more to the tune of, *'Well fuck you, this is my country not yours. I was born here. And if you don't like me or my style, why don't you just get the fuck back to Vietnam?'* Being the gentleman I am, of course, I did not tell her to tell her mother this, but it did tick me off more than a little bit.

We arrive at this little place over on Atlantic Boulevard. Out of the ride and into the movement motion of the inner sanctum of Vietnam central.

On the way in, preceding us, were these two more than seriously fine specimens of Vietnamese women, both clad in long stylish skirts, the colors dark like the night. I could not help but give my comment(s) of approval to my white mini skirted lady in tow. (I hate miniskirts). She punched me in the arm.

In, it was *no-charge*. She apparently knew somebody. The place full, massively full; packed to the maximum full, way past fire department occupancy limits, no doubt. A band played. Her friends, so she claimed. Vietnamese, singing the current hits off of the New Wave radio station. The musicians, *'all a family,'* so I was told: ages ranging fifteen to forty. The music, actually very good copies. The atmosphere, sucking big time.

Now, imagine yourself in a crowded room, crowded to the extreme, being six foot one, with long blond hair. Six foot one and surrounded literally elbow-to-elbow, or should I say elbow-to-shoulder by a thousand plus Vietnamese who averaged the height of my biceps. I felt like the fucking *Jolly Green Giant.*

She asked me if I wanted to dance, as we stood there in the masses. *'Where,'* I wondered? But she tried to make a few moves, so I gave it the old college try as well. Let me tell you though, when I dance, as you now may know, I do like to get-down, and there wasn't even enough room to breathe let alone *boog-a-loo.*

So, the music went on, the evening went on, with more than a few serious babes giving me the AOK eye. Me, being the only white boy in the place, and all... Believe me, dreams, they were set in motion...

The vibes in the atmosphere, sent my direction that evening, all felt right. That is to say, except for those of the *X,* you know the one, who had arrived with the family late, in all of his short hair white trash glory, and was sitting at the reserved family table where we, my babe and I, were shunned by a family giving the silent treatment to their daughter because of their disapproval of her man, his, *'do,'* and who he was. Fuck that and fuck them!

She wanted a drink. I bought her a drink. Whiskey and milk; uck. Me, I dosed down a soda water. Keep it clean, keep it simple.

The dance, the people, the crowdedness, the music, the New Year's Eve countdown, the New Year's Eve kiss, simple and one pointed. Came up and went down. Not much to mention in a mentionless world. We were out of there 2:00 A.M.

As we drove back into the more or less central city, *love,* it was in the air. In the air, and her hand in my crotch. Now, I do mean literally in my crotch, no lie. My canary was ready to fly from his cage, if you know what I am a talking about?

I mean, man, I could not figure this whole thing out. Was it going to be as easy as all that? Well, A.O.K. my way, nothing to complain about here in this direction.

"You know, when you looked at those women tonight, on our way in, I was jealous."

Now, had this been a white bread sort of chick, I would have thought nut case to the max. But her, she was: this brightly dressed, valley girl glasses on, serious babe of a Vietnamese chick, laying these words of intimate love upon me.

"How do you say, I love you, in Vietnamese?" I inquired.
"Ing eoh am."

I practiced, the words of love to her, as her hand remained stroking the penis of passion in love center central.

Here she was, a woman in need of a relationship.

And the nighttime rings of its whispers, as I can tell her all of my lies. Is it this, is it that? I do not know. I never knew. All I know is love. Spell it with a capitol, *'L.'* And watch me, as I run away.

"Oh, I forgot my keys!"

She tells me as we are driving west on the Santa Monica Freeway.

"Well, what do you want to do?" I ask.

I thought that the play was definitely in motion. You know how chicks like to feed around the bush. Me too, if you know what I'm talking about?

"I am tired, I need to take a nap," I have heard that one more than once as a prelude/interlude to an AOK let's-get-it-on-session.

Well, a long story made short, something that I do oh so well; we ended up at the IHOP on Sunset B.L.V.D., complete with all the faggots, all the late-night bros, and a waiter who was both, and had one killer 1970s sized afro.

I didn't push it too hard, thought I did oh so casually ask the question if she wanted to chill on over to my place in Hermosa Beach. But, that was that. A little late-night food, passion, and poison session. Then we made the drive, her hand in my crotch, back over to her almost central city crib.

"Drive slow, your car makes so much noise."

Her parents were home, she could see the lights that were on. I walked her to the door, a basic good girl/good boy kiss. Good night and a promise of a date in two days. So much for life...

*   *   *

Day two: not the date day but the one following this one, in and of our discussion; a loving little evening telephone call and a, "I am so interested in you. See you tomorrow."

A dinner date at my favorite Italian restaurant, over Santa Monica way. A drive to, a drive from, hand in my crotch, of course. A drive to, a drive from; kisses on my neck. A drive to and a drive from, her place to my place—if you know what I mean.

Now, don't let me get ahead of myself here. Picked up at her crib, basic uck from her parents. I even got to shake the old man's hand. An old dude, obviously a late bloomer in the have a family *departmento*. He obviously had a stroke for one side was chill factor zero, but *fuck 'em*. I had what I wanted; namely, their daughter in the palm of my hand. Or, should I say, she had her palm in my crotch.

I know this sounds weird, a chick who would go straight for the kill zone. It was more than a little strange to me, as well. But then I have had some even stranger experiences in my day and time. Like way back when, I was maybe eighteen, up Santa Barbara way. A chick who had done time in the psycho ward and she was still out there somewhere. Anyway, we begin to get down to it, and she wouldn't let me deposit my coins unless she got to stick her finger up my ass. I mean hey, *'That's no man's land.'* But she kept going at it, saying no-go to my *mojo* until she got to stick her finger in my ass. Well, fuck that! Finally, I just rolled her fat ass over, which was no easy task for she was more than a bit plump. But, I got her in a *po-sit-i-on* where none of her hand action could be gotten down to and gave her the quick wham bam, thank you ma'am. My backside, still a virgin from a chick's finger or otherwise. I got mine. She got what she deserved. And, I was out-a-there.

But, back to the story at hand. So anyway, as you can see, I have been with some real melodrama weird ones. No pain, no gain. So, I can play along.

We did dinner, as previously stated; a little walk in the park overlooking Santa Monica Bay. I always take the babes there post my little *rendezvous* at my restaurant of choice.

A promise here, a promissory note there. "Oh you are the only one, the only woman, I have ever come here with." "Really?" "Yes, really. I come here alone, alone a lot, but I have never brought another girl." Yeah right...

We take a little walk and she discusses her story, her lies. She tells me how she had met up with this dude back on the Illinois side of the picture. He joined the navy. She joined him.

234

Latched up at the love shack down Florida way. *There went my hopes for Vietnamese virgin meat.* Actually, I had little doubt that it had not been previously chewed on, with the aforementioned hand in crotch and all.

It was a rather interesting story, I thought. I always meant to ask her but never got the opportunity, *'That wasn't it a little strange cribbed up with a GI on a GI base where no doubt many of the dudes there had been over killing her county's kind a few years the previous?'* But...

I wondered, as well, what her overly conservative parents must have thought of the shack up and get down situation that be going on with her and her *love'n* man?

One thing obviously led to another, as the shack was no longer latched up. But, actually/truthfully I didn't even really care.

So, post the park and some romantic little glance, some romantic little kisses, she wanted to see my Love Station Zero. So, down the coast we head, her hand in my crotch, of course.

My H.B. apartment; I pull up behind my pickup truck. Cool and slow. PS: Aside from my 356, I also have a truck.

"Let's go take a walk," I suggest.

Never push it. Let them beg for it.

A walk down The Strand: look, listen, and feel, the now full winter ocean. She was cold, cold wearing a bright yellow secretary style mini dress. God, I hate bright colors.

Cold, we head for the crib,

"Oh, this is so nice."

Yeah, right. Slobs they were exchanged.

A little passion passed back and forth for a time. Love in the making, lust for the taking. We sat there on my maroon/red couch; purchased for $175.00 new, over there in the gutters of Van Nuys at a discount house. It looked like a Mexican couch. It felt like a Mexican couch. But no, it was velour, and it was mine. Placed artistically atop my 1960's green shag carpeting.

Now certainly, I am one of those dudes who likes to go back and forth with a little basic fore-play to the aft-play romance. And laying slobs, well that is AOK too, but when push comes to shove, sorry there babe, I want more. I want it all. And enough is never enough.

I made the move. Well first, let me tell you, all the kisses, all the love, complete with her hand massaging the wild animal down below. He was up and ready for action; really ready. I move in for the kill, hands on her boobs, shoved away. Hands on her legs, moved away. Then, to her privates, pushed away. Me, never being one to give up so easily. I kept at it as her hand continued to massage my pleasure zone.

Let me deviate here, if just for a brief second... Had that sweet little Vietnamese hand not been full-on in action, I would not have been so forward in the frontal assault; thinking there still may be a bit of a good girl left somewhere inside of her. But...

So, I go for the breast again; finally/finely left to play. I go for the, *'Let's unbutton this dress top.'* Playing with the exposed, golden small, perfectly firm, Vietnamese breast. Oh, yeah.

Then, out of nowhere, complete shutdown.

236

"What are you doing? Stop that!"

Well, needless to say, the mood was broken. She went on to tell me that she was not that kind of girl. I went on to tell her that she was a fucking prick teaser.

I drove her home, nice and being the gentleman that I am. I thought, *'Well, fuck this. I do not need it! I have a hundred Korean sisters, of my young dude martial arts students, just begging for a chance at my pants. I do not need it!'*

Back in the almost inner city, home she was. I decided to hit downtown for a little food session at the late-night Pantry—eat too much steak and potatoes session. That real American food that kills you softly and slowly. Dinner down, no real action happening. Some loser wanted to make a bet with me on some upcoming fight. I went home, thinking, *'Never again.'*

*　　*　　*

10:00 A.M., the day next, me still way far gone in sleepy time *never-never-land;* a telephone call. Yes, it was her. Her and here. She wanted me to pick her up at work, 4:00 P.M. "I love you," she exclaims. Yeah, right.

Never let it be said that I am not one to be compulsive, addictive, self-destructive, *et cetera-a-mundo.*

I rolled around in bed for a few more hours. Pulled myself out more at my time, the early afternoon. Hit the shower, even caught a shave. Got dressed, headed for the P.O. Box; a letter from a female friend of mine in Burma. Hit a little over looking the ocean, local *java* shop I like, *'The Kettle,'* and then on to the LAX pick-me-up.

There she stood, dressed in pink. Uck pink. A mini skirt, naturally. Tourists and travelers moving behind her, around her, in all of their blatant glory. The glory I dislike: moving to some distant location, location to nowhere, everywhere being all the same. She stood there, pink. In pink, as the winter crowds moved around her form in grays, in blues, browns, in suitcases the colors of the night. The sun it was setting, setting over the buildings of LAX. It, the sun, was in my eyes when I looked ahead. She was a vision far less pure, to my side. *Tapasya:* purification by fire. In the movement, the continual movement. The sun, and the crowds. She wore a pink, mini dress.

Into the car. Into the South bound, on Sepulveda Blvd., afternoon traffic, she kissed me and said, "I missed you." Yeah, right. A kiss for a kiss. I laid some serous tongue action upon her.

"Everyone is looking."
"Good!"

We discussed her day, her day of exchange. Exchange by any other name.

"Do you know a Filipino girl who works there, her hair is a bit longer than yours?"
"No, there are no Filipino girls that work for the company. I, in fact, am the only girl."
"Was there one working there maybe two months ago with longer hair? She tied it back."
"No, that was me, stupid. You thought that I was a Filipina. I used to have longer hair. I used to tie it

back. I remembered you. I can't believe you didn't remember me."

The story being told, once upon a time, a few months back, I remember going to the exchanging, seeing this to-die-for, what I thought to be Filipina.

So, there it was, a dream laid out before me. One of those looks that you get, a glance, a stare, from an unknown face. Eyes that pierce your soul—make you want all that they have to give. The promise of promised love. You know, she will be the one. She looks, you see, you move away, never to be known, never to be had. How many of life's glancing experiences are like that? How many, I do not know. But, here. But, now. This one I was handed and I didn't, did not even know—didn't see it coming.

Dumbfounded by the reason, lost in the images of my mind. A gift in the hand. A gift from the gods. A dream answered, here in my car.

"Yes, I cut my hair shorter the day before I gave you my telephone number. You should have heard what the guy in the booth, who works with me said about you when I gave you my number. You see, I have never given my number out, never given it out before. And he, the guy, has been asking me out forever. And I would never go."

She continues, "I have to cut my hair shorter again now, because my mother wants me too."
"Why, you are twenty-six years old and your hair, it is beautiful. I don't think you should cut it anymore."

I never understood a person of that age getting the told what to do by the *madre;* but then to each their own. I had other things on my mind. Much more important things…

*   *   *

So, we did dinner, Mexican food. I killed about *tres* double margaritas and was feeling oh so fine.

Then, she wanted to take a little l walk down upon The Strand. Well, my interests were aroused again, to say the least. So, I drove over to my crib. I pulled the ride up and in. She decided that it was too cold to walk. No doubt in a pink summer mini dress, it was. So, she wanted inside. Well so did I, *if you know what I be talking about?*

Into my crib we go. She plants herself. This time not on the maroon velour couch but on this big round bamboo framed padded center chair I had. I offer her something to drink, "No thank you." We make small talk, "No thank you." What she wants and asks for is a kiss. I, being the gentleman that I am, have no choice but to answer her needs.

Now I must tell you, I was a bit more than apprehensive about the full-on let's go for it again session. Beings how I was rejected the night before and rejection is not one of the things that I take oh so well. But, put the pedal to the metal and burn rubber on me, I went for it again. This time it was more than accepted.

She gave me the basic, "What are you doing?" kind of stuff, but I was sure that she had to know what I was doing by this point. So, I gave no apparent answer, just moved on in.

First, I exposed her small: perfectly formed, previously described boobies. I lick a caress here or there. She obviously was going to let me go for it tonight. I moved on to her legs, up between her thighs. Pull down the pantyhose. A feel, a touch, down goes the underwear. Her beaver sparsely haired, but oh so alluring. I began to kiss her legs, move to between her legs; tongue in, touching that special spot. She dug what I was dishing out.

"Oh, it feels so good."
"Your beaver is nice. Some chicks have some real stinky beavers. I won't go near them."
"Well, I take care of myself, keep myself clean."

I almost wanted to laugh when she said that but instead move my way up and moved her, hand-in-hand, oh so fucking romantically into my bedroom. I lay her down on my futon bed. She helps to remove my remaining clothing and we dance on.

I give the basic, let's play 'em move. I put my dick by the passageway to passion; moved in around, but did not put it in. Then, just barely in, immediately pull it out. Do that about five or six times and they are begging for the full-on insertion. Leave it sit just barely inside a time. Take it out. A little bit deeper, a little bit more. Play on, play on. Finally, full thrust, she dug my form. Her pussy was tight, shallow. I could see why some white trash navy Midwest boy wanted her on the crib side.

I went and got a rubber out of my bathroom drawer. Back in, literally. But now, she felt protected. We played it this way and that way. I let her roll on top. She huffed and puffed, came big time, in no time at all. So, I roller her over, her soup drying up. One of those one cum chicks. I tried but that is just the problem with those bad plastic capes, sometimes they just wrap the dick way too tight and cuming is a fucking no-go situation.

I explained it to her, went and got another bad dude to place upon my meat. I put the pedal to the metal again but still no-go. The fucking rubber got too tight again.

One more new one. This time I had to go grease it up with the local cooking oil, as per her request. Her pussy dry. Still no luck. Finally, she sat there calculating period dates, and period times. She let me just do her bare-back.

By this point I was ready to say fuck it to the rubber(s) anyway. The main pupster in action, he had a wad to blow. And a wad was blown.

Thus, lust being out of the way, actually quite uneventful for me, we lay there exchanging the basic LOVE comments. Then, onto a shower, back in the sack-jack. I wanted her to spend the night, but she said that she had to go home, parents and all. So, I hit it one more time for the road.

Outside into the night, I dove her to LAX. I drove her into an LAX parking lot. Drove her up next to her car, Florida license plates. A gift from her one-time navy dude. The chick always comes out ahead...

"He made good love, that's why we stayed together so long," she said.

Like I really fucking wanted to hear that. But, I am sure he was dropped down a notch in the lovemaking *departmento* when I had gotten done with her.

"What do you think about getting married?" She asks me.

"I don't think about it."

Talk is cheap. Life it is cheaper. Words they say nothing to me. Live and love. Running to and running from. Nothing means anything at all.

She told me I was only the second man she had ever gone out with, only the second man that she had ever made love to. Funny, I had heard that, those lines, somewhere in some lie before. It didn't really matter much. I really didn't care. You're only a virgin once.

So, we parted, she had a class to go to tomorrow, she said it was at USC. Then, she had to go to work but she would drive over at about 7:00 P.M. Nothing to lose, not much to gain, I consented.

She drove off in a yellow Firebird of a dude's gift; Florida on the license plate. Me, I moved in the night, my night. My car black, black like the lies that are hidden deeply in this nocturnal realm. This is where I come alive.

As I drove into my time, my place, the depths of the pagan night, I wondered why it had been so easy this evening and such a no-go the previous night. Had she taken to heart the words of, *'prick tease,'* that I had spoken to her. Or, did she instantaneously love me more? Which/what?

As I thought of the subject for a time, it came to me that this, not then, was our third date. Now someone, somewhere had come up with the foolish premise that getting down should not be gotten down to until that third night out. Foolish bullshit if you ask me. Personally, I believe in why waste time? See it, do it, live it, the first night around. But, that must have been it though. I never officially confirmed it, however.

I moved on, out to some nighttime haunt, seeking not to be left alone through the evening.

*   *   *

Daylight comes, in my afternoon. In my ride I find a notebook that she had left from the night before. Naturally, being the inquisitive person that I am, inside I look. LACC the school, not USC.

Now, it's really no big deal. At least not to me, for I have told more than a few lies myself— thrown in the *di-rec-t-ion* of a babe I had my lust vibes upon. A player in a player's world, right? Somehow though, what begins in lies can never lay the foundation to the truth. Thus, only her second man to plant the power pup in her vaginal canal—I had definite disbelief.

*   *   *

P.M. Next. Seven fifteen rolls around, she is late. Usually, I do not wait at all; fifteen minutes though, it seemed fair enough. Seven twenty, telephone call,

"There have been a lot of international planes that have come in. I have to work late; I'll be there by 8:00 P.M."

Well, I was a little *tick'd,* but only an hour. I can paint…

Eight o'clock, no show. Eight fifteen, I was on my way out the door. Telephone call,

"Still very busy, they won't let me leave. I can't be there until after nine. I am so sorry, but then I will spend the night."

"Look," I told her, "I live in a world of totality, either this or that, no in between. So, I want you to come over now."
"I can't, they'll fire me."
"So what, then quit."
"I can't quit my job, what will I do for money?"
"Then forget me."

I hung up.
Now, of course, you are probably saying that I am a power tripper, etc, and so on. Sure I am. I want to be the center of attention and the center of the world. And, if things aren't going in that direction, especially with the babes, well then it's *asta luaga* on the flamenco guitar.
So, to wrap this little long bit of verse up; I sat down and wrote her a letter that night. One of those ones I used to do, thinking that they were so artistic on the typewriter, spreading the words here and there across the page. Unfortunately, I didn't make a photocopy of it, so I don't even really remember what it said. No doubt, just the basic, *'Fuck off, you are a liar, bullshit person, etc,'* type of letter.
Due to my writing said letter, I was still in the pad. I get the call at ten o'clock,

"Do you want me to come over now?"
"No,"

Click, I hung up on her. Me, I was/am a pure and simple mid-twenties child.

*   *   *

I sent the letter and her notebook to her the next day. A day or so later, I get another telephone call,

"So, do you want to talk it over, work it out?"
"No," I hung up.

I could see this was not going to be an easy bail session, she was going to keep hanging on. And, with me being the self-indulgent anything but spend the night alone kind of person that I am, I again changed the old telephone number, for the ten millionth time.

Keep the new babes new and unscathed by the past.

Now, if it had been another chick, another personality, not so forward, demanding, and expecting of another lifetime, I may have been more forgiving. But, when zero is only equal to, and not more than zero, what is a guy supposed to do? Exit, stage left.

So, that was basically the end of the adventure. Unfortunately thought, post her, my dick had gone into hock, and the money had run out, so I spent the next eight months with no new pussy and no travel; no fun...

We did pass each other, in the Torrance Sears store, *once-upon-a-time* however, maybe two years back. This story transpiring about three years ago.

It was almost funny. I had gone in there to buy some tools. Craftsman being by far the unparalleled best. I was kneeling down. I look up and there she stood with some homeboy of a Latin

246

dude. I wondered if he was the second one ever to make love to her? Or maybe, it had gone down to the first. Depends how stupid the guy was, I guess.

Anyway, our eyes met. We looked. We moved away. She, obviously not wanting whatever story she had told the dude, blown. I laughed to myself.

Then, once maybe a year and a half ago, in the depths of one of my returns from Asia jetlag sessions; with no new pussy on hand, I thought to write her a letter. Well in fact, I thought to write a lot of old flames a letter, to see what may come from them; the letters, not the old flames. I mean, I knew what they each individually had to offer and well, I was interested in a smorgasbord bite. A step up from a, *'wish sandwich,'* huh?

Anyway, though the letters were basically all the same in text, a little word here, a little phrase of remembrance there was added to make them personal. That is except in the case of the aforementioned lady of desires letter, which for some reason came out much more in depth and longer. But, I never sent any of them. I got some new babe(s), some new chances, and some new money to head back to where I feel the best; Asia, so…

For whatever it is worth, I have a copy of the unsent letter, here upon computer files. Perhaps by placing it here, it will make the time spent writing it somehow more worthy. So, anyway, so here it is:

Dearest Lin Wa,

Well, it has indeed been quite a long time. It is almost funny that I am sitting here writing you a letter. For it had been two years since I saw you last. Many times you have come to mind, but life and its situations lead us on, doing what we do. A few days ago, I came upon your address that you had written down for me so long ago and it inspired me to write this letter to you.

You were a dream. I remember that first time that I saw you at the LAX currency exchange booth, a few months before we actually met. I even remember the fantasy of love that you conjured up in my mind at that time. When you gave me your phone number, I did not even realize that it was you, the same beautiful woman, for you had changed your hair. But ah, what a dream lived.

Do you remember the first time we went out? To the New Year's Eve dance at the nightclub in Monterey Park. Remember how your parents got so upset because you had gone with me, a guy with long blond hair. At the time, I though how small minded. That is the problem with the world though, it only sees the external. It is so dominated by what is acceptable within society. It was an interesting evening though, to say the least.

Hey, I even cut my hair really short about six months ago, it had gotten very long. I mean it was one of those battles with, "I'm getting old," and it has become so fashionable to have long hair and, so you know, I hate trends. But I just don't feel natural without it, after having it long for most of my life. So, it was a lesson learned the hard way. It has thankfully grown back.

Well, my life has gone on. I have spent a lot of time in Asia and a lot of time dreaming and living the life of the mystic artist that I am.

I recently also just moved from my old apartment. It's funny how sometimes we end up staying at a place for so long and never intend to. Me, I was there for three and a half years. Now, I am right on the water. It feels good to move; a change. So many things have gone on in my life it is hard to write them all in just a few short lines. I am sure the same is true with you.

Sometimes, when I have thought about you, I have wondered about your connection with a guy in the Navy. Vietnamese girl and U.S. Navy dude? America is so full of Wonder White Bread sort of people it is quite sad, for illusion has so much more to offer.

You know, it is funny writing this letter. There was a time when I thought that I never had any reason to contact you again. For the truth is, you and I are very different people, very different minds. Me, I live in a totality where nothing matters but the feelings of the moment and forget anything to do with the world. Perhaps I have been given the opportunity to live that dream. You, on the other hand, at least when I knew you, believed the lie and illusion of the material world. Well, to each their own.

So here we are. Can you believe it, we are twenty-eight years old. In fact, you may very well be married by this point and have children. If you are I hope that this letter causes you no problems. If it does, I am sorry. Other than that, I hope that your life is happy and things are going well.

When I have been at LAX exchanging money to take some distant journey, I have sometimes looked for you. But I have never seen you again. I do not know if you still work there. But anyway… As stated earlier, I hope this letter finds you well and happy and I just wanted to tell you that I remember the special lovemaking session that we had together, your beautiful golden skin against mine. And I remember the love and infatuation that we both felt. It is sad that it did not last longer. Ah, love...

So, if you ever feel like it, drop me a line or give me a call. If not, I will always hold you in a special place in my memory.

Love,
Sandy Shaman

CHAPTER 13
MELROSE P.M.

It was late. It was Thursday night. No women, no one, nowhere, with no place to be. Nothing to do. The alone was closing in on my head like a vice clamp in heat. I was a little stoned, a little drunk, and sex it was on my mind.

'How can I facilitate the fulfillment of this desire,' is the question that went through my head. Melrose, yes Melrose. There was a new little *'Oriental Massage Parlor'* that had opened, up there. A Melrose *may-sage* parlor.

Melrose it is funny, like West Hollywood in general: rejuvenation, renovation, style and culture in the works. I remember when it was a sleazy old street that no one even went to, except to pick up a dose of written spiritualism at the Bodhi Tree Bookstore or some used clothing at this one little garment shop. Now, there are many-many of them, the *way too expensive* used clothing store. Many of this, many of that. So fucking hip, I hate it.

I mean, let's put things in perspective, I grew up in the gutters of Hollywood. Now all the tourists fill its streets: West Hollywood, Melrose, in particular. Indiana, Idaho, Minnesota, Texas, hicks. I mean, they are all fucking hicks and tourists and they think it is so way cool to be there/to live there. Live there in what they think is happening. Where the dollar signs have gone up and everything else has gone down.

To a *local* like me, it's a fucking joke. To all the trendy, who are a day late and a dollar short, it's a-happening. Fuck 'em all.

Occasionally, I will pass its bounds, *en route,* on route over to catch one of those mystical written doses at the said bookstore.

I caught a glimpse once, once well maybe twice; one of those fleeting glimpses, a passing vision of later indulgence and possibility; a whorehouse on the Asian side of the picture, if you please. Now tonight, the aloneness permeates the air: dick-hard, dick-ready, dick-holiday, dick-in-hand. I am out into the Porsche driving away from the beach and into the god-forsaken city, Hollywood.

I pull up, I pull by. Should I park in front? There is a space of availability. Paranoia wins out. I hit it over to the side.

The side streets, *the back streets,* where all of the visionaries hide. Where they all dance. Where they all live. With no need for the view of the city, for the breeding bullshit insanity that makes man's mind tick. The side streets...

Out of the car, I put my long coat on. It is cold; a tail end winter evening. I stroll down the street. There it be, there it lie: what it is, what it was, what it *ain't.* Nighttime fantasy, nighttime nothing; paid for on their back with the dollar green. All the men who have nothing better to do than chase the escaping nothing into the zone of the forbidden and the foreboding. I am a blood brother with them all. I am one of them.

'Oriental Massage,' the light blinks on and off. The sign on the door, says 11:00 A.M. to 12:00 A.M. I look at my watch, it's five minutes to twelve.

I laugh to myself, early hours. I don't usually hit the streets until one or so. The nighttime life on the extremities, it is sure folding up early these days.

I reach into my pocket, pull out a glass vile. In goes my fingernail—my pinky nail—up it goes to my nose. A momentary wake-me-up in an already sleeping world. I am ready for the dance.

As I walk in, the girl behind the front desk, a more than beautiful Asian object, maybe twenty-five or so, she looks at her watch; almost time to go home, but it is not yet the witching hour. She will have to hang for a few more.

"May I help you?"

I look directly into her beautiful eyes, the kind that are so tightly closed that they are barely open, almost like they cannot see at all. Just the way I like them, just the way I liked her. The kind of girl that I could have married, given a chance in the dance.

"Hi," (not *'hi,'* like in English, but *'hi,'* like yes, in *Nehongo;* Japanese). It was my answer and just as I was about to speak to her, in her native tongue, I realize, best to keep our conversation of the evening simple; no explanations asked for, thus one not needed. So, I said,

"Yes, I would like a massage."

Looking at her watch again, she said, "But it is late, most of the girls are not giving anymore."

I laughed inside as she used the word giving. *'Giving me what,'* was and is the question. In a world where nothing is free and love is bought so cheap. Well baby, just spread your love disease upon me. Leave me no room for escape.

Life is all what you make of it...

"I would like a massage from you," I voiced, as I stared deeply into her eyes.

Instantly we understood each other. She looked at me, glanced at her watch, stood up; ah what a woman: five foot six-ish, thin, long hair, and even appeared to have some boobies. She walked over, hit a light switch, obviously to turn off the *'Oriental Massage'* sign. Yelled to someone in Japanese that she was going to work. Locked the front door, turned to me and said,

"Thirty-five dollars at the desk for a massage, the rest we will talk about in the room."

Now the *may-sage* parlors, they all do this. I mean, they want to get a dude in the room and naked to make sure he's not a cop. Some even make you whip your dick out to the front-man at the front-desk. But, there was no front-man obvious tonight. Probably in the back, watching through some hidden camera.

The street whores are the funny ones. A drive by form of fashion, passion, and love. When the heat is on, and the cops are heavy, they make you pull the pup out in the ride before they get in, but that is all another/other stories; a few hundred or so.

She opens the door to the hallway, a darken red/brown space full of doors that lead to rooms. I walk in; the adverse of a phallic symbol, vaginal symbolism. In, not out. In the doorway to the perils of the night. Oh, kiss me deeply, deep inside your treacherous form. I am inside. She closes the door behind us and leads us on.

I looked around and realized that this is basically the kind of whorehouse that I do not really dig. It was obviously once a retail store, so the ceiling is way high and the walls, if you can call them that, are eight feet on the topside. So, you can hear all that is going on in the room next to you.

I prefer a little privacy when I fuck, if you know what I mean.

As we walked to our given space of static redemption, I heard no action going down. That was/is a good thing, I thought. As we passed one door, down the hallway to hell, my sweet young, newly found friend, leans against the door and says in Japanese, obviously to another working girl, "I'm going to work. Let your man out the back door." A very deep raspy voice reply, *'in Nehongo,'* "Okay we are already finished. He's a quick one." I wanted to laugh, especially when the smile came across my young loves face, but I didn't want to give my dialectic capabilities away, so I held it deep in my gut waiting for a further time, a later place for it to explode. I settled for the anticipation of that oh so fine feeling I knew I would-be-a-having when we were alone.

We waltzed back-Jack, to the last room on the left; number twenty-three it said. By my count, there were only maybe eight rooms. It was interesting, I thought, numbers and all of their forms. But, I decided to leave he number to its own perfection and explanation. We went inside.

The door is opened. I step in, 8 X 8 X 8. Eight foot, by eight foot, by eight foot. Our palace of pleasure, our dreamland of the night. Step into it for a moment. Live it for whatever it is worth. And, the moment of the dollar sign is so easily forgotten when love is all that you feel. I do love, love…

Wood paneled walls, red carpeting, a dresser with a mirror. A massage table stood front, stood center.

"Oh fuck, we have to fuck on one of those," I said out loud.

Actually, I really dislike those things. I mean, they are cold imitation leather and there is no room to move, groove, or anything. And I mean, I do like to party fuck.

"I'm sorry," says my love bunny. "But the police have been trying to close us down. They don't believe that we are a real therapeutic massage parlor."

I walk over to plant one on her, she steps back. I realized that I had committed the cardinal whoring sin; I tried to get right down to it, lay my love tongue down her love throat. Experience it all, as if it truly were cast to the realms of spontaneity. And, in a world where most hookers won't even lay the slobs, call me a sinner supreme.

I looked at her, she at me.

"How much?"

256

"Take off your clothes."

Which I naturally began to do: feeling fine, looking fine. As I am going about my business I ask,

"Where is the guy who runs this place?"

For you know all massage parlors have some dude in charge. Either some big buff homeboy or some little greedy wimp packing a thirty-eight. Sometimes a little bit of both: the brains and the muscle. Personally, I would just as soon slap up those little dick heads; give them the gagster slap. For they think they are so fucking cool and tough, bouncing women around to bake their bread and then butter for them. But, anyway…

She said, "Oh he's here watching."

Now I, at least hoped, that she was only being descriptive in her description. I mean, it did bring up all of my paranoia(s) of observed sex, videotape cameras, and the like.

Like the *may-sage* parlors in Bangkok—the big ones, not he small ones; at one end of every room, there is this large mirror. I mean, really big, full wall size. And, you know there is some dude or dudes sitting there, *watch'n, talk'n, discss'n,* and *size'n* the *sitch* up. All for the sake of babe-protection. I mean, *'Hey, I understand.'* You don't want the women getting *jacked.*

I have always expected to end up seeing myself on some, *'Hot Girls! Straight Out'a Thailand'* Video Tape. But, as I never watch porno,

257

never was really into it, I guess I would never know if I was or was-not...

But hey, come-on, I mean, show it to anyone, for I really don't care. No wife, no family, and all the like. I am OUT and partying free. And, come-on, I mean whores; they are the perfect passion—no harm, no foul. A dollar paid for an unforgettable memory—a moment in worship of the divine perfection of the female form. A moment given to the goddess.

So, there I was, I was naked, *bare-to-the-bone*. I placed my butt upon the *may-sage* table. Yeah, just as I thought, it was cold.

She placed a white, what looked almost to be a nurses' robe over her clothing and then began to slip her dress off underneath. It was the game, you know what I mean, get the dude's dick all hot and bothered; steaming on a cold imitation leather massage table.

"A hundred dollars," she said.
"Why do all you lovely ladies of the night have to play the fool's money game?"
"No game," she exclaims.

So out of my pocket (well, I was actually naked, so out of my mental pocket), I pull the old line, willed to me by Saturday Jim before his days of wedlock.

"I don't want to buy it, I just want to rent it for a little while."

It got us both laughing a bit.

"Seventy-five dollars," she said.

258

"Okay."

I mean, I hate to negotiate: barter, bargain for the pussy price. And I mean, the cold air was getting to me and my dick was beginning to shrink in size.

Here hold this one baby, warm it up.

So, I got off the table, grabbed my pants on the floor, tossed her, her pussy price; out of the pocket *d'matrimony.* I sat back down with my pants across my lap, I mean it was a little cold in there. Reached for my sport coat, pulled out my little vile; opened the lid, reached in for that feeling, it had begun to fade.

"Want some?"
"What is it?"
"What do you think it is?"
"Is it good?"
"Of course, it is. But what the fuck difference does that make, you are getting it for free."

She reached over and with a long painted red fingernail pulls out a load. I'm thinking that she should be paying me. None-the-less, the moment of love is in action, as I ask her,

"Do you have a mirror?"
"Sure."

She reaches into the drawer of the dresser. All reminiscent, I am sure, from a time back then, when the police actually believed that they were a therapeutic massage parlor and they could get away with such unholy contraptions as a bed. Heaven forbid, a bed in a therapeutic massage parlor.

Out of the drawer come the mirror. She hands it my way. I lay down a load. She grabs a razor blade, we are set.

With the feeling back in, and the movement in motion, life begins to, once again, embrace its perfection. That feeling that tickles the mind, that dances on the soul. The play is on, the movement forward, the dance of the sinners, the passion of and only for the fools—never let that cocaine feeling slip too far.

About then, I hear the rear door open and slam, my heart jumps a beat or three. That full-on high hysteria when you're too ON, but then instantly OFF. I realized though that it was just that short-lived dude, of the price conscious evening, checking out the back way if you please. The other girl calls thought the door in her sultry Japanese voice,

"I'll wait for you out front."
"Okay."

It was funny how all languages seem to adopt the expression Okay.

"But, it might be a while," she mentions.

They both laugh, thinking that I do not understand. I just look and smile.

With a few lines up our noses; up with a rolled ten spot, I say,

"Well, shall we do this *thAng?*"

I could see in her eyes that she wanted me to dish out some more of that bad powder white so she could chalk up again. But, I mean hey, fuck that, let her buy her own. I have to pay for what I am get'n here and the common laws of trade, supply, and demand; well hey, they do apply here, as well...

So, I take the remains on the mirror and gum it. Look up at her, in fact, I must add that she did look quite poetic with her long black hair and nurse white, almost sheer, almost see-through robe upon her Asian form.

I toss my pants on the floor and lay myself down on my stomach upon the table. She comes over with a bottle of oil in hand. How I do love this treatment, not so different from Bangkok where you actually do get a bit of a massage, if you ask for it, in the bargain. She lays down a few slaps, a few movements.

I roll over, open her robe, ah what a body. Nice little tits, a beaver with just the right amount of Asian pubic hair. She even had a little scar near her ribs. Probably someone, some *yakuza,* had tried to carve her up once-upon-a-time. *Perfection within the imperfection,* my *mantra.* I love it.

My dick started to get hard again as I removed her robe. Though with the *toot-ski* up the nose, it does take just a bit more of the pay-ed/paid attention to activate its love stream. But none-the-less my *'Wild ThAng,'* it was move'n.

"Don't you want a massage?"
"Sure, in a minute."

I pull her close to me, her body next to mine. Ah love, I do love, love...

That moment lived in the extreme(s). The totality of the supreme. And, for all those people who fuck only to fuck and for all those who claim you can only love a good girl; fuck them. I mean, just let your heart soar, and you can love anybody. Oh, that feeling, it even tingles in me now.

I kissed her. She kissed me back.

I guess the coke, opened up her love realms.

I liked it. I guess that is when my cocaine bought me, a night times session with nothing held back.

There was a hand on my rod: waxing the banana, giving me that extra incentive that my wild pup needed. She dropped a bit of oil on my body—its initial coldness made me jump. But, with her body placed atop mine, warmth was in the air.

She knew what to do, where to place her finger, where to place the movements of her body. Shimbashi district of Tokyo, Edo, or Kyoto: from a long-line, a ten-thousand-year-old tradition of women trained to please a man. Or maybe, she just took some massage courses at LACC, Los Angeles City College. Who knows?

Love potion number nine, her juice flowed onto my genital regions. She slaps my dick up her love canal. I am in heaven: the love, the woman, the sex, and the cocaine.

I look at the ceiling that is slightly chipping and needs painting. She pumps on and on and on.

"How long have you been here?" I ask.
"Awhile."
"How long have you been doing this?"
"Awhile."
"Will you marry me?"
"I'll be your wife anytime you want."

'Yeah, for a price. A price and some lines,' I thought.

Her body moves up, sits up. Her legs straddle the table we are upon. She starts throbbing and huffing and puffing, making the screaming fuck noises that only the Japanese whores seem free enough to make. Free, when nothing is free. Not here. Not there. Not anywhere. For everything in life, there is a price to pay.

She is enjoying it. *'Fucking unbelievable,'* a whore enjoying herself. Usually they are dried up DM, (dead meat), too confused to enjoy the pleasure. Too tied up to feel the pain. I don't know, maybe it was me; I like to think so. But probably, it was the coke that freed her soul.

I think to move this LOVE-situation down onto the floor, where I could really get some power action moving. For this fucking session was ever so fucking fine. But then, I think of all the scum that has come into this place. Businessmen with spit-stained shoe soles, gutter tramps on vacation, West Hollywood hip moved in tourists. "Fuck it," I say to myself. I let her pump on.

"Are you going to cum?" She asks.
"Are you?"
"I am about to."
"Do it."

Now, I had to work myself up to it. I mean, for those of you that don't know that the main rod does get a bit numb with the induction of the *caine* into the system. And sex, thought the heavens may be haveable—cuming at times, well it is almost like you have to work at it/force it.

I let her movements caress me a bit more, a bit more radically if you will. I licked and sucked a little boob. Let the love motion, the love action pump me up and down a bit harder: a bit harder, a bit harder, a bit harder. The pleasure strategy was a moving. I was wham bam'n hard from the underside.

She got her hers a-screaming. I, a few minutes post, got mine.

Her beauty and the perfection of this night did hold my pagan soul bound. I looked at her and in Japanese I tell her, "I love you."

I told her, because I do love the nights, the streets, the simplicity of a whore. Their sheer spiritual perfection, non-attachment perpetuated. I hold them close. I held her close. Life that long lost love, the girl next door. The love that one has forever been awaiting but has until now been denied. Yeah, I did love her.

She looked in my eyes. I could see that for her too, it was the perfect moment in a far less than perfect world. She had lost herself, like I, in the passionate excellence of this momentary nothingness recorded only in the *Akashic Record* and the bounds of literature.

Perfect love forever, as momentary as life is. As short-lived as existence. I give a kiss to the night.

She said, "I love you, too."

We got up, wiped a bit of the remaining oil off. Got dressed. I powdered my nose one more time, if you catch my meaning, put the *toot* back in my pocket. Opened the door, walked with her back down the hall.

At the first room, abode of bliss; door opened, sat a lady. Plumper, yet equally as Japanese, as my love catch of the night. Her deep voiced friend, I assumed. In a chair, a blue suited wimp. Obviously thirty-eight carrying pimp of a massage parlor owner; our eyes met. He looked away. Their eyes met, my babes and his. He was pissed and wanted to go home. He's lucky I didn't blaze him up right there, just for being the power-tripping loser that he was.

She walked me to the front door, opened it. I gave her a kiss on the cheek goodbye. The door closed behind me. That was it. The end of a new beginning for neither one of us. Her nor I, had the slightest idea of what tomorrow may hold.

I stepped back beyond the walls of that sanctuary into the blatant realms of the truthful, the pure, the acceptable, the saints and the sinners.

Perfection: perfect understanding, in an imperfect world. We all end up where we all end up and a lot of times we do wish that it were a different way. But, it is not.

So cast a blow for the devil. Cast a blow for the spiritual perfection of God. Cast a blow for the night for it is what caressed my soul.

And when there is no further use in pretending, no further reason why and when; all that is bad becomes all that is good and all that we wish to change becomes that way. Then our dreams, they may be answered. The dance, it may well be known. And tomorrow never means anything at all. As today just passes on by.

*   *   *

I think that they should change the rules for the saints; first they must live a little sin. It is the only way that you know anything at all.

265

I looked at my watch, it was about 1:40 A.M. Hey, the night is still young, what should I do? Maybe go over to Tommy's, catch a burger. Maybe down to the Pantry for a T-bone steak. Maybe to Full-House Seafood, eat some Chinese cuisine...

I walked to my car. Got in. Drove off. As I find spiritual enlightenment in the streets, on the streets. Directed by the fading glow of the old streetlights.

And you never know what you will find...

CHAPTER 14
TOO MUCH THAILAND

I had been in Thailand a long time, too long. *'Too much Thailand,'* as my mind had put it. I had decided that it was way time to leave. I caught the next plane back and on down to Bangkok.

I had been North, up North of Chang Rai. North, where the wild opium poppies grow free. Well, not free—cultivate by machinegun carrying goons. But, it is beautiful, as far as the eyes can see; poppies, opium poppies; nourishment for the soul and a promise of death in the veins.

I had to hustle a bit, the flight was fully booked—no seats available. But, I was in no mood for playing games; I got on.

I cruised back into the city from the airport and was asked the typical Bangkok question by the typical Bangkok taxi driver,

"You want massage? I know best place in Bangkok. Clean, not dirty like Pat Pong."
"No thanks," my typical response.

I pulled into my usual hotel where everyone knows me and kicked back for the evening with the intention of hitting the airline office come sun up and setting myself up with a flight to Taipei then on to Japan. Get back into a bit more civilized culture.

The next morning presented itself. I pulled myself out of bed, eleven-ish, went down and had some breakfast and some of the basic *java*; finished and started my walk to the airline office.

It was a nice day, why not walk? Why bother taking a *tuk tuk,* the little three wheeled taxis

Bangkok has to offer. And besides a little exercise and all...

So, I strutted my bad self out, walked down Suriwong Road. As I walked, I was, of course, asked the usual questions,

"Need a girl?"
"You want massage?"
"No," and/or, "No."

The airline office intact/in tow, completion *par excellence.* A little rap with a babe I knew there named A.J. She had done some time on my side of the world and on my actual turf, down the South Bay way of L.A.

I remember the first time that we had met: she tried to impress me, give me the rap of this cool little singles bar, as she put it, down Manhattan Beach way. Singles bars, I don't dig them. But now and then, out there in the Bangkok night, well that is a different story. Anyway, that was awhile go and dreams and destinies they do move on and they do die hard.

I was back a moving upward into the deeper realms of this city that lives by the ways of the night. *Too much Thailand,* and my *danero* or should I say *bhat* had gotten short.

I thought to myself, as I walked in the heat of the streets, if I still had some mega bucks, some more passages into this dreamer's realm, that I would probably step back, step deeper in, take another long deep breath, and move again somewhere out here/there into the lost realms of Southeast Asia. For out here/there on the *hard road,* I could be anything, anybody that I wanted to be. And though I hate lies, life it was becoming more and more of one. For when I walked the foreign soils, I was it, the one that drew the eyes—a big fish in a little pond. Long blond hair, full of style, in a black-haired world, where fashion-passion has not yet come on. I, the dream every woman wanted to live. They would look at me with a dollar sign in one eye, a green card in the other.

A falsified dream, a contemptuous lie in a blatant land where *white was still right*. It is all so haveable, so knowable, so loveable. A lie, yes. An ego stroke, sure. No one who has lectured me as to my reasons for wanting to be in Asia is telling me anything that I do not already know. It is a dream, a lie, a supposition supposed.

My money situation and hiatus from culture, well it was pointing in the direction of home, however. Home, such as it is. Home, such as it never really was. For now, here: Asia; the Southeast quadrant of, had become far more my home.

Pumping down the street in the Bangkok heat. Direction, my hotel of a love crib. The walk, oh yeah, it did do me right, it did do me good.

I don't know if you can understand humidity. I know that I never could. That is until I hit the far side of Southeast Asia. I mean, it is more than N.Y. Never did really dig the Big Apple, anyway. It is nowhere near So. Cal. It is far more than even Mother India. I mean, it is so hot; it is wet hot. Walking, yeah, I did have the tendency to work up a sweat.

Powering down about in the vicinity of Lumpini Park, I see this little econo box of a four-door Japanese sedan, parked roadside; gray in all its glory upon my proceeding approach. No mention, no call, *'Though a funny place to park, on such a busy street,'* I thought.

Movement in motion: fashion and passion. I am proceeding by,

"Hello, hello, excuse me."

Well excuse me, if you please, what is there to say. This serious, serious, serious babe of a street sweet was hanging out the window, calling me into her web. She wanted me to go to her/with her. *Anyway, that was her way, would suit my way just fine.*

"Come in, I want to talk with you. It is so much cooler in here."

I mean, what's a guy like me supposed to do?

Now my initial street kid paranoia kicks in. In a car, a way babe riding shotgun; a uck of an, *I don't know what,* I do mean ugly to the max, female at the helm. Now was I going to get *Shanghaied* here or what?

What or why, and the passions for reason. Never really knowing the reason why. A kiss of death, a kiss with the tongue, right down its throat. Well, it always means more than no kiss at all. In, I got.

Now there was some of the little basic *convo* going down: where was I from, where was I going, was this my first time here; no way. Who was I, what was I, why was my three-day old beard so much darker than my hair; ask God.

Now, *helm-ster,* the captain, the ugly, didn't say a word, but this other sweet little thing, and I do mean that she was *kill,* she had turned around, spoken the words of the rap, took my hand, held my

270

hand, stunned me like only the purest form of a whore can do.

That touch that caresses the soul, that touch that knows no mind. It has been learned. It has been practiced. It has been mastered. Kill me one time, kill me twice.

"Yeah, I am bailing, too much Thailand, heading out and on Taipei way."
"Is that your passport in your pocket?"
"No, I am just happy to see you."

She didn't get the joke.

"Can I see it?"

They compared notes in Thai, as they reviewed my places of *de-part-ure.*

"You have been everywhere."
"Not everywhere yet."
"Do you travel alone?"
"Yeah, would you like to marry me and travel with me?"

Passport back in pocket, her hand back in mine. Oh, steal my soul one more time. Do it all the way.

"Would you like to go and have some orange juice with us?"
"Why?"
"Just to get to know each other better. No money, charged," she concludes.

Everything has a price baby. I knew it then, and I do know it now. Pay it, live it, where is its source, where is it born, and where does it go?

Now let me explain the situation here. You know, like the way all the pseudo artist literary giants have so aptly attempted to do: I am in a car, with a one hundred percent kill vixen of a babe holding my hand and bartering for my love. It is a million degrees outside, and it is oh so cool in the gray realms of this ride. The sun is out there. The *air-con* is in here. I see the Bangkok world passing by me: the cars, the buses, the *tuk tuks,* the walkers, and the drivers; nowhere to nothing and what does life really mean anyway. Now she is obviously a whore, come-on... What her game is—is the question. Now I mean down L.A. way, I have had my session with a few *women-of-the-night* riding mobile: hookers and harlots, princesses of the day and of the night. But here on the Bangkok side of the picture, well it has never gone down that way; as-of-yet.

I mean, the massage parlors; sure. The streetwalkers; sure. The babes that hang out in front of the clubs of the Patpong and try to pull you in; of course. But mobile???

So anyway, push comes to shove. I could have bailed like any good boy would have done. Good boy, well... Not really my flavor.

"Do you want to party," I ask.
"Party?"
"I mean you are seriously beautiful, and I would love to love you. So, let's quit playing the game here and get down to the business."

She looks over in 'Ugly's' *di-rec-ion,* says to her in Thai, thinking I don't understand, a basic let's DO IT type of statement.

"Do you want to go to your hotel?"
"Why, this ride is fine."

Post a minor debate as to the practicality of the realism of a FUCK, (as they like to say in Thai), in the backseat. We were on. Love was in motion and let me put it this way, I was up and ready to go.

She parlayed herself from the riding shotgun position to the riding my shotgun *po-sit-i-on* in the rear. Out the front door, in the rear door. Ugly drove us over to this little semi dirt infested street a few blocks away.

Now people they were around. The tinted windows shaded us; making by-passers, passing by, keep going into the nowhere of the sheer Bangkok heat.

The ride over; she had been on me leaning/laying slobs on my neck, my face, my lips the whole time. Oh, so right, oh so tight. *En route,* on route, my hand up her black dress.

All the best whores wear black.

I had grabbed a little *poo-say,* just to make sure I was on the right side of the coin, if you know what I mean. I was, it was, all AOK.

Now Ugly sat there watching, I told her to take a hike,

"But it is too hot out there."

Let it ride, let it flow. She got to watch the wild kid in action.

I had the skirt up, my brown baggy pants semi down. The wild thing, it went in the far side of her underwear. Her top, I about ripped it off getting to those oh so fine, Chinese Thai, pale skinned boobs.

Now this was no *make-love* session, and there is little left to prove. I *wham-bamed, thank you ma'am;* one of those butter the muffin stroke it till you choke it sessions. Power thumb on the fast hand side.

Done and out, my pants they were pulled up and on. She was getting her shit together; said something to the effect of price consideration to Ugly, riding up front. They discussed, *'saam loy',* three hundred *bhat. 'Fuck that,'* I thought to myself, though it was the going rate down Chao Praya II's way. But this was not there, no bath, no massage, no deal.

I open the door, I stepped out.

"Thank you, bye."

I close it. I began to walk on. The babes; well one babe, one dog, they naturally are out and after me. Yelling things to the effect of, 'they want their money, they want this, they want that, I owe them…'

Yeah right…

"I gave you what you wanted baby."

I'm walking a bit faster than they. They jump back in the ride and begin to follow. I move, grove over to the busy street. Keeping everything obvious, if you know what I mean. They had to deal with the traffic, the coming and the going. I had a

274

few blocks on them by the time they caught up. A few blocks and right by the Tourist Police Stand, the one that is situated right across from the Dusit Thani Hotel

They pull up, they start screaming. I walk over, tell the residing cop that these hookers, they are bothering me.

Maybe it was my speaking Thai. Maybe it was the twenty bhat spot which I laid in his hand. I mean Thailand it is seriously corrupt. It could have gone either way. But, for whatever it may be worth, he gave them the word to *am-scray*—bail. I walked on, they drove on. Freedom and passion, there always seems to be a dollar sign attached.

Back to my room, chill back from the heat. I worried about getting the clap, syphilis, or something from not wearing a rubber for about five seconds or so. Then, had a cola, a soda, a mineral water, an iced coffee, and a nap... I went to sleep laughing.

Nighttime, my time it always does seem to roll around. Dinner in Thai. A walk through the spheres of the night. I was waiting time, killing time. A later hour when I could go dance. It was to come.

My Bangkok disco, of that time. A hot little jumping spot: downstairs, down center, dance the night away.

I hit it a bit earlier than usual, a bit past 9:30 in the P.M. It was still *chill-factor-zero,* no one really cutting the rug, or tripping the light fantastic, as the old folks used to say. Sat back, had myself a Perrier. Still nursing one of those three day mega maximum amount, I mean *'Whoa, so potent dude,'* kill hangovers.

In over my shoulder, as the new wave disco beat pounds, *strutt'n* up to the bar, comes this semi fine, semi *strok'n,* what looked to me to be a Thai bitch of an elegant whore. I sat there, at my usual table, in all of my perpetual style: listening to the music, watching, with an occasional glance over my shoulder; as she moved, as she grooved, cigarette in her hand. Did she want it, does she, would she turn me down? You know, all the pounding questions of the pounding disco beat. *'Could I, should I, ask her to dance? I don't know. Disco sucks.'*

Finally, in a non-intoxicated swooping motion, before anyone else, of the arriving crowd, had the chance/got to her first; I asked, "Do you?" She did. I did, we did, a little dance upon the disco floor.

I even forget her name now; you know that I would probably tell you if I could remember. Her name and the music. Her name and the dance floor. I don't know, what do names mean anyway?

So, we took and we shook. She had those basic sucky Thai moves. I don't know what it is, a bit hard to describe in words, but Thais *just-aint-got-no-soul.* It is like, have you ever watched like a sixty-five-year-old dude try to *boog-a-loo;* tight and old. Anyway…

A bit of a dance; but me, I like to get on down. But her, with no moves to my liking, well, I slid off of the dance floor. We slid over to the bar. I look deeply into her eyes,

"I am the one that you have been waiting for all of your life. I am talking serious matrimony here."

The same old line, same old time. They buy it. I sell it.

To make a very short story even shorter, she was all up for the Shaman love treatment. We hung, we danced a bit. I light her cigarettes, though I hate smoking. I told her she had beautiful long hair, though it was kinda stringy. And I made her all kinds of non-intoxicated promises in the disco night. Remember, I didn't want to re-enter the realm of the drink due to my just curing a three day hang over.

Now up pulls her friend. White jumpsuit: permed, curly, long black Thai hair. She had a dude in tow, so I didn't pay it, or the possibilities of the situation, much mind. She was far more of a babe, even in an ugly jumpsuit, than the one which I was spending my time a-romancing. But you know how it goes, *a bird in the hand...* Or is that a hand in the bush?

Pushing past eleven, I am asked for a dance with the secondary lady in tow. Lady of choice, if the choice had been given. Lady of chance, and by far my best reason to want anything of this night at all. I mean, my new found, first found friend, is talking of children, love forever, and she is fucking serious...

We dance, the friend and I. She had a few better moves than my first love, but nothing to brag about. Her name, I remember but I think I will not say it clear. A poetry book I wrote about Bangkok is partially dedicated to her. If you are all that interested, read it there.

Post the floor, her obviously Chinese Thai dude in a bit of jealous mode tries to lay the slobs on her. She defers payment and looks over at us, her friend and I, with the gag motion painted upon her face. Well, my chances are looking up.

The first love squeeze of possibilities and I dance for a while more. Off the floor the secondarily reason is gone, has left, oh well...

Maybe twenty later she, however, reappears, riding solo. Solo means *A-Go-Go*. She stood there behind me, drinking some *java* at the bar.

Well, let's waste no time here, in a timeless situation. The move is on and the preferred passion placed. Her friend, my lady, you know the one: stringy hair, looking like a bitch of a Thai whore and all, is *out-of-it; Game Over*. My cravings have shifted definite direction. Thus, she, curls and looks and a jumpsuit, invites me for a drive in her car, a drive around Bangkok. Now, being someone's friend and all, the elegant whore was all for us going for a drive. She was tired, so she stated, and had to go to work early *manyana*. We, her and I, made dinner plans for the evening next, she was out-a-there. We, the other her and I, were out-a-there, into the hot Bangkok night.

We made it to the parking lot. She had this way supped up VW: cut down low, flared back fenders, a tail fin, and a Porsche engine. Now I almost would have laughed, but knowing Thais as I do, they do love their supped-up rods.

So in on the left side, out for a ride. *Burn rock, Fred.*

"What do you do?"
"Nothing. What do you do?"
"I'm a travel agent."

Then came the basic rap of life and love and no, this was not my first time in Bangkok.

"How old are you?"
"Twenty-seven."
"How about you?"
"Oh, I am twenty-four."

Words are cheap, lies even cheaper. I am a
pretty good judge of age, and I would have placed
her thirty—certainly not twenty-four. But what is
age anyway?

A drive through the night, nowhere left to
go.

"You have seen it all?"
"Yeah, more than once."
"I will show you my house."

She drives up to one of the biggest mansions
I have ever seen in Bangkok.

"Oh, that's nice."

Then she goes into a long discourse on:
chauffeurs, butlers, maids, and the like. We do all
have our dreams. And lies, they are easily spoken.

Thirty minutes post, post.

"My car is having trouble; my clutch is not working
right."
"Let me feel."

My leg over, felt all right to me. But she
played it off. I actually believed her, but I played it
too. We drove back to my hotel.

"I need to get home, you know a place where I can call someone."
"Sure, my room."

Past the guard at the elevators; can't let too many lame women of love prowl the nighttime halls. Into my love abode. Love abounds in the love abode.

2:30 A.M. to 3:30 A.M. the basic say nothing get her into the sack *con-ver-sat-I-on.*

"Well, it is late. You can stay here if you want. Don't worry, if you can't trust me, you can't trust anyone."

How many times have I used that line?

Teeth brushed; she wore one of my shirts. Into the sack-jack.

The lights from the distant reminisces of the flagrant pale Bangkok night echoed into our vision field and danced oh so slightly upon our eyes; just barely enough light to see.

King size bed: her side, my side. I put the move in between.

"What are you doing?"
"Just sleeping next to you."

Arms entangles, I will dispense with all the other, get here to get there bullshit. Holding her tight, all right. A touch, a feel, a kiss, my tongue moves into blatant action.

"Was that an American kiss?"
"What?"

"What you just did to me, was that an American kiss?"

"Well, we call it a French kiss."

"Oh, it was so exciting."

Now naturally this puts a dude into the motion of love. I mean she, someone who has never been love-tongued before/had a tongue shoved down her throat. Come-on, there is serious room to educate, regenerate this little feline.

The moves back on, I realized there was no underwear in place. Oh, this was going to be so easy.

The fact is, if I can jump to the future facts/facts of the future here; she never wore them, not even with skirts. So, my initial incentive was just a fool's delusion of thinking she wanted, IT. But nothing now known could ever have robbed that moment.

So, off comes my shirt, the one she is wearing. In goes my dick: power pump, maximum thump.

And the days, they seem to mean nothing and the nights they seem to mean so much more. Deep in the realms where there is barely just enough light to see; see me, oh see. Feel me, yeah, feel me.

In and on, the session continues. As I kiss her, I feel the wet of her cheeks, wet from her dripping eyes. She pulls me out, pulls away, lays her face into her pillow and cries.

"What's the matter?"

"I have never made love with a *falong* (foreigner) before."

"But, I love you."

And all the lies that I have told, all the dreams that I have shattered. All the meaningless nothingness, which I have spoken, it makes me sad, too. And I always wonder why I meet the players, the players and the liars. Those with nothing left to lose. I always wonder why I break the hearts of the virtuous. Why my heart gets broken by the tough, by the ready, by the fools.

A promise, a lie, a touch, a feel; we began to make love again.

Now, it was not that she did not know what she was doing. For you see, she had been married, had a kid, a son, so I had been told. She got down; went topside, back and forth, round and round. Nature moves in circles, don't you know. She was about to do, it. Cum, by another diction: Thai, English, or the otherwise. Me, I was about to blow it…

*   *   *

Let me subtopic here a bit if I may; Dudes, you want a rock-hard dick all the time. You want to power fuck like you never could state side. Then join me over here in Southeast Asia, Southeast Asia and the dream. I don't know what it is: the heat, the humidity kicking the circulation, the position of and or on the planet, or simply the dawning of the Age of Aquarius, but I do mean, and I am no amateur, if you know what I mean and I think that you do, I fuck here/there like nowhere else.

                    *   *   *

So, I didn't really know her: her moves, her scene. One-eyed Jack in the fresh seafood store, I rolled her over to keep me hammering awhile longer. My mistake, I had to way far pump it, to re-get her to that previous cum point.

So, it was a session for the memory, not necessarily one for the textbooks. Somehow though, somewhere though, a woman who had never been French kissed, only plowed by a former husband. I don't know, I was laying down flat, sunny side up, somewhere out there on the serious side of love.

Another session or two; four or five in the A.M. until sleep.

Morning *java*, good morning. I love you in the afternoon. A session up the love canal or three. Breakfast in bed, giving me head. And the day and life, it does seem to tick on and on.

She had a job to go to. A travel agent with a car to repair. I walked her to it, kissed her,

"You're way late for work. See you later."
"See ya…"

The day ticked on in the progressive winter heat. I like Thailand in the winter. Well, winter such as Thai winter is. Time to kill and money to spill, I walked the streets with my too heavy camera bag in tow. I looked around me, time to leave? I just couldn't decide. Why did I have to find her? Why here and why now?

*   *   *

A knock at the door; yes, perhaps it is a vision, a Thai vision; one like the one before. The evening it is here; yes, it too has come. The time, my time. The love of the love, the love of the flesh, (only a sinner can know of its pain), the love of the night. Compounding the pounding, the pounding in my heart. Yeah, she was beautiful.

A drive in her fixed car,

"Would you like to drive?"
"I guess so."

Behind the wheel. The car did have some speed behind it.

Chinese restaurant, over by the park. She didn't know how to eat with chopsticks. No lie.

Waitress not paying us needed attention. There it was, a bowl full of Thai peanuts, table front, table center. Her hands, her fingers, yes, they reached around them. She grabbed one. A throw, a miss. Grabbed another one. A throw, strike two. Grabbed a third time. A throw, it was a hit. Attention; well, we got it.

Back then, I was different. Different than I am now. Maybe, I would call it stuffy. You see first I wasn't, then I was. Now, I'm not really. But the throwing of the peanuts, well, it did put a blush on my face.

Everybody makes their statement. I once had a professor; undergraduate, a field trip up the Eastern side to the North of the state, Cali. He said it first, he said it well. Yeah, he was right. *'We all want to make our statements.'* Well, most of us…

Dinner done, hotel room again, love session on the wild side. Damn, though she didn't have any tits and though I may like them small, but something as opposed to nothing, she was a serious catch. She had that something. The something that was not nothing. Nothing equaling, not a thing at all. We fucked, big time.

The phone rang. The memory, a date. Time set, tried and true. Her friend. The first catch on the disco floor.

"Where are you? You are late! I have been waiting fifteen minutes!"
"Oh, sorry."

Oh shit, I forgot. I didn't want to go. Why go with that long straight-haired Thai chick of a lousy disco dancer, looking like she was straight off the far side of the Bangkok street, like a bitch of an expensive whore, or stay here, with impending, impeding lustful love.

Well, the debate went on, with my new love and I.

"If you have something going, if you and her are together, I will walk away."
"What about last night? What about just now?"
"You must go to dinner."

I didn't want to go to dinner. I already had dinner. Dinner and dessert.

"Why don't you tell her about us," I asked.
"I can't, she's my friend."

With friends like that, you don't need enemies...

You know it is just like my bud Saturday Jim and I. It's like the old code of honor stuff. We don't fuck, never would, each other's old babes. We don't move in on each other's action. Don't fuck family, etc. and so on. I mean, it keeps it clean, we have been bros forever. Keeping it clean, lead to bros forever.

You know, he has got this cousin, we will just call him Johnny Boy. But the bad soul boy Saturday Jim once, way back when, had this Saturday night fling, with a *love her one time, love her two times* sort of babe named, (named, I will leave that out. You know, for the mentally ill or the weak of heart, or the soon to be bound by the chains of wedlock). Anyway, I remember it well; he would sit around discussing what a bushy beaver this chick had with all of the boys. "Hey, isn't that the way you like them there, Sandy Dog?"

We were all bros back then: Saturday Jim, Venchenzo, Johnny Boy, and me. The drink would flow and the talk would go, you know all that stupid macho dude sort of shit, of how you fucked a chick this way, how you power pile drive her that way.

About a year back, it came to pass, Jenny, (oh shit, I said her name), available, Johnny Boy hot-to-trot. Well, a long story made short; now her and Johnny Boy are on the serious side of love...

Now, I know all you self-actualized, modern sort of, head-up-your-ass, because you are so fucking liberal sort of *in-di-vid-u-al mutha' fuckers* are going, "Hey, *no problema.* That was then, this is now." But we people, my people, my bros, now we are from the streets, not self-actualized. And remember, *Self-Actualization is not Self-*

286

Realization. We live where a push is shoved. And that shit just does not go down.

So S.J. and Johnny Boy, now there is a tension. A tension of remembrance. All over what? Stupid love! Stupid sex. Who had been there first.

Love is for suckers. A dick in a cunt. Dudes *rap'n* vile intoxicated shit and all that stuff. And Johnny Boy, no matter how hard he may try, will always have in the back of his mind the thought that Saturday Jim had tasted the fruit, plucked the flower, long before he ever got there. If he marries her; the words of a drunkard will forever ring in his ears.

I mean, I once had this bitch who used to talk to her old dick-list, love stallions on the telephone lines, because she didn't want to hurt their feelings and tell them to fuck off. I got that stopped *pronto* when I found out. But I never forgave her, eventually dumped her ass when I was done using it. And believe me, payback is a *mutha' fucker.*

Keep things clean, keep things simple. Life is easier that way.

*   *   *

So forced out, I had to go to dinner.

"Where have you been? I have been waiting half an hour!"

'Who the fuck cares,' I wanted to say. I got a babe happening up in the love crib. Your best friend, baby. But instead, the love doctor came on.

"Sorry, just had to shave and make myself attractive for such a beautiful woman as you."

She drove, air conditioning Japanese made comfort in gear. Love central had the hopped-up V-dub and no *air-con.*

Arrival location. Dinner in the dining room. A touch of class. Yeah, she certainly was different than her counterpart. No tossed peanuts, manners and all. Complete with, so she thought, style.

"You know, I live life by feelings. I could feel it the minute that you and I met. We were meant for each other, love forever. I am the one that you have been waiting for all your life, baby."

Thick, bad dude, thick. My rap it was in forward motion.

She discussed all of her desires, all of her needs. Talked of, as she put it, *'Her baby.'* This one claimed, thirty years old and was a-planning to have, *'Her baby,'* with me. Her baby?

She wanted to know why I had long hair. Same old fucking stupid question. Why did she? Told me, she would *State-side* it with me, just because of our love. Inside, I laughed.

Though no love was in motion on my side of the picture, bullshit certainly was in the air.

My mind, it was on the other side, over there, on the other side of town. No class, I know, but so un-kissed. Somehow she had really touched me, though I thought maybe she was just dealing me in, and playing a game.

My words were clean at this *lo-cat-i-on* though. Clean and thought out. Cover my ass in all directions.

288

"No, nothing happened, just a drive. I don't like her. I was in love with you from the moment I first laid eyes upon you."

Lies to lies, why do I try? Nothing man, they mean just nothing.

Post the eat. Check please. A hundred dollars plus tip, in the form of Thai *bhat.* Out-a-there, early dinner, middle-dinner, we had some time to kill before the disco dinner. I, well you know, invited her up to my room. I mean like, what else could a guy like me do, I you catch my meaning?

From there, it is cast to the realms of sexual pagan history, where any dick reached its form and is placed in the love trap. I let the wild power pup sink into her quicksand. She fucked like she walked, like she ate, like she spoke, like she danced, like she acted; *fucking stiff.*

I mean, I could not even get that feeling of false love: that little tingle in the heart, pretending infatuation to myself.

I had more with that whore, that whore of the day before. But, I suppose, I have had those tingles of infatuation with more than a few whores.

Love, it is easy: easy to feel, easy to do. Just get a form, a warm form, a female one for me. Dress it right, let it be tight. A kiss of illusion equals a thousand years of false meditation.

Done and out, nothing even worth writing about. Down to the disco, let me rock. Oh yes, I do love to rock.

I had to dance the first few dances with her, though my *pre-fer-ence* would have had it another way. Then sitting down, talking all that love bullshit: a promise here, a lie there. Sometimes, I am serious bullshit, far-too-far of the player.

We are sitting in the dimly lighted distance, at a couch of a table setting, little Miss, oh I mean Ms. Stiff and I. I chilled backed a Perrier, she had some alcoholic concoction.

Out of the darkness, into the lightness of the dancing feet comes my Thai dream demon, real-true-love. Movement, motion coming our direction, I ordered her up a whiskey and coke, her drink of choice.

I sat there, dark and in between them: disco music pounding, colored lights flashing. I would lean over, "I love you, only you. I need you." Then I would do it, say it the other way, on the other side; the flip side. I mean, I played it well. Well, as well as it could be played.

It kind of reminded me of this once-upon-a-time, a-long-time-ago, in the never-never-gutter-land of Hollywood: you see, Saturday Jim, Venchenzo, and I, come Saturday night, we would party down. And I do mean inebriated party down.

There we were, there we would end up, his Hollywood aunt's apartment, if you please. Our crash pad, Saturday nights. Way too fucked up to move onto any other realm of possible passion, post the sessions with the drink and the streets.

Saturday Jim boned Jenny there the first time. Right there on Johnny Boy's mother's bed.

Oh, did I mention, they are related? Saturday Jim and Johnny Bob are cousins. See, the plot gets even thicker.

Johnny Boy, he lived there full-time, we were just there on the sly. But anyway, on this one over-night session, soul boy Saturday Jim's sister was there. Johnny Boy's sister hanging tough, sliding in on the side wat there too. I sat there *rap'n*—both of them engulfed in all of my verbal excellence and style. I promised them love, lust, twelve inches, and forever. Everything that I do not have to give.

But it was us; we from the gutters, a small Hollywood apartment, dressed in 60s long shag carpeting and off-white walls. The air was smoky, the smell was of booze. I slide onto the floor. I would think of a line, then whisper it to one. Then drunkenly thinking the other one didn't hear it, lean over and whispered it to them. Things that only the drunken fools can do.

Nothing to lose and time to kill. I was far younger back then.

But it was just *rap'n* practice, the code of honor held tight.

But, back to the story-line…

*   *   *

Well, the move in the motion, it had started. I think Stiff, had figured out what had gone on, gone down, if you will, the evening last. Though my friend of the actual love, continued to deny it. But, Cat-Fight it was on the horizon.

"I am going to kick you!"

Yelled, my love babe in Thai. Not to me but to her; Stiff, you know the one.

Now I don't know why I do this kind of thing to myself: ego gratification, the ability to play with people's lives, based in the male macho and all; whatever… But I love to play, play it. I play 'em so well. What a fucking fool, yes?

Finally, it was about to get nasty. I do mean really nasty. Up, I stand,

"I don't need this!"

I was out-a-there.

Leave it to them to fight it out, for I had a plane to catch tomorrow: places to be, people to see, and there is always another illusion waiting on the horizon. But damn, did I blow my chance with such an un-French kissed Thai passionflower?

To my room, I hung the *'Do Not Disturb'* sign on the door and packed. Done too early to crib down. Not drunk, so no spin. Out the door, hoped that they were not waiting. They were not. Hit the streets. Did I really want to leave Thailand? Damn, I love Bangkok.

I walked down to the Patpong; past the whores, past the guys trying to sell me the whores. It was hot—hot night. Too hot. I was upset, mega upset. Too in love, too fast, too infatuated. I needed more.

Too many lies; I tell them all the time. Women, are they people or just simply my toys?

The heat pounded on my head, the feeling pounded in my heart. I was sweating. I was walking—walking back; back to the hotel. Nothing more I wanted from this evening, this session of *Too Much Thailand!* No, not tonight. No, nothing more.

I walked. Up there a bit, a car pulled to the side. I watched. I saw it. I thought of the *stiv* in my pocket and the potential for my having to use it.

It was a bitch from the backdoor. Her driver, a dude. Driver-side, the outside; they were out. An

Anglo and a Drag Queen. *'Hey fucker, go back to San Francisco,'* I thought.

"Do you have the time," I was asked.

Though I didn't really want to, I looked at my watch. As I did, the homo-sex-u-al, took a soft hold of my wrist.

"Get your fucking hands off me!"
"Whhhaaaaaat."

Bam! I gave the *mutha' fucker* the famous Saturday Jim, put the nose on the other side of the face, Saturday night punch.

I guess that I should tell you the story, if I may again paraphrase, subtopic, indent, content, of how this punch came to be titled as such.

You see, Saturday Jim, Venchenzo, and I, well, we go way back: ten, fifteen, twenty years, I don't know, I lost count. Somehow, we were always out there on the extremities.

At Hollywood High, we had our own private wall with our *'DM,'* (Dead Meat Babes), listed upon it. You know, the one's we hit and quit.

Long hair, yeah, we had it. Drugs yeah, we took them. Drink yeah, we did wet our lips more than a bit. But I don't know, I think our best days must have been the punk days. We did have a look, did have a dance.

Anyway, Saturday Jim, Venchenzo, and I were doing a session at the Starwood. Tight black pants, black sport coats from the thrift store, black tee shirts, and black necks tie around our neck.

Now, there at the Starwood, they had the, how should I put it—the cultural side if you will. I mean, you know, where the art was being played lived, experienced; the new... On the other side of the place was a discotheque, where all the long hairs, the geeks, the Mexicans, and the assholes, in general, went to Saturday night party down. Anyway, 2:00 A.M. rolls around, out the door we all go.

Venchenzo and I had been slam dancing, so we were covered with sweat. Pneumonia in the making. Saturday Jim, just recovering from introducing face-to-pavement on, or should I say off, his bad motorcycle; he had spent the evening making love to the barstool.

It had been my turn two months the previous: head encountering concrete, breaking it in a dozen places. So neither one of us was full-on. He was fucked up though, way fucked up. And further fucked up were his legs, arms, and head: banged, bruised, broken, and bandaged, if you know what I mean and I think that you do.

Out into the night, walking to the car; cold winter, just past the point of the first of the year. Up comes a longhaired group.

Back then, we all had distaste for one another; long hair, short hair; it set up apart. They were them, we were we.

The longhaired group: a chick accompanied by two dudes, another lady on the side.

"Can I have a cigarette," asks this one chick of Saturday Jim who was more than happy to oblige.

The one dude, not her dude, post her lighting it up; grabs it from between her lips, throws it upon the ground. Intoxicated Saturday Jim yells out, "You bitch!"

Now, if there had been time for explanations, I would have explained that he had been referring to the dude, hand in her mouth, not the babe, cigarette in question. But that asshole of a dude, who had pulled the cigarette from the lips of the girl, well he, like a pussy, just walked on. She, the wanting to smoke chick, just walked on, as well. But then/there, back comes this longhaired Rod Stewart looking *mutha' fucker*. At least he had the balls to stand up. His mistake...

It all happened so fast; as he moved forward to fight. He was thinking the, "You bitch," commented was pointed at his girlfriend. It was not. But, as he rapidly approached, a Saturday Jim cigarette was flipped in his face.

Then/there, I see out of the corner of my eye, a black and white—a police car coming. Police car vision, out of the side of my eyes.

"No," I try to say. But the word did not have a chance to leave my lips. Bap! The forward waking dude, he got introduced to Saturday Jim's fist. He went down, went down hard.

The cops, they grabbed S.J., threw him upon the hood of their car. There he was, all smashed up from a motorcycle accident. Fucked up to the max from the drink, and tossed upon the hood of this cop's car.

Now this sat none too well with Venchenzo,

"Let's kick their ass," he said to me.

"You don't kick cop's asses," I continued to tell him, as I tried to keep pulling him away.

"Get him away from here," a cop, with his hand on his gun, yelled at me; seeing I was holding him back.

"That's my brother!" Venchenzo yelled back.

Secondary paraphrase here: Now in the clubs back then, it generally did get a bit rowdy and fists, they often did begin to fly. Us and our bros, we did hang tight: *one for all and all for one and all that shit*. Especially since Saturday Jim always did like to pick out the biggest bar brawler in the place and start a fight with him and/or his friends. Other stories though...

"Let's kick their ass, Sandy."
"Hey man, they've got fucking guns."

It is taking all my strength to hold Venchenzo back.

So, to finish it up; the Rod Stewart looking *mutha' fucker* turned out to be a true man. Post his shaking off his being knocked out and his nose being strategically placed upon the other side of his face, he wouldn't press charges.

"It's my fault, man. It's all my fault..."

Saturday Jim, thus released. He always wanted to buy that guy a drink, but the guy never showed his face again. And for the pussy of the other guy who started the whole thing and couldn't back up his friend and just walked away, "Fuck him." He is the one who deserved the facial rearrangement.

*   *   *

Back to the story at hand...
The bitch of a Drag Queen was lying down on the ground. The punk of a pimp began to move

towards me. I just stuck my finger out, pointed at the *mutha' fucker*. He got back in his car, drove away. I walked away.

Back in my room, I lay in bed. Torn between my love for Thailand and heading back in the direction of the stateside way. Torn between my overwhelming infatuation for this sweet little, never been French kissed before, Thai sweetheart.

I tried to sleep. Sleep did not want to come.

Then/there, a knock upon my door. Do I answer it or do I let it ride? Would it be two bitches wanting to kick my ass? Or???

I answered it. *'Do Not Disturb'* sign in her hand,

"Does this mean me?"

There she was, my love of the former night. My choice, in a world with far too many choices. She had come back; come back even though. Come back complete with a glazed look in her eyes.

In the dark, into bed, I kissed her. Her breath tasted of whiskey; whiskey, and *ganga*. She had obviously gone and got high. Make love, only love. Stay or leave, what can a bohemian fool do?

To sleep, finally to sleep. It now came all so easily. Dream and desire, where does one end, the other begin? Damned if I knew.

I woke from my sleep; deep, lost into the late hours of the night. Deep and lost, deep inside her. I awoke and we were making love.

It is funny, as I reflect. Maybe it is Asia. Maybe Bangkok. Maybe I was a younger man back then. But there have been a few times, younger times, other times, deep in sleep, awake making love to the form lying next to me.

In this case, she was there, she was high, she was drunk, she slept through most of it. I guess I could take that as an insult, now as I think about it. But then, I have been way too fucked up too.

Morning call on the telephone, my taxi is ready to take me to the airport. Thanks, but no thanks, I have a ride.

"They will keep the money, which you have already paid."
"Who cares?"

It was a heavy session, a heavy feeling; leaving or not to leave. Down to her car, she pulled in the bad little V-dub—up in front, up center. She drove me, with a few tears in her eyes, to the airport.

Inside, it was all in motion, for I had planned to go; I was to leave. Back then, I hated to change plans, not just for flights, but I would get a thought in my head and believe it to be gospel. Now, a whole whooping two or three, more like two years later, I try not to hold onto the belief system so tight. I try not to believe my own lies.

She kissed me goodbye. I invited her to L.A. I walked away into the international sky: Taipei, Tokyo, Kyoto. Feeling happy for the freedom. Feeling lost for the lack of love and for whatever else it was all worth, which basically is nothing.

I remember her. I remember the love. I remember her excitement at her fist tongue kiss. I remember the tears she cried on our first night of making love. I remember the infatuation that I felt.

I guess I should not have left: should not have left the love, the lady, the memories, and all that. But, leave I did.

Yeah, I did catch a splinter or two on that one.

And all that this experience has added up to is just another story told in the already staggering volumes of unread literature.

CHAPTER 15
INITIATION

Well, there is no doubt that I was in a regressive period, stuck into a regressive weekend as I headed up North to San Jose for a religious ceremony, where I was to be initiated into the final level of the Rosicrucian Order. I mean hey, let's remember my focus in life...

I pulled myself out of bed at the crack of noon, on this Friday morning, and got it all together. Threw myself and my cameras in the car, put the top down and on the road I went. I cruised North up Highway 101 listening to some tunes, smoking a pipe, and generally just watching the sights and feeling the moments of the ride.

Up past Santa Barbara a bit, it started to chill down on the serious side. I had some trouble with the downed top. So, I had to get out and deal with the foolish realities of life along the side of the road.

In a mechanical world, there are mechanical problems.

FYI: Jeep tops are not easy to put on.

Having that fixed; my bones more or less warmed by the heater, the drive continued up the coast into the sunny, yet cool, autumn afternoon.

Highway 1, up through Big Sur, was closed due to rockslides. It had been closed often over the last few years for similar reasons. Mother Nature taking her revenge on the impositions of man into her realm.

With Highway 1 closed, I was stuck going up 101. Now 101 isn't bad, it does have its own type of beauty. Yet, there is something spectacular about Big Sur. It always has been that way and it always will; whether man has the opportunity of viewing it or not.

As this was Friday, and the ceremony didn't begin until Saturday, I decided to hit my favorite hotel over Santa Cruz way and crib down for the night. This would of course give me the opportunity to cruise into my second favorite bookstore and take out my usual two or three bags and/or boxes of books.

Over-all the night remained uneventful. I got some books, drove the Santa Cruz coast, went out to listen and commune with the Diving Mother Ocean of the North, and walked around a bit and looked at all the Santa Cruz hippies. Which way to the sixties? And, all of the Santa Cruz punks. Which way to the seventies? But, anyway…

The morning was an early one for me. My cool, been all over the world with me, credit card size calculator/alarm woke me. I got up: drained the lizard, showered, went and had some *cappuccino,* and headed over the hill on the forty-five-minute drive to San Jose.

Now San Jose is an interesting town. A nice enough place to visit, I guess, but I wouldn't want to live there. But, somehow, it was almost fitting that this conference and ceremony was to take place in this city. For everywhere you drive, you see all these churches, of all these faiths. Not that churches have much to do with faith and spirituality, but the city is full of them.

San Jose is a city that has more or less recently sprung to notoriety and success with the influx of the computer into the modern mainstream of society and the placement of what is now known as Silicon Valley. The place where all these computers are formulated/are made. For with this has come the computer nerd yuppies and the computer nerd yuppie *want-a-bes* from all over the country. All the computer and business school graduates dreaming of fruitful employment and an easy, early retirement.

Me, the illusion always held so much more than the nine-to-five.

But this trend has definitely poured new life into a culture that was vastly dominated by Mid-West transplants bringing all their beliefs and religious superstitions with them. Combine this with a vast influx of post-war Vietnam refugees and definitely the city has grown a flavor all its own.

I arrived a little early, so I drove around a bit viewing the sights. Stopped in and had myself a few pancakes at a *java* shop. Slice me up another cup of that bad *java*. And generally realized that I should probably be some-where else, doing some-thing else. Yet, the dream it does tick on.

As it neared time for the ceremony, I drove on over and allowed nature, fate, and illusion to take its course.

Now, since my youth, that being my late teens and early twenties, I have had little use for spiritual groups. Having had more than a few bad experiences with them; it has left me stale. Yet, my knowledge of, shall we call it, another truth, another reality as continued to grow. This, without the aid or assistance of those so-called keepers of the truth.

This group, however, though stuck deeply in its own illusion of symbolism, ceremony, and structure had caught my eye and interest on my first journey down to Singapore. As little actual in-person group activity was required, it did fit into my hectic schedule of spending someone else's hard earned day(s) quite well.

After the proper passwords and symbols were invoked, the ceremony it did begin. And as all ceremonies go, it bored the fuck out of me.

As much as I tried to make it a deep and meaningful experience, it simply was too sugar coated. And, as sugar eventually makes one fat and diabetic, it held little interest. I mean come-on, realization can only exist when the eyes are open. My truth lives in the streets.

The ceremony continued and the twenty or so people who were present were asked to get up and walk into this other room where the look: the look of life/the look of impending death came to us. How fucking melodramatic. A bunch of *want-a-be* actors. They should move to Hollywood.

But there, in the walking group, she was. I hadn't even noticed her. Must be getting old.

She, however, had obviously noticed me. For her eyes were full-on glued my direction, painted with lust to the maximum, gazing upon my form.

The first thing I noticed about her were these turquoise blue flooding pants. Though they were semi out of vogue, yet they were still worn by some. They fit her, they fit her right. Looking up; her hair it was blond, long. Her eyes, blue and available.

My glance met hers; illusion in the making, love for the taking. The line walked on.

The bullshit continued for the next hour or so. Me, I was antsy, ready to get out-a-there and go get my dinner on.

Dinner, at a Vietnamese restaurant. Food for the gods, food for the fools like myself who dreamed something more may come of a casual, possible chance meeting in the language of love, spoken in Vietnamese. Or, should I more properly say, *Tieng Viet.* (Sorry, I don't have a Vietnamese typewriter, so I can't turn the e's upside down or place the proper accent marks).

The ceremony came to a conclusion for the evening. Everyone was out in the main hall, *a-rap'n.* Now me, I'm a reclusive introvert for the most part. I don't really dig people, with the exception of babes, of course. And it would have suited me just fine to hit that old front door. But, as I entered the main hall, standing between myself and said door, was this lady of blond. Her stare pulled me to her like a magnet guides itself to a steel wall. But when the encounter comes, it hits, it hits hard like a brick between the eyes.

She said, "Hello, how did you enjoy the evening?"
"So-so," I answered.
"What's your name," she asked.
"Shaman, Sandy Shaman. What's yours?"
"Bonne Mae."

'Bonne Mae,' I laughed to myself, obviously a hick.

She immediately said, "I have to ask you a question right up front."
"Well, I have nothing to hide. I will tell you anything." My rap already kicking in…
"Are you single?"
"Of course. Are you?"
"Yes, I just have to know that first."

My mind immediately begins to see the writing up-on the wall. I got it. She wants it. It was almost too easy. Easy; where there is sadly no illusion, no conquest.

304

In most cases, I would have already lost interest. Well, for the most part I already did. White is, in my case, just not right. Not my flavor. I am just not into white and fluffy. No, not for me. Wonder white bread just isn't exactly my cup-of-tea.

Give me that Whole Wheat, that French, that Rye. But, I was in a different town, San Jose. A watering hole for the computer set and me, I was just a mystic on the loose. So, I stayed. I spoke with her. I let her live her fantasy.

We stood around and talked for a while. She was from Montana and had come down for the ceremony, leaving her three children with a friend; her mother, or someone. Who the fuck knows? Her age was thirty-three. She looked more like forty plus, but I didn't want to say that to her. She had been divorced for about five years and was obviously on the serious prowl for a new love stallion. In my mind, as she talked, I said to myself, *'Well fuck that, a party is a party, is a party, and you look like a party girl.'* But don't you know that you never take a party girl home to mom.

Five minutes turned into twenty as we exchange stories. I was *really* getting ready to bail, for I wanted to hit meat that was more to my taste, more my scene, namely some *Ori-en-tal*. In San Jose, specifically Vietnamese. But her magnetic pull was tight. Not so different from other women, *seeking women,* that I had met, known, and then left them standing out there alone somewhere until the next possible husband material pulled up and pulled in, if you catch meaning and I think that you do.

Finally, she invited me to dinner and though it was not to my actual plans, I accepted. What she did not tell me is that she was engaged to have dinner as well with one of the High Priestesses of the Order; with whom she was staying in San Jose. As I made the comment to exit stage left, she informed me as such. Uck, this is just not my scene!

So, about this time, the Priestess comes out, in all her two hundred and fifty pounds of glory. In tow, she has another little playmate friend about five feet nothing and more than a few pounds over herself. The three of them basically decide where *'we'* wanted to chow-down; a uck steak house. And me being the can't say no, non-dynamic gullible fool that I am at the times said, "Sure, whatever..."

With this, my first lesson of the evening was learned. Don't give in!

They had all decided it would be nice if we drove together. *Yeah, really nice. Fuck me.* So, we all piled into the Priestess's little two door Japanese econo-box of a yawn mobile. Bonne Mae and I in the backseat. The two *plump-kins* in the front.

Immediately, as our drive began, Bonne Mae was all over me. She had slid to my side, had one hand in my crotch, the other holding my hand. I mean this babe was seriously desperate, if you know what I mean.

Now, I like lust as much as the next guy, if not more than many, but comes on... I have to admit at feeling a bit of the *un-com-for-table-ness* in the presence of two Mid-West transplants that knew that we had just met.

The ride cruised along. The Priestess, obviously full of her own self-worth, and her status; not different from most people of a holy position or otherwise, and she was yapping her head off about metaphysics and the group. The other lady, mostly reserved, due to her newness to the cult, just sat in the front seat and politely listened.

306

There I was feeling fucked, saying to myself, *'Well, fuck me.'* I was out of my environment*, riding bitch* in the backseat of a car; something I never do. Getting lusted on by a Mid Westerner or North Westerner, whatever… And wishing I had just not let the magneto's pull suck me in and had headed on out of that big beautiful front door and onto a Vietnamese restaurant full of desires, where with every dance, there is another chance.

The drive, surrounded by Mid Westerners. Me, a Californian; L.A. native born, it was lost in their elixir of self-righteous talk of self-righteous nonsense. I had left this world long ago and yet, there I was forced to endure it again. Hell on Japanese wheels, powered by Arab fuel, surrounded by Mid-Western accents and morals, with a lustful hand in my crotch. Where is the way OUT?

We pulled up in front of the steak house they had decided upon. The driver had to look and search for the closest parking space. Man does that annoy me. People who can't fucking walk a few extra feet. She must have picked up on my vibes for she said she used to like to walk until she got fat.

'Well, then get skinny and healthy bitch,' I thought.

We made our way in. I was embarrassed by my company.

They ordered their desires. Me, I had a salad bar. Steak had done the Priestess no good. I wasn't going to follow her lead. Bonne Mae looks over at me and asked if I wanted some wine.

"Well, now that you mention it…"

So, I ordered up the best bottle of wine they had. It cost a whole five dollars. So, you can imagine what a great level of the grape it was.

We sat down and I, well I had a drink.

They all sat around and talked about the group religion. Me, I had another glass of the grape.

I mean, how could I talk to these types of people? Their reality was so different from mine. They had bought into all the lies and all the bullshit that religion has to offer. How could I explain to them that I had become a monk at sixteen and saw through all of that egotism? That I had spent all this time in Asia and realized that the ultimate illusion is that there is no illusion at all. How could words say that to ears that would not hear and minds that were already made up? How could anyone open their eyes? So, I chose to remain fixed upon my wine. For the only sage is the silent sage.

I listen to mostly the two of them, Bonne Mae and the fat Priestess talk. The other lady, whose name was Missouri, or Iowa, or something like that was much more into her food than the rap.

Bonne Mae kept her ever-present hand on my leg. Her possible leash on the bounds of eternity and the factors of maternity. Sorry babe, I'm not buying. A foolish plan, at least in regard to me.

The Priestess commented how she could always know a person by the flavor they were. She said, she sees people in flavors. And that every time she met a person, she tasted them, thus knowing everything about them.

I asked her, "How much of your tastes are influenced by your own mind?"

She had no answer. But asked, wasn't I going to eat my salad. By this time the *vino* had taken hold, and I had no interest in food. I just laughed.

As I had just about killed the first, I suggested another bottle to Bonne Mae, as she was the only other one drinking, her whole one glass; the other two being much too holy, but she declined. She was basically just in the mode of kissing whose ever ass was the most high and, in this case, at least so she thought, it was the *fat ass*.

So, I killed the bottle. Sat there dreaming of Vietnamese love, Vietnamese illusion, and being anywhere but where I was.

Finally, it was time to go, thank God! So, the car filled up and back to the temple we drove.

Now there was this little game going on, for the Priestess realizing Bonne Mae's attraction to me asked questions like, where was I staying, etc. Then reminding Bonne Mae that tomorrow the ceremony began at 6:00 A.M. sharp! And she, the Priestess, had to be there at 4:00 A.M. to prepare. And since she was staying with her, she would have to get up early and maybe it would be nicer if she could stay with me in my hotel and all that…

Well, the only way out was the way in. And a bird in the hand was worth two whores in a bush so… I said, "Sure, no problem, you can stay with me."

By the time we return, I had begun to sober a bit and the desire, or the lack of it, were showing themselves to me. So, as Bonne Mae and I stood in the parking lot talking, the other two had driven on, I laid it out.

"Look," I said, "I have nothing to offer you. I am a dreamer and I am into Asian ladies, and you are probably a much better fuck than I am anyway, and you would probably do me in."

"Oh," she said, "I can't believe that you are not good in bed, just look at your body. And please give me a chance to change your mind about white women."

So, what could I do? I had tried, but no results. My *karma* was clean. I had warned her. So, I put the proverbial pedal to the metal.

I began by laying slobs on her right there in the parking lot of the temple. How holy is that? The illumination of the streetlamps lighted the vision.

Then, I went straight for the breast and eventually my hand was down her pants. She was soup city: HOT and bothered. I suggested we go for it, right there in the parking lot, in her car, which we were leaning up against. I mean, how fucking cosmic, in a religious parking lot, and all. But she was too uptight and suggested we go for a drive.

As there was no way out for me that night; I, *how-you-say,* went along for the ride.

We got in her car, a Volvo, with Montana license plates. I was almost humiliated as we cruised San Jose. She opened the sunroof, let the night air in and tried to discuss the novelties of this particular religious group's philosophies.

I told her, "Look, from what I see, these people are full of shit. I feel no spiritual energy from any of them. Just a bunch of housewives and businessmen who have never stepped outside their own head long enough to witness any of the things that are really going on in this and other realities. They just want to belong to something, like a social club. They want to feel that they are holy. It's the same problem with all religions. They're so caught up in their ceremonies and titles that they never see the illusion of no illusion. They're just trapped in their own righteousness and holiness. The ancient foundations of this group obviously has their potentials but the people who reflect these foundations are full of shit."

"Oh," she said, "I see what you mean."

Obviously, she was a *'Yes'* person. Said *'Yes,'* to anything just to be accepted. Especially when she saw a potential husband in sight. So that was the end of the spiritual conversation for me. Now my mind and destiny were clear, time to get fucked up.

About this time, we passed a liquor store, and I suggested we go in and get some more liquid to wet our lips with. If you know what I be talking about.

She insisted on going in and paying, for I had paid for dinner. ...Yes, for all of them. But, she wanted me to come along for it was a very bad area of San Jose and there were all these rowdy looking Mexican guys out front. *No problema.*

We went in and she grabbed one bottle of the grape. I said,

"That's it? Come on, we need more than that."

So, she grabbed another bottle and was ready to pay.

Behind the counter they had the hard stuff and my eyes, well, they opened up. I suggested we pick some up, but she said, "Do you have to be drunk to be with me?"

'Fuck'n-A,' I wanted to say. But, I chilled back. I mean, my mind said 'Yes,' but my mouth said, 'No.'

So, she paid for the two bottles. Two bottles of wine, I thought to myself, 'It's like fucking soda pop.'

We went and got back into the car to the looks and comments of the Mexicans around us and she drove off. As we crossed the intersection, there was another liquor store on the other side of the street and I said,

"Stop the car here, I forgot something."
"What, cigarettes?"
"No way, I'm a healthy guy. I don't smoke. Just wait."

I jumped out, went in and grabbed a bottle of the bad vodka. Paid for it and back into the car I went.

"Drive on," I said, "Now we're ready to party."
Bonnie Mae looked at me and said, "Am I so ugly, do you have to drink to be with me?"
"Say what?"
"The two subjects are not the same, you know. This is *soma,* the elixir of the gods. And no, in fact you are really quite pretty."

Though she was only on the so-so, on a good day, or the bottom of a shot glass, side of pretty.

"Because if you don't want to be with me…"
"Well, in fact, I had planned on a Vietnamese dinner and then you never know."

312

"Oh, you like Vietnamese food? My father was in the army, and I lived there for several years."

Now we had something to talk about. Something of interest; She had lived in Vietnam. The evening wouldn't be a total waste.

The evening went on, we talked, she drove. First, the wine was consumed. I, in my drunken stupor, would toss the empty bottles out of the sunroof. Then, I cracked the real stuff; the vodka, my main drink.

Since I had drank three bottles of Jack Daniels solo awhile back and no longer could even deal with the smell of it, the vodka was my new love potion.

We eventually got to the hotel. It was 12:30 A.M. or so and I was fucked up; way fucked up. The manager of the motel, I could see was still up, and I was a bit concerned that I had only rented the room for one and he may be pissed. But, in my condition, how concerned could I be?

We got into the room, and I immediately put all gears forward, all plays in motion. And went for it.

She said, "Sandy, I really love you. I have never met anyone like you before."
"Yeah right," I said, "All the babes tell me that."

By this time, I was laying serious slobs on her and most of her clothes were off.

She said, "You're not just doing this because you're drunk are you?"
"No," I said.

But the truth should it be known, was... Well, you know.

She then asked, "Have I convinced you that white girls are okay and Orientals are not better?"
"I don't know, I haven't fucked you yet."
"Oh Sandy, I love you. Do you love me?"
"Love is so temporary, baby."
"Oh, but we can make it last."

'Yeah right,' I thought. *'You with your three kids and desirous of more.'*

I pulled down my pants and realized that I had a pair of boxer shorts on. I wore them more or less for a joke this journey, instead of my normal bikini underwear. I was almost embarrassed for a second and then,

"Oh Sandy, you're wearing boxer shorts, they're so in style."

I wondered how a forty-year-old; oh yeah, she had claimed to be thirty something: divorcee, who lived in Montana with three kids, could know anything about style.
Just before I was about to plant the power pup, I asked her, just to check it out,

"You don't have VD, active herpes, AIDS, or anything, do you?"
She said, "I haven't had any new lovers in years."

'Yeah sure,' I thought.

She asked, "You don't have AIDS do you?"

314

"No, but my boyfriend does."

"Oh, are you Bi?"

"No, I'm a fag. I just fuck chicks sometimes."

See took me seriously. She didn't get the joke…

Finally, I just said, "Shut up and let's fuck."

So, I put the major power pile driver to her and I mean major. The pup was in his rare intoxicated form. And I did get down. I put it to her so hard that the bad headboard on the bed broke off of the wall.

We were going at it full-stroke-on for quite a while. Then it came to my mind, this scene in a Bukowski book, made movie script, that my main L.A. babe and I had seen the week before. So, slap, I laid a good one on her face. She dug it. I slapped her up some more, she liked it more. So, we kept at it: the fucking, with an occasional slap here and or there for good measure.

She said, "That's why my husband used to do to me. I love it."

'You're a fucking nut baby,' I drunkenly thought.

As I lay there fucking in one position or another, I began to realize, white bread, wonder white bread, uck. Now I mean, they all look alike, think alike, and their pussies smell alike; stinky. This one even had stretch marked tits. It was at that point that I realized never again would I go for this halfway white bread love. It simply is not worth it—has nothing to offer me.

I eventually, too drunk to cum, rolled her over to go for her backdoor, but she declined and so I just said, "Fuck it." (Fuck, being the favorite word of an intoxicated drunkard).

At about 3:00 A.M. or so, I rolled over and ducked into drunken sleep, knowing there was no way in the fucking world that I was going to wake up at 5:00 A.M. to be at the place for the continuation of the spiritual convention by 6:00 A.M. and receive the final part of my initiation into the deepest realms of the spiritual order.

*   *   *

How she did it, I do not know. But she was pulling my ass out of bed at 5:15 A.M.

I said, "What the fuck are you doing? I usually don't even go to bed until this time."
"Come on, come on, we have to go."

So, I dragged myself up, still very drunk. Took a quick shot of the leftover vodka and brushed my teeth. I used the vodka to rinse my mouth out. She mentioned that she would sure like to brush the taste of nighttime, love-time out of her mouth.

I said, "What and have me risk getting some disease from you? And besides my main chick in L.A. would get way pissed off if she knew I let another woman use the toothbrush that she uses."

I grabbed my stuff and staggered down to her ride, and we got in and headed for impending enlightenment.

On the way, Bonne Mae asked me,

316

"Do you love me? I love you."
"I don't believe in love. I believe in desire, infatuation, even attachment. But love, what do you mean?"

Bonne Mae leaned over on me and said,

"Can we be together forever?"
I said, "Look, I got a Korean chick down in L.A. and she's a virgin and wants popped big time. Up in San Francisco I have this babe of a Chinese, white powder princess, who longingly awaits my every return. And Asia, I'm not even talking about the babes I have a-wait'n in Asia. And that is not even to mention My Main L.A. Babe. Forever! Fuck forever! It only lasts a second."

As we continued, she questioned,

"After today, I will never see you again, will I?"

I felt like saying, *'You called the play baby, so now you gotta live it.'* But, I just sat there in my sickening condition. I knew I was going to have a major fucking hang over seriously coming on strong.

*   *   *

We arrived at the spiritual abode, and I tossed my stuff in my car, which I had left there the night before. I headed in for further sermonizing.
It went in, and it went on. On and on.
You cannot believe the experience of sitting there surrounded by mid forty-year-olds, Mid

Westerners, all into this bullshit and my having to puke like you cannot believe. The hang over pouring over me like so many cheap drinks mixed out of expensive bottles with false ingredients placed inside of them. I was one tattered man.

I was sick, bad; really bad. The lights were low. I was falling asleep. Bonne Mae and some old lady, riding the other side of me, kept nudging as I nodded out. This, while the placid music and the chants keep going on, and on, and on. I thought it would fucking never end.

While all those around me: the tranquil, the holy, the believers of the lie, sat there, taking it oh so fucking seriously. Believing they were inheriting the truth of the ages, the gospel of the gods. There I sat in the arms of the truest religion, the highest enlightenment, PURE EXPERIENCE. There is no substitute. Nothing left to gain, nothing left to lose. I was sick as a *mutha' fucker.* It went on and on and on.

Finally, it ended at about noon, and all the people paraded out into the main hall to discuss what a religious experience they had. Me, my experience was boredom and pain. I was sick. I was trying to figure a way out-a-there without having to deal with and/or give my number to Bonne Mae.

Walking out of the sacred sanctuary, I noticed Bonne Mae heading for the head. My escape plan was made. I just saw that front door and walked straight out of it this time. Into my ride and off I drove. Leaving all the holy and all that is holy behind me.

There was a liquor store about a block away, so I hit it and purchased a six-pack of 7UP. They didn't have the hangover size bottles that I usually buy at times such as these. So, the sixer would have to do.

As I got back in my car, the thought came to me, should I go back and say goodbye to Bonne Mae. Then I realized, come-on, three kids and from Montana. And after all, she had called the shot. She realized that she would never see me again.

Back in my car, I headed North up to the *Gayasia,* the Gay Bay, or simply my old haunting grounds, *San Fran-cis-co.* I drove along 101 hoping that I wouldn't get pulled over for speeding or swerving, or anything, for I had a *deucer,* DUI, drunk driving, a year or so back, you know. And if they got me again, I would have to do a few days County Time. I was careful, though I was still noticeably fucked up.

I got up there about two or so and headed for my first intended stop, the Museum of Modern Art. I flashed my membership card and headed on in. I was still sick as a *mutha' fuck'n* dog though, its intensity was an up and down feeling.

It finally hit me. Hit me hard. I had to throw up. The 7UP helped but there was no way out now. So, into the head. I just barely make it and puke I do.

That's one of the worst things to have to puke in a public toilet. Though there was thankfully, no one else in the bathroom. All the thoughts of all the airborne spores or all the AIDS infested San Francisco faggots came to mind as I clinched the toilet bowl. But what can a guy like me do, you know?

Afterwards, I was in no mood to view any more art, nor to eat, drink, see people, or *nada.* So, I just decided to head on back down to L.A.

I got out there, *on the road,* and the lack of sleep caught up with me. It was all I could do to keep my eyes open. That raging battle when they shut and the conscious mind says, *'Open! Open!'* But they don't want to open. They won't, but they must.

Finally, with my head throbbing, my stomach churning, and being too tired to even sleep while driving, I pull into one of the little Mexican crop picker road towns on 101. Hit the local convenience store, pick up some aspirin and go and whip out the plastic money and rent me a motel room.

The old lady gives me this funny look, like she doesn't like my kind. But she obviously digs my plastic; platinum. So, she does what she must and rents to me and directs me to a room, way around the back and hard to find. I pull up, in I go. Kick down a few aspirins and lay out. Asleep in maybe three seconds.

I couldn't have been asleep ten minutes and at my door comes a knock, what *karma* I thought. It's the guy who is painting the building and he wants me to move my car, so he won't get paint on it. So, out I go and move it, I do.

Back in the sack-jack, his painting compressor kicks on. Fuck! Too burned out to do anything else, I bury my head in the pillow and try to sleep. I just pretended I was in Hong Kong.; as the noise was reminiscent of the pulsing pounding that goes on there constantly.

I got up five hours or so later and back on the road I go. L.A., coming up none too fast. I hit my usual, along the way drive-thru fast-food places, and pick up my usual two large cups of the *java* at each stop and around Santa Barbara I can again pick up L.A. radio stations.

As for Bonnie Mae well, the High Priestess must have given her my permanent address, my Post Office Box, for I still to this day get letters from her; telling me when she is going to be in L.A., inviting me to her hometown, and to spend Christmas with her and her kids because she still love me. Plus, Christmas Cards, always Christmas cards. Have I ever answered them? Fuck no!

*   *   *

Life and its dance and its secrets to enlightenment. Its secrets to reality, and its impending illusion full of all the lies that the masses love to believe; love to hate to believe.

The kiss of passion, the kiss of death. What a dance.

And me, I think that the Japanese word *Satori,* referring to sudden enlightenment, says it best. Literally translated, *'A kick in the eye.'*

CHAPTER 16
SOUTHEAST ASIAN NIGHT(S)

Hong Kong, it pounds like a headache, like a hyperventilating heart attack; a hundred billion people going nowhere at a million miles per hour. New York, I don't like it. Detroit, Chicago, you can keep 'em, too. They are like Hong Kong, kinda. No, not really, nothing is like Hong Kong.

I don't know, maybe it's because it's the first international port that I really explored. Maybe it's because I keep going back: have come to learn, come to see, come to live/understand the underside; a place where those bargain shopping tourists that have flocked there over the past few hundred years never could/never will. Maybe it's the babes, I don't know. I like the place.

Summer, for some reason, I have ended up in H.K., as I refer to it, for the last several summers. Man, the heat it does pulverize your soul. The heat, the humidity, the rain, the booze; yeah, I do have a bar that I like to hit there. A lot of local-living Westerners go there. I don't go there for them. I don't even want to talk to them. Occasionally, one hits me with a *convo*. I just chill back. There are some of the more pricey locals hitting the stools there as well. Even a few H.K. fags on the flip side. Me, I just like the drink that flows there; like it to wet my lips.

Kiss me one time, kiss me two time(s), kiss me three time(s), kiss me five; but usually you gotta kiss me more than ten.

Out there on the Southeast Asia side, H.K. being barely within its geographical bounds, I tend to hit the discotheque. Disco dolls for rent, for hire.

White lies, white eyes, they seem to speak so loudly to them.

My game plan usually is to hit the bar 9:00 P.M. or so, wet my lips with a few, then go and catch the subway over to the other side, under the bay, the Kowloon side and dance. (Dance, with a firm period of exclamation).

The discos seem to bang harder over on that side of the paradise. And then the if; the return to the crib side with a lady by my side/lady in hand and in the bush.

For the basic discussion sake of the night in question: the words being spoken, the *sadhana* to be performed, the lesson to be learned, whatever... I hit the nighttime walk to my bar of passion, "Hit me with a greyhound, if you please." They all love to see me there; all the bartenders. I guess I'm different looking than your average Westside H.K. yuppie type who rolls in on the Eastside. Yeah, whatever...

I dose-ed down three, well maybe four; tried to ignore this tourist looking dude of some sort of a furniture import/export loser; Bermuda shorts on, and a camera bag in hand. He had a story to tell. I wasn't interested. Believe me, I've heard them all. Since I had to listen to it, you may as well have to hear it, too... 'In H.K., from N.Y.; moved here, too much business on the line. Left his fiancée. (Who would want a N.Y., 'JAP,' anyway). Came to make his fame and fortune. Didn't know his way around yet.' Dude, you never will if you have promises to make, promises to keep. Leave that shit to the perspective family—MEN, not the men who, 'LIVE,' in H.K.

"How long have you been coming here?" What a question to ask.

"Ten years. Yeah, ten years. And yes, I have lived here, too."

Finally, as he wouldn't shut up, I had to slide on *out-a-there*.

"No, they won't let you in. No, not dresses like that."

Man, that's all I fucking need, you know, some pudgy New Yorker in plaid short pants tagging along.

Down the street, down under the street; yes, I had enough coin in hand to subway under the bay. Sometimes short in the change department I ride the ferry; but in the night, the tourists, they all come out to play.

Outside again, up the stairs, the heat, it pounces on me once more. The humidity, it makes me sweat. Oh yes, I am readying for the night.

Disco sucks, well at least in L.A. Here, H.K., it pounds with a passion now that it's not all glitz and glam but post wave/new wave. The drum machines they pump through its veins, thus it pumps through my veins; like a drug of addiction, a passion too full.

Up to my seat at the disco-bar. A new Bar-Keep, he didn't know my drink.

"Greyhound."
"What's that?"
"Vodka, and Grapefruit juice."

Oh yeah...

So, he poured it up strong, mega strong. I let it slide on down. Another, if you please.

Dose two, stronger even still, as he tries to lay the *convo.* on me. Now he wasn't a bad dude, all things being considered, young maybe nineteen, tried to tell me how to pick up the chicks. Believe me, dude, I don't need any lessons. By round three, the drinks were getting even stronger and I could feel my head moving on.

You know bartenders, well sometimes they try to be nice guys, try to pour them strong. I mean, you know, if you just wanta get fucked up, that's fine. I mean like, I do the same thing, like when my buddies Saturday Jim, Venchenzo, and I are having a Jimmy-Jam session over at his *crib de matrimony.* But out here, out on the *hard road,* I mean like out here in the field, it is just not what a party sort of dude, like myself, wants to taste. You want to come on slow, come on easy, keep a little bit of move for the dancing.

So, post about round five, I was about down for the count. No dancing action, nothing really find-able. A dead night in dead-meat land. Too chilled to really care by this point, anyway. I was out-a-there.

Grabbed a taxi. As I just recently flew in from Japan, stupid drunken asshole me, I tried to tell the guy where I was going in Japanese.

Anyway, back at home, *Love Station Central,* I always go into this little late night of a H.K. city hang out *java* shop on the ground floor of my hotel. It gives me the fool's food for thought and the nighttime protein to keep me from a kill hangover on the serious side come morning time. And when there had been no dancing on the right side and/or no women to fill my night, well it is true that I have even met one or two, well maybe three, of the how you say, *pavement princesses* or even the good girls (well, how good can they be), in there to take to the chill off of my hot Southeast Asian night(s).

Burger and a *cappuccino,* how poetic, as the late-night world did spin around in my head. There were some ladies: some loose, some single, some in groups, some out for the KILL. But it was crowded, my vision none too clear. "Give me the check." Sigh it. Get up to my room, I was out-a-there.

My room, it was nice. I stayed there so much they usually give me a suite for the price of a single. I sat on the floor in the bedroom, wrote some poetry, drunken style. The kind I can never decipher come the morning time. Watched some T.V. Thought of some lust.

*　　*　　*

Damn, wasn't it I who once was a yogi, who would force any thought of desire from his brain! Yes, I remember, it was I. For I passed through this port on my first trip to India. That was a long-long time ago. Ah, but this is far more simple, at least far more truthful, if you will. Far more honest if nothing else. For even the most holy is controlled by desire, the desire for no desire. And who is to say what is truly holy anyway?

So, wrap desire up for me, place it in modern fashion-passion aluminum, no plastic foil. Call it what you will. Call me a sinner, if you have religion. But don't you know that I have religion, too. Call it whatever you want. I call it the mystical path of enlightenment. But words they don't mean anything anyway.

Morning comes: my head hurts, my stomach hurts, it was that fucking *liqueur* that the bartender suggested be placed in my Greyhound. Oh fuck, I am sick. Go choke down a little breakfast. Slice me up a cup of the *java.* The hostess that is cute, who always tries to pick-up on me was there, but nothing seemed to help.

I had to get out, get some air, oxygen in my lungs, in my blood. The streets, these are the streets of passion. Oh fuck, that fucking hangover pain. Here comes the promise, the promise I never keep, *'Never, never, never again.'* As there is always an again.

Life and the streets of desire and the passion of the dance of the fool. It leads one on into the arms of the goddess whose passage takes you deep in the realms of the night. But, the price for the passage is high.

I walked around, nowhere really to go. I am not going to describe H.K. to you, read the *Tourist Guides* if you want to know what it looks like.

I ended up at this little park I know of on the far side of town. I wasn't feeling really any better, so I sat back, had an un-cola; something/anything for my stomach. I had an idea or two for one of those books that I have been meaning to write for years, jotted it down in my carry around portable notebook. But my stomach pumped on in its pain.

Walking again, I felt like I was going to pass out, up and over by the tennis courts. Needing to sit back again; sit for a little while. I pulled up my place front and center and watched as these two babes of H.K. women take one another on, tennis style.

Damn, they were pretty. Golden skin that pasted itself against the green of the park planted H.K. trees, the dark gray blue of the, about to rain, H.K. sky. Full black hair peeking out from under the underarm sleeves of their white tennis outfits. If I were not so sick, I would have gotten a hard-on. The love of the lost, passion in a flower, please place it in my hand.

Maybe ten or fifteen into the game, into the day, I guess one of them had won. Open the gate, close the gate, sit down, talk it over; two levels down on the bleachers below me.

"Weren't you at the disco, last night? I think I saw you there." A question asked of me...

Oh, hand me the dream. This form, it will do just fine. How I do love Asia, me being a big fish in a small pond.

"Yes, I was."
"I thought that I remembered you," said her words with a smile.

My vision was a little clouded on the evening last, if you know what I mean. I wish I could have placed her but...

"This is my friend, May Ling."
"Oh, nice to meet you, and you?"
"I'm, Sue Zi."
"Nice to meet you too."

Did I like tennis, did I play? Well yes, a little. Did I live in H.K.! No, L.A.

"I would love to go to L.A!"

Sometimes I kind of fumble around, not as cool as I like to think that I am. A lot of fish have passed through my hands that way. Then I lay there wishing, dreaming my nights away. But it was her, actually she, who inquired as to my whereabouts for the evening to come.

Did I like the ballet? Yes, I love the ballet. Would I like to go? Well, time to kill and money to spill; A.O.K.

She didn't want me to pick her up that night; wanted me to meet her there. I walked back to the hotel, feeling like hell but full-on lost in the dream.

Why haven't they invented an immediate hangover cure yet?

Several hours to kill, I took my usual afternoon nap. Happy, I did go to sleep happy. I awoke to the rain coming down and the city bopp'n. My hangover, well it had taken a turn for the better. Watched some T.V., took a shower, caught a shave. Dinner alone; our pending date was to be post that. Ready and out, out the door. Taxi and a ride, arrival a little early.

I stood there, suit and tie. I usually am in one anyway. I watched the cultured as they moved, casual cultural on the H.K. side.

Now L.A., it is stuffy. The cultured are the culture. The low, the beachy, the hippies are whatever they are, but here it all mixes together. A guy who dressed like shit might well drives a Rolls Royce.

Up she comes, I am numb. I mean god, what a babe and human in form. Dressed in black: lace and long. A black *sky piece* placed perfectly upon her head. H.K. and a woman who loves ballet. I may never leave.

The ballet, Canadian; I don't know, something was missing. Afterwards, out to late night *cappuccino,* late night pie.

The night available, only left to the dreamers.

I took her home Kowloon side, taxicab, a kiss goodnight.

She lived on the tall-side, one of those complexes of flats that rise into the H.K. sky in the night. A million of them, there are a million of them built a top one another. Like the city, like the country: too many, too close.

Back to my room, far too infatuated to dance out further into the night. Just lay back, dream of what is to come.

I passed a fine young specimen of a wild thing in the passageway to my hallway, didn't even give her a second thought.

A day or three: dinner, dancing, roller-skating, walking in the rain, and in love. She was like me, no place to be (you know me, I have no place to be). Daytime, nighttime, anytime, freedom in the passing caress of the wind.

Ah, how I love people with no better place to be.

So, I won't bore you with all the details of love, watch any old movie and you will see it upon the screen. In her arms, our lips did meet. Yes, this was, *'The Night.'*

"Would you like to come up?"

The building was white, Hong Kong white, stained by the weather, by the rages of time. The hallway was white, dirty off-white like in Thailand; Southeast Asia and the dream. The walls of her apartment were white, placed strategically a cockroach or two. I won't go into that, they are really big there, there is no getting rid of them, and they gross me out.

Simply furnished, a one bedroom: blues and greens, a plant or two. Kiss me again; a touch, leads to a feel. I was in her arms; she moved us to her bedroom. We lay down upon her bed.

Her clothing off, she took mine off, like the gentlest of professional love. All ivory, pale white, upon golden yellow. She took my dick, inserted it in her.

Ah, what a grasp, if you can catch my drift. Love and in the inside and out of the outside of the subject discussed. Small breasts, firm. Hairy underarms and legs. Damn, everything I look for on the Asian far side of love, on the Asian far side of the earth.

That little bit darker complexion, they seem to grow more hair: beaver side, underarm side. Maybe it is the black of the black hair. I don't know? But I sure like something to lose myself in.

She knew what she was doing, definitely did me right. I could not help but remember this joke I heard from a comedian, *'Did she fuck you good the first night? Yeah, well where did she learn?'*

She, up on the topside, she came: one time, two times, three times, four, way fast. Way, the way I like it. A play here, a move there, it was the moment in motion.

I lay there in her arms; you know one of those stupid fucking in love sort of feelings in true love sort of scenes. The heart gurgling, like you feel oh so right.

As you know, I have a way of saying what the women want me to say. I said, to this sweet long-lost love of a momentary dream,

"Oh, this is what I have been looking for all of my life."

I don't know, some call it pillow talk. The *rap* you give them between the sheets. But the sheets, they had been kicked off in all the heat. I mean hey, let the sweat roll free.

"I don't think so," so she said, "I'm not what you are looking for. I love you but you don't know me."
"You don't know me either."

I had to throw it in. Never let them get the last word in.

"No, but you really don't know me."
"No, but you really don't know me either."

I mean, you know how it is, I like to lay the feelings of love, live the feelings of love, even me being the cynical dude that I am. And certainly, when the love words are being a-spoken, a *nagatory* response is NOT what I want to hear.

Anyway, another session in the mummy bag of love. I slept in her arms throughout the night. Morning comes, love in the vagina central. The wild power pup is up for action again.

Breakfast done, breakfast had, I split. To have and to hold and time to let go.

Doorman, door scene, *Sikh;* my hotel in the H.K. sky. I return(ed) early afternoon,

"How much is she charging you?"

"What?"

"Is she charging you by the week?"

"What!"

"I see her here with a lot of guys, but they never stay as long as you. You must be very rich. It must be expensive for you to spend all that time with her."

So, loved wrapped up in a dollar sign. Well, it had happened to me before. In love with a whore.

I guess I could have gotten upset at all my foolishness. I guess I could have let myself have all of those bullshit broken hearted pains.

Me, I just laughed. Booked a flight for Bangkok. Packed, caught a taxi. Got to the airport just a few to spare. I mean, she did try to tell me...

I used to consider myself a *mys-tic,* now I think *mis-take* is a better description.

Words and love, what do they mean? I guess they mean nothing.

But, anyway...

CHAPTER 17
THE PASSIONATE KISS OF ILLUSION

I do not believe that the average person can ever truly understand artistic frustration. The gut-wrenching feeling when you know that you have so much creativity inside of you but the world in all its bullshitness keeps robbing your time, your energy, your moment until all is lost into a life that is allowed to be lived far too shortly and there is never enough time to accomplish all that needs to be done. This feeling cannot even be put into words, but it leaves one knowing that death is a far better option to the continual reoccurrence of an unworthy life.

Here lies the worst paradox of artistic frustration, for it's at this junction that many an artist duly takes their own life. If this be done however, then all the creativity and art is truly lost and the world has won.

But in a world where nothing really matters anyway... Where whatever you can do can be equally accomplished by another. Who knows what holds the ultimate lasting truth?

At times of artistic frustration, lost deep in the not knowing what to do or where to turn, many a frustrated artist turns to alcohol, drugs, or illicit sex. But what does one turn to when the allure of all of these has worn thin? This is where I was. No friends worth turning to, money was tight, way tight, and acceptance nonexistent.

I had spent the last long time with my pud in my hand: no love, no babes, not even a night on the town, or the money for, to sooth my nerves; nothing, *nada*.

334

The average fool tells one at this point that they should forget all the art, all the mysticism, and fade into the mainstream, becoming a normal functioning part of society. But how can one with vision ever do this? Once the illusion is seen, one can never return to it.

The world it is an evil master. It takes everything leaving the artist at times with no strength. It keeps knocking one down and getting up is harder and harder, until finally it takes all the inner energy one has to complete the simplest of artistic endeavors.

The term frustrated artist has become quite *cliché* these days. Yet, most of those who claim that status are simply businessmen, egotists, attempting to gain money, fame, and fortune through the arts. Some obtain it, the few that do however are virtually never the artists that they claim to be.

Most humans, here in the western world, wish simply to complete high school, maybe college, find a mate, have children, work until they are sixty-five, retire, and die. Then, there are the claimed artists; of one type or another, who are willing to work nine-to-five to support their supposed habit. Eventually these art enthusiasts usually end up fading into the melancholy mainstream and wind up as a functioning member of society, as well. It's difficult to call that type of person an artist at all. For an artist is forever an artist. Live or die, that is what they do.

There is an occasional person who succeeds in their chosen art and lives to make millions at it, but I have found, that for the most part, those are the ones who are either pushy businessmen themselves, have family money behind them, or there are others who drive their business bus for them. A better name for this type of so-called artist is an art-business-person.

The majority of the mystically creatively inclined die mad and broke. And leave it to the businessmen to buy and sell their creations for profit once they have died. May those entrepreneurs be damned.

Each of us makes our own choices and most humans have the allure of fame, fortune, and power; developed undoubtedly by the stimuli placed in the mind by society. There is, however, those out on the extremities whose artform is their life and to compromise their time, energy, or space for anything but that seems totally futile. Death is a better option than that of a life surrendered to the mindless mainstream.

The pain out on this edge can, at times, become quite severe. I know, for I am one who suffers that pain.

My life had been cruising along as it normally does but my time and energy were all being robbed from under my nose. There were people and family that needed my assistance and that demon of the world was trying hard to suck me in: taking my time, making me do worldly things that I would prefer not doing. Money was mega tight, *as mentioned,* and I had the thought to bail myself out by selling my long-time buddy, my 356. I was deep in the trap that had engulfed me and though I waited for a sign, there seemed to be no sign coming, no way out.

The world, well it is a funny place. If one's only dream is to get a job, it's not so hard to accomplish, if one is not too picky. And if one's only dream is to settle down and get married, that, as well, is not so hard if one is not too choosy. But how do the dreamers of the world, who refuse to accept second-best, finance their livelihood, if they do not choose to live on the streets; a *sadhu* in America. How does the mystic flow into the ocean of life when the devils of the world keep building dams? And how does the artist show his vision when he is not, nor wants to be, a businessman?

Questions are always questions in a reality where all who claim to know the answers never know the answers and all who speak would do better to remain silent.

The wind blows and the birds find what they need to eat. The waves massage the shoreline and the fish are all fed, but man, the jokingly highest creature chooses to create a destiny alien to all that is, and binds himself by walls he chooses to create. I had no vote on the placement of those walls.

*   *   *

I was feeling a bit drained. It made me sad to have my energy zapped by the world and not have enough left to do my chosen vocation, *artistic nothing*. But, I needed to get out of the four walls of a prison known as an apartment. So, I pulled myself together enough to head on down to Long Beach to a sleazy little Cambodian restaurant I knew and chow down.

I hit out to my car, gave the ocean a wave, 'Hello' and breathed deep the semi-pure L.A. beach air.

It was a bit cool this Thursday, but Spring was in full bloom and I knew that it would not be long until the heat and the smog of the Summer would be upon us. I thanked Mr. Weather for hanging tight in all its coolness and hoped it would remain so for a while longer.

I debated taking the freeway route or heading down PCH, (Pacific Coast Highway). I choose the latter and cruised on. I drove below the estates of the multi-millionaires of P.V., (Palos Verdes), and wondered how many of them had gotten their money through their art. *'The art of deception,'* I thought, and laughed to myself. I drove on through Lomita, then on to the factories and the stench of Wilmington. Finally, I came into Long Beach.

Long Beach definitely has a bohemian side to it and though its neighborhoods are racially interactive, and most are not that much on the safe side, I find myself there time-and-time again studying the streets: in the day, in the night. Myself being the cultural researcher that I am.

Long Beach, it has an abundance of relocated Southern and Mid-Westerners within its boundaries. As well as virtually every ethnic group on the face of the earth. Rents are cheap, but sometimes the cost for cheap rents is high.

I had finished my Ph.D. dissertation on the Cambodian refugees who lived in Long Beach eight or nine months previously, so I had made an acquaintance of one or two places I liked to dine at and take my health into my hands. Well, we are all going to die anyway.

As I turned right onto Long Beach Boulevard, I decided that maybe I should head on to the Long Beach library *en route* to lunch. It is always a nice place to kill some time, walk around, and check out the large ethnic, cultural, and social mixture that frequent it.

I made my way there: pulled up, parked, and in I went. I headed over to the very large section of current magazines. As I was going down the aisle, to get the weekly magazine on Asia, just beating me to the punch was this young, beautiful, and oh so stylish Asian girl taking it from out of my grasp. She wore a long dark skirt, a white shirt, low heeled black shoes, and black nylon stockings. A cut, shoulder length, black *'do.'* Classic looks placed perfectly into their place of perfection. Just the way I love them. And to think, I once thought drawstring pants were cool...

She glanced at me for a moment, smiled and walked on her way.

Ah life, love, desire, and all the rest of the words and feelings that have absolutely no meaning. There she was, the perfect princess, grabbed as the magazine was from my reach. A new focus, far more important than the magazine had come into my reality, my field of vision; a new desire had risen.

The magazine of choice had been taken, so I grabbed another one with a given Asian title, but my real interest had shifted to the babe in possession of my magazine of choice. I mean, *fuck the reading, I prefer the living.*

It was that same old basic feeling of desire, that one which makes you chase. Knowing that/believing that this one: it will answer all needs, all desires, heal all open wounds. But, the truth being known, the truth being told: it/they, the desires, rarely accomplishes anything. Am I being too cynical here?

*　　*　　*

There I was, more than a bit lost in the midst of life and all of its non-allowance for the artist. And, I was alone. I had been alone for quite a time, and nothing seemed that it would feel better than falling in love. What a fine time to fall in love for I had nothing better to do.

With magazine in hand, I headed out of the aisle in search of the previously described young lady.

A stupid macho dude in all his glory, seeking enlightenment in the arms of a stranger. Seeking a cure for the artistic blues but seeking none-the-less.

An object by any other name. Who was the fool?

I saw her sitting on one of the library chairs but the one nearest to it/to her was occupied. All I could do was sit as closely as possible, within glancing range and hope.

The time went by; she read, I pretended to read. She had to know I was there; I mean I could not help but stare at her.

I'm not a very forward person by nature. Some may laugh at this statement, upon completion of the reading of the previous pages, but it's true. I'm very reserved and introverted, almost to a fault. This condition is, of course, momentarily cured under the influence of various substances or in the presences of such friends as Saturday Jim or Venchenzo.

The question was, how to make contact? This is, of course, the point in fact of all pursuit in the gentlemanly approach to love.

I think now of Japan and how it is like a child in a candy store for me. For there, the women in their long skirts and long hair and beauty make me almost go mad in desire: desire for one, desire for more, desire, generally unfulfilled. I needed love, what was I to do?

It's hard to say if it was my playing into destiny's hands or a movement of the spirit, but I had finished all of importance in the magazine, which I eventually had forced myself to read. And having become bored with no returned glances—I hoped she didn't think that I was some *perv*. And, in general, becoming quite pessimistic of the possibilities of knowing this love, I returned the magazine to the shelf and had decided on the dreams of possibilities of love and whatever may come to me in that Cambodian restaurant I was progressing towards.

As I was to walk, she came to put the magazine away with a smile.

It is definitely a moment of extreme tension, at least in my case, when I'm about to say the first word to a new-found person. That is, of course, unless I am parlaying a substance feel or riding the wave in the presence of my macho friends where if they, the babes, don't want to know, then forget 'em. But I was alone, and I was straight.

I said, "Hello."
She replied, "Hello."
I inquired, "Interested in the study of Asia?"

As my heart pounded a million beats a second.

"No, just the article on the Philippines."

"Is that where you're from?"

"Yes."

"I've been there several times myself. What part are you from?"

"Cebu City."

"Oh yes, I have been there. It's very beautiful."

"Did you go there on business?"

"Do I look like a businessman?" I joking reply. "No, I went there for the dream."

"The dream?"

"The dream."

I will not bore you with the proceeding conversation for the foundation has been set. Perhaps as other autobiographical writer have done in the past, I may at a later date pull this incident to memory and recap it further and more precisely in other pieces of literature. But, for now, at this time, that will do.

We walked from the aisle together. Walked to the doors together. Walked out of the doors together.

"What are you doing? Are you hungry? Would you like to have lunch?"

Yes, she would.

She was far more dynamic than I. She was far more trusting than I. She was far younger than I.

We walked to my car. The day had become cloudy. Cloud, fog, haze, smog; I really do not know which, or the mixture there, of but the color of the day had changed. It had moved its way from blue to gray but that, quite in-fact, was alright with me.

I unlocked, opened the door, and allowed her entry into my realm of need.

I walked to the other side of my black Porsche, reflecting the presence of all color in its now, semi-unclean, shine. I removed the parking ticket, which I had received. I seem to collect them. Opened my door, entered and moved into her realm of need. The one that I did not see yet. I started the car.

We did not go to my predestined Cambodian restaurant, for I felt it a bit to funky. I instead chose this rather *nuevo-hip* small little hut that opened nearby within the walls of re-developing downtown L.B.

The food was acceptable. She, Christabelle, (those ladies from the Philippines have some of the most beautiful names), had lived in the U.S. for six years: was attending the local Community College, liked reading, dancing, roller-skating, was nineteen. I was twenty-eight.

As we left the restaurant the feeling almost came over me to simply take the 44 magnum semi-automatic pistol I had stashed in a draw, in my apartment, awaiting its destined call of separating my brains from body, my life from the bounds of this world, and blow my brains out. For there she was, this perfect creature. Perfect in the sense of the world's imperfection. There she was. There I was. We had met and I, though I already knew I loved her and sensed she loved me—I, I had absolutely nothing to offer her but a dreamer's dream in a dreamless world.

She had a part-time job at a bookstore and had to be on her way. I gave her a ride, of course. She stated how she was so happy to meet me, an artist, and with a Ph.D. Her mother, so she said, would love that.

*   *   *

Is this Asia or what? No, it is America. It is the land of a fool's power-plays in a fool's powerful world. I don't know, maybe it's nature. I really haven't a clue. But the outside and the rap/the bullshit is all that is respected and all that is seen. What is it, tell me why, all women want to marry, settle down with what they deem as acceptable. They want what their mother wants, the perfect son-in-law. How could I ever be that, even with a Ph.D? Asia and America, once I thought that there was a difference. No longer do I believe such a lie.

*   *   *

I dropped her off, love in her eyes. I hoped it would not spill out and onto the masses occupying the bookstore in which she worked, rendering her powerless and seduce-able to the spell of everyday life/everyday man. I dropped her off; it did not mean that I wanted to.

I was happy I met her and I wished I never did. Both at the same time. I had found instant love, like instant coffee, for those, who unlike me, do not choose to grind the individual grounds freshly before each cup. Instant love, perfect love in an instant and far from perfect world. It all stunned me/it lost me.

I drove home and thought never to trouble her life with my confused presence again. I ran to, the only place I had to run to, the gym, the health spa. Where I did run; three miles. I lifted weights. I hoped for another illusion in the form of a woman; a not so perfect woman, etc., etc., etc.

I went home, post the gym. Took a needed nap, with my headphones on; silencing the world around me. The kind that they wear at the shooting range. I wear them when I sleep in the day, and when the morning light calls. When all the alarms of the world go off to be someplace important, of no importance. When the coffee machines are switched on or in the case of automatic timers, switch themselves on. I wore them when I slept to get sleep from my hours—hours away from the realms of the normal world.

They/the people of the world, are all going somewhere when I'm trying to sleep. Somehow exchange never seems to work. I guess because I'm a considerate person. But, the facts being told, they/the world, and the people thereof and therefore, always seem to have no consideration and believe it is their right to bother me: their noise, their starting cars, their driving cars. At their times, not mine.

Me, I am an all-night guy; different times/different world. Yet, I'm strapped to the *turbojet* of their world, and I cannot function in mine. For I try to be quiet in the hours of the late night/early morning; my hours for them. But then there I was napping five o'clock or so, they were coming home in their cars; parking their cars, making noise.

I wore my headphones, trying to sleep. Why do they, the masses, the mindless masses always seem to have control?

*   *   *

I woke or was woken. I got up depressed/upset. No one to call, nowhere to go. Blank canvases stared at me with all their emptiness from my kitchen where I paint. The paint on the floor, several inches thick. They stared at me with their empty eyes. I was frustrated. *Remember me, the frustrated artist stuff and all...* I wanted to paint, I wanted to love, yet I could not call the new woman/girl in my life for all I would do is mess her up. That's all I had to offer, a mess up. So, I stared at the walls, stared at the T.V. And life's time ticked on. Sometimes you just wish it would hurry up and reach the clock's end.

Maybe it was nine o'clock, maybe it was ten. The telephone rang, as it now seemed so rarely to do. It was her, Christabelle.

Though my rational mind told me there could be nothing, my desire, of course, accepted her call with a passion. I invited her out, the next day.

It was dinner. It was love. The dinner continued on to dinner the next night. Out the day after that. The day after that, again and again and again...

I think the details are best spared for they are not so flamboyant in nature, or so whimsical in rhyme. It was simplistic and encompassing, infatuation to the maximum degree.

Her nineteen-year-old mind had found what it thought it was looking for: a Porsche, a platinum card; a promise for her, and a Ph.D. for her mother.

Myself, I was lost, lost in the middle, as so often happens to those like me; *the lost in general.*

I do have a bad habit of falling in love. She had it all though. Perhaps she could have stood to

346

drop a few pounds but in the imperfect world and perfection in its own sense; all-is-all.

There she was handing me, *love on a platter.*

But, somehow I could not distinguish it from all the insane necessities that made up the rest of my life at that point in time. It's not that love combined with lust had not crossed my mind with those considerably younger than her. And truth being told; it, lust, did perpetuate my thoughts of her as well. But somehow her perfection, her young elegance, rendered it impossible. Impossible for me to lose myself and act out my desire of lust upon her nineteen-year-old, dreaming of marriage, youthful form.

It was our eighth time out, dinner in just the right sort of very elegant restaurant. Completed, we made our way back to my apartment near the ocean. We walked along the seaside, hand-in-hand, arm-in-arm. She leaned up and kissed me, oh so perfectly.

It's not that we had not kissed before but this time it was different. It had all the fundamental makings of love in the third degree: pure passion/burning passion.

We walked back to my apartment. I knew what was to happen. I knew what my body wanted to happen. It began to happen.

We moved from the embracing upon my red couch, to embraces upon my futon bed in the next room. She unbuttoned my shirt. I helped her. I slipped her blouse over her head. She helped me. Soon all clothing had been removed; so artistically.

We lay there naked in bed. Her golden skin shined in the dimly lighted nighttime hallway light, turned to low position on the rotating control switch. Its shine reflected in my eyes.

We lay there kissing, holding, loving. Yes, it was love by any pragmatic definition of the word.

I was on top of her, then to the side. She said,

"Sandy, do you know this is my first time?"
"No, really?"
"Really, I have saved myself just for you. I love you so much and want to give you my everything."

Now, in truth, I had heard these words more than a few times before. But in the taste-test, the proof is in the pudding, the good housekeeping seal of approval had previously been tampered with, if you know what I mean? Christabelle's words, however, rang too true.

She places herself atop me. As she did, I could feel the soup beginning to flow upon my leg; that sweet cherry wine. She moved closer, tighter, I could feel my dick at the appropriate entrance cavity for the realms of passion.

I wanted in, but...I rolled her over and off of me.

"I love you so much Christabelle that I want to prove to you that I respect you and save this moment for our wedding night."
"Oh Sandy, you are so perfect. I love you so much!"

We hung for a few minutes with the main power rod, the sword of destiny, un-sheathed. It tried to convince me to go in for the kill. I had to get—get out. I did not, could not watch her dress. She did, I did. I took her home.

As I pulled up in front of her Long Beach home, I exited the car, opened her door, as I had trained her to expect.

"I love you so much Sandy. You are so perfect."

The words, they rang again in my ears again. If only she knew...

She hugged me, hugged me tight, put her head on my shoulder. Then removing it she, lifted herself upon her tippy toes and kissed me. Our lips met deeply with the soft impact of touching human form, touching human skin.

That was it, the final,
Passionate Kiss of Illusion.

The next day, the very next day, I went out to this apartment building which I had long seen adjoining the ocean a few blocks from where I had been living. I had long dreamed of living there/here, right on the ocean. Though the rent seemed too high, I rented an apartment. The price no longer seemed to matter, my financial condition a mess at best anyway.

I called the telephone company, disconnected my telephone with no forwarding number. I moved out. Three and a half years at that place had been too long anyway.

I have never seen Christabelle again. I gave her the only possible gift, the best gift I could; that of saving her, opposite to spoiling her, for the next perfect son-in-law that may come along. *I trust he will be more perfect than I...*

Sometimes I have thought to call her, especially in the enormous number of lonely nights

I have spent since I last saw her. Sometimes I have thought to telephone her, especially in nights of drunken stupor, when I would be out, partying down. But, I have not.

My life it has... Well, I have continued to struggle with intensive artistic frustration, though I have come to dislike that term even more since the time of Christabelle and I—eight or nine months ago.

They say artists must suffer to create, I never understood why. It seems everything, *'they,'* have to say is so negative.

Some canvases have lost their emptiness in this time period. But, I no longer have a suitable place to paint late into the night. The words, somehow though, they have come to be written more readily, at least in the terms of the autobiographical since.

I guess all life has its flow of necessity and it is simply the observation and consciousness of the spirit which lets us arrive at our given perfection. *All in our own season,* as it is said.

For years I played music for hours a day, so fulfilling. Now, it is as empty as it was once enticing. When I can, I paint... Yet, it now seems all the paintings have been done.

There was a time when I wished to photograph the world and all my artistic visions. Now, after having spanned the globe many times and trapping the souls of so many salient beings; too many of the photographs have emerged not quite in focus, and it seems they have all been taken, all been seen before. So now, I sit here at these keys whenever I can break from the spell of this world and, at the ripe old age of twenty-nine, relay my experiences.

350

It may be my flow, it may be my destiny, it may be neither of the above. Who knows, maybe tomorrow the music will all come back.

The dance of the artist, who is the art. The dance of the mystic, who is the mysticism, it does have its flaws. But if the consciousness can be fine-tuned, just for a second, then all the illusion leads to all the ultimately perfect form of reality.

Find the reality in the illusion. Find the truth in the lie. And you will know enlightenment.